Not even the most beautiful widow or expensive incognita had ever made him feel like Becca did. Certainly not this warmth that spread through his chest at just the sight of her.

Phineas took one of her gloved hands and bowed over it. "Lady Rebecca."

"Lord Nonesuch."

He couldn't help but grin at her again. He could get used to smiling. And Phineas was more aware than ever of her luscious curves and recently bitten lips. "We had better start walking, for if we don't, I will push you against that tree and kiss you senseless."

"I daresay that I should like that very much—if only I knew your surname."

Shaking his head, he laughed and offered his arm. He was enjoying their little game and he didn't want her to know that he had proposed marriage to her sister-in-law. "Oh, Becca. So should I. But I am not yet ready to tell you my name and I have at least fifty questions to ask you about yourself."

"Only fifty," she said, attempting to scowl at him and failing miserably. "I should think I was a fascinating enough individual to warrant at least twice as many questions."

Author Note

I'm delighted to share Lady Rebecca Stringham's story! She is the youngest daughter of the Duke and Duchess of Hampford. Becca has been a favorite of mine for several books and I am so excited for her to be the heroine this time. Lord Norwich, Phineas, was first introduced in *The Marquess and the Runaway Lady*. Norwich is inspired by real dandies like Beau Brummell, who had considerable power during the Regency era.

In 1810, Miss Mary Anning (1799-1847) and her brother found the first known Ichthyosaurus specimen near Lyme Regis. Mary excavated it. In 1817, Lieutenant Colonel Thomas Birch bought several of the Annings' collection of fossils, bringing them to national attention like in this book. In 1842, Sir Richard Owen coined the term "Dinosauria".

Unfortunately, dyslexia and other learning struggles were not understood in the early nineteenth century. People like Becca, who had difficulties reading, were thought to be a "dunce" or unmotivated, and in some cases, medically deficient. In 1887, Rudolf Berlin, a German ophthalmologist, coined the phrase "dyslexia".

Like Becca does in this story, I have struggled with my weight and self-esteem based on the measurement of my waist. Persons of size often experience microaggressions by friends and family who think they are "helping". Becca's feelings are similar to my own and as such, everyone experiences body perception differently. I hope that no matter your size, you will realize that your worth is great and that your possibilities are endless.

BECOMING HIS BLUESTOCKING COUNTESS

SAMANTHA HASTINGS

Harlequin
HISTORICAL

If you purchased this book without a cover you should be aware that this book is stolen property. It was reported as "unsold and destroyed" to the publisher, and neither the author nor the publisher has received any payment for this "stripped book."

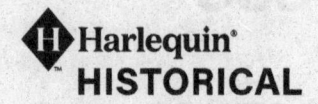

Harlequin®
HISTORICAL

ISBN-13: 978-1-335-83140-8

Becoming His Bluestocking Countess

Copyright © 2025 by Samantha Hastings

All rights reserved. No part of this book may be used or reproduced in any manner whatsoever without written permission.

Without limiting the author's and publisher's exclusive rights, any unauthorized use of this publication to train generative artificial intelligence (AI) technologies is expressly prohibited.

This is a work of fiction. Names, characters, places and incidents are either the product of the author's imagination or are used fictitiously. Any resemblance to actual persons, living or dead, businesses, companies, events or locales is entirely coincidental.

For questions and comments about the quality of this book, please contact us at CustomerService@Harlequin.com.

TM and ® are trademarks of Harlequin Enterprises ULC.

Harlequin Enterprises ULC
22 Adelaide St. West, 41st Floor
Toronto, Ontario M5H 4E3, Canada
www.Harlequin.com

Recycling programs for this product may not exist in your area.

Printed in U.S.A.

Samantha Hastings met her husband in a turkey-sandwich line. They live in Salt Lake City, Utah, where she spends most of her time reading, having tea parties and chasing her kids. She has degrees from Brigham Young University, University of North Texas and University of Reading (UK). She's the author of *The Last Word*, *The Invention of Sophie Carter*, *A Royal Christmas Quandary*, *The Girl with the Golden Eyes*, *Jane Austen Trivia*, *The Duchess Contract*, *Secret of the Sonnets* and *A Novel Disguise*. She also writes cozy murder mysteries under Samantha Larsen.

Learn more at her website: SamanthaHastings.com
Connect with Samantha on social media:
X: @HastingSamantha
Instagram: @SamanthaHastingsAuthor
Facebook: SamanthaHastingsAuthor

Books by Samantha Hastings

Harlequin Historical

The Scandalous Stringhams

The Marquess and the Runaway Lady
Debutante with a Dangerous Past
Wedded to His Enemy Debutante
Accidental Courtship with the Earl

Visit the Author Profile page at Harlequin.com.

To Summer Larsen

Chapter One

London, England—1818

Shivering, Lady Rebecca Stringham came to the melancholy conclusion that assisting in a romantic assignation wasn't enjoyable at all. Firstly, it was cold. There was a reason that Hyde Park was near empty at the early hour of eight o'clock in the morning in March. Frost covered the tips of the grass and the leaves on the trees glistened with dew. Secondly, she counted off on her pointer finger, it was dull. Since her tutor, Mr Alonzo Lawes, was off flirting with his secret fiancée behind some obliging trees, Becca was all by herself after purposely leaving behind her groom and lady's maid.

Thirdly, her tummy rumbled. She was hungry and a bit irritable. All she'd had to eat or drink so far that morning was a cup of hot chocolate and it had been bitter. And fourthly, she wiggled her ring finger, she was tired of always being the supporting character of the story. Becca was twenty years of age and finally going to debut in society, but all she had accomplished by coming to London so far was enabling Alonzo to meet secretly with Miss Cassandra Betrump.

Touching her little finger, Becca was trying to come up

with a final complaint when the sound of a horse's hooves caused her to turn around. Astride a magnificent chestnut horse was the most beautiful man she had ever clapped eyes on. His golden curls escaped from underneath his tall black beaver hat. His eyes were the light blue of an afternoon sky. He wore a dark green riding coat with several capes.

Such ostentation would have looked ridiculous on any other gentleman, but it seemed appropriate on this Adonis of a man. Even his Hessian boots gleamed in the sunlight as if they'd been newly polished with champagne. The only thing to detract from his pale perfection was his thin lips—they appeared to be in a perpetual sneer. Becca nearly turned away, for she'd been caught staring at him. Not that there was much else to look at besides the frozen grass.

A mouse darted from behind the tree and ran in front of the beautiful gentleman's horse. The chestnut whinnied and reared up, causing the man to be thrown. He flew off his horse elegantly on to the cold ground of the park.

Becca started forward to stop his chestnut from bolting back to his stall, but her movements only further spooked the horse and it galloped away in the opposite direction. Sighing, she continued until she reached where the handsome gentleman lay on the ground. His hat was a few feet away from his head and his golden curls were even more lovely up close. They were the bright yellow colour of amber. She had to stop herself from giving into the temptation to touch them.

Removing her glove, Becca knelt down on to the wet ground and picked up his wrist. His long, slender fingers were encased in kid leather gloves. She couldn't help but wonder if there was any part of this man that wasn't polished perfection. Touching the inside of his warm wrist, she felt a faint pulse. Exhaling a breath she hadn't realised she was holding, Becca let out a little laugh of relief.

He wasn't dead.

His complexion looked very pale though. The cravat around his neck was intricately and tightly tied in a design Becca did not know. This gorgeous man was clearly a dandy.

A tulip of the ton. *An out-and-outer. A Bond Street beau.*

She'd never found the dandy set attractive before. Her sister Helen called them 'man milliners'. Yet, her pulse raced and her heart was beating unnaturally fast. It didn't take a woman, or man for that matter, of a scientific background to realise that these were the physical signs of attraction. No doubt, if she could see them, her pupils would have been dilated as well. There were slight lines around his eyes and she guessed that he was in his late twenties. Older than herself, but not too much.

Shaking her head, she laughed again. This time at herself. She might have been the daughter of a duke, but she considered herself the least attractive of her three living sisters. Two of her sisters had married dukes and the other a Scottish earl, the handsomest husband of the trio.

Becca, however, was plump, even after losing a stone this past year because she had restricted her intake of sweets. This golden man would be interested in a willowy young lady who matched his own slender fair looks. Becca's hair was brown and thick, her eyes blue and her complexion had thirteen freckles. She knew that they were not fashionable, but she liked them anyway. She thought that they gave her rather boring nose a bit of character.

But the real reason this beautiful man would never be interested in her was because Becca was unintelligent. No matter how hard she tried, she could not read very well.

The words did not stay in the correct order. Last year, her mama hired Alonzo, who had received a double first at Oxford, and not even he could teach her to read like other people. Through a great deal of effort, Becca *had* improved. If she held her finger underneath each word and sounded it out slowly, she could read a letter in twice the amount of time that it took most people and get the majority of the words correct.

Slow witted or not, she needed to wake this man. If she couldn't get him conscious, she would need to fetch him a physician immediately. Sitting down, she eased his head into her lap. The hem of her morning gown was already a bit muddy from kneeling. His golden locks felt like silk to the touch and her breathing quickened—another sign of animalistic attraction.

Becca had always wondered why women lost their heads over a handsome man. She'd never understood it before. Such giddiness had seemed foolish and stupid. Now she was the one being stupid. Even in the animal kingdom, *like* attracted *like*. And she and this dandy were nothing alike. He was a golden lion in the sun and she was a brown mouse that hid in the shadows.

Placing her hand gently against his soft lips, she could feel him breathing. But it was shallow. Becca hesitated before further investigation. He was a stranger, not a brother, and social conventions stated it was improper for a young woman to be so close to an unknown gentleman. But she was also a naturalist and she needed to make sure that he was all right.

Becca moved her hands to his exquisitely tied cravat and undid it, as well as the top few buttons of his shirt. Pushing back his high-pointed collar to each side, she exposed his chest underneath his chin. It was pale like the rest of him, but with lovely muscular definition. His frame was more beautiful than the marble statues of gods in Greece.

If she were in a fairytale, a kiss would wake him up. But as a woman of science, she knew that such stories had no academic or historical basis. Still, she felt warm—no, feverishly hot all over. Another sign of desire. Females of many different species became overheated when they were near a handsome male. Becca needed to wake him up and walk away.

Moving her hands to his cheeks, she gently caressed them. 'Sir? Sir, you've had a fall. Please wake up.'

His long, golden eyelashes fluttered and he slowly opened his light icy blue eyes.

Becca couldn't help but smile down at him. 'You're going to be okay, sir. A mouse spooked your horse and threw you. I trust that your chestnut ran home to its stables. When you get a little more colour in your cheeks, we will get you home as well.'

Phineas could almost believe he was still asleep. His head was in the lap of a beautiful young woman with just the sort of figure he preferred—one with a magnificent chest and generous curves. Her hair was brown and shiny. Her lips were red and full, as if she'd recently bitten them. The skin of her hands was warm and velvety soft against his face. If it weren't for his pounding headache he would have been in paradise. If only she would kiss him, his dream would be perfect.

He closed his eyes.

'Sir. Sir, you mustn't go back to sleep,' she insisted in a pretty voice. Clearly, the diction of a lady. He supposed if he looked about him, he would see a footman and maid accompanying her. Rubbing his face against one of her gentle hands, he decided that he didn't care. He liked being precisely where he was. Her lovely hands moved to stroke his hair and he enjoyed that as much as her caresses.

'You have to wake up, sir. You have hit your head and injuries to the brain can be quite grievous. The best thing you can do is to stay alert until you have seen a doctor or a physician.'

He shook his sore head. 'I don't want to wake up.'

'You're not asleep, you're concussed.'

Phineas opened one eye reluctantly to look at the demanding Venus. 'This is a dream. You are a dream and I intend to enjoy it.'

She laughed, a light, merry sound that warmed his heart. 'How can I prove that this is not a dream? Shall I pinch you?'

His other eye opened. Dream or not, he desired this lovely young woman. 'No. Kiss me, instead.'

His retort was met with another giggle. 'I can't kiss a strange gentleman. You might already be married.'

'I'm not. Kiss me to prove you are not a dream.'

The beautiful young woman shook her head. She smelled like temptation—spicy and sweet. 'There is no scientific method or theory for using kisses to wake humans up.'

'Write one.'

She smiled down at him, surrounded by sunlight. She looked like an angel. A nymph. 'I'm afraid that I am too busy studying Muridae. The largest extant rodent family and the largest of all mammalian families. Did you know that there are over one thousand species of mice and rats? Just like the mouse that spooked your horse.'

Phineas shook his head, now remembering his early morning ride and the rodent that had run in front of his new horse, Chesapeake. 'It was a rat.'

The young woman tutted. 'The creature was not large enough to be a rat. It was a mouse. A wood mouse to be precise, also known as *apodemus sylvaticus*.'

Rubbing his eyes, Phineas could almost believe that he was still in a dream. What stylish young woman talked about rodents in Latin? He was certain that he'd never met one before and doubted he ever would again.

'Do you think that you might be able to sit up?' she asked in her sweet voice. 'I could help you.'

Leave her soft lap? *Oh, no!* Dream or not, Phineas liked being precisely where he was. 'I believe I need a few more moments to collect myself.'

Her gentle hands caressed his hair again. Despite his raging headache, he'd never felt better.

Phineas might need minutes before he could sit up.

Hours, even.

Days, if possible.

Her delicate hand touched his cheek. 'Do you remember your name, sir?'

'I am no sir.'

'A mister?'

Scowling, he shook his miserable head, making her giggle again. It was a light and lilting sound.

'A lord, then?'

'Yes.'

'Which one?' she asked, moving her hands back to his cheeks and caressing them softly. Phineas thought that he might be dead, for her touch felt divine. 'Or do you imagine that I have memorised *Debrett's* guide to the peerage?'

Clever angel.

His lips twitched. 'I hear that all debutantes do.'

'And how do you know that I am a debutante?' she countered.

He'd clearly guessed correctly. 'The Latin gave it away.'

'Truly? I speak Greek as well. But I am more interested in your name.'

Phineas rarely smiled. He never grinned. It must be his head injury from the fall, for he was grinning back at her. He hadn't given her his name, therefore she refused to give him her own. In the ten years he'd attended the London Season, no debutante had intrigued him more. Nor had they made his pulse race and his heart thud against his chest. He was half tempted to pursue her in earnest, but she would eventually bore him. Everyone did, except for his ward—she kept him perpetually on his toes.

'Very well,' he said. 'I will give you a small hint. My given name is Phineas.'

'Becca.'

'A lady?'

She raised her eyebrows and shrugged her shoulders. 'I do try to be one. Most of the time.'

He laughed, a low, unpractised sound. More air than anything else. He liked her wit almost as much as he admired her figure. He was a man after all. 'Is *lady* in your title?'

'Yes,' she said, her finger tracing the angle of his chin in a caress that sent chills down his spine. 'And it is difficult to live up to the expectations of being a duke's daughter. I inevitably disappoint people.'

Impossible.

This gloriously angelic creature with her giggles, generous curves, wicked fingers and sharp intelligence could never disappoint. But he racked his pounding brain. She was the daughter of a duke. There weren't too many dukes who had marriageable daughters. The Duke of Richmond, but this young lady did not resemble Lady Georgiana. The only other Duke whom he could think of with a great many daughters was the Duke of Hampford. But weren't they all married? He vaguely recalled that Lady Helen Stringham had wed the Earl of Inverness the year before. He'd danced with her once or twice, but he had found her to be strange and distant.

Taking a deep breath, he guessed, 'Are you a Stringham, by chance?'

She awarded him with another breathless smile that set his pulse racing even faster. 'How very clever of you, Phineas. Now I wish that I had memorised *Debrett's* so that I might be able to guess who you are.'

'Lady Rebecca Stringham,' he whispered her name, tasting it on his tongue. He liked it. He liked it a lot.

Phineas only hoped that she did not know that he had once proposed to her sister-in-law, Lady Louisa. He'd only been twenty-one at the time and in a great deal of debt. He'd planned to marry an heiress to reach solvency, but after the lady in question married a man whom she loved, he'd rethought his plans. Sweeping economies and no gaming had allowed him to rebuild his fortune and now he had a strict gambling amount that he did not go over. His other financial indulgence was his wardrobe. He would rather die than dress like a country squire. His fine clothes kept the world and polite society at a distance and that was exactly where he liked it.

'Have I rendered you speechless with my magnificence?' she asked, her eyes twinkling down at him.

'I'm still waiting for your kiss.'

Her warm grin melted his cold heart. 'My Lord, as you are well aware, there is nothing *proper* about a kiss between an unmarried lady and a lord. Besides, I don't even know your full name.'

'Kiss me properly and I will tell you.'

'You should tell me your name because I saved you,' she said pertly. 'You were a dandy in distress.'

Phineas couldn't hold back a bark of laughter. He doubted that he could play the invalid much longer, so he slowly raised his head from her lap. Alas. He would have stood up, if Becca hadn't placed a restraining hand on her shoulder.

'Give yourself a few minutes to sit before you stand,' she said. 'I shouldn't wish for you to swoon again.'

Phineas raised one eyebrow at her, giving her a quelling look that would have caused many a duchess to quake. 'Gentlemen do not swoon.'

She shrugged one lovely curved shoulder. 'So you fainted.'

'Men don't faint either.'

Pushing back a curl from her face, Becca smiled. 'If you prefer, we can say that you were rendered unconscious. Although that does sound a little bit pretentious to me.'

His lips returned to the usual sneer that he wore in public. 'I should be pretentious. I'm a lord.'

'Then be a lord and not an ass,' she said, no longer smiling at him. 'Put down that exaggerated eyebrow and stop sneering at me, Phineas. Despite not knowing your surname or full title, I am not scared or intimidated by you at all.'

He was being an ass, although, no one had ever stated it so plainly before. Phineas was used to being perceived as an indolent and fashionable fop. He preferred it that way. His sneer usually kept society from coming too close, but he knew instinctively that he didn't wish to keep Becca away. He wanted nothing more than to drag her back into his arms and kiss her until her toes curled. He noticed that she wasn't wearing one glove. He could almost feel her wicked fingers caressing his face and hair again.

'Where is your glove?'

Becca pointed at it in the mud. 'I took it off to feel your pulse. I wanted to make sure that you weren't dead. You gave me quite a shock.'

If he didn't back away from her on the grass, he would be giving her quite another shock. Gulping, Phineas managed to say, 'How thoughtful of you, but did you have to destroy my cravat?'

His teasing words did exactly what he hoped for. Becca grinned at him again.

'I was trying to help you breathe better.'

'It was a work of art.'

Phineas also noticed that his collar and shirt were unbuttoned. His clothing was never untidy in public. He was always dressed to the nines. He didn't like appearing at a disadvantage. *Ever.* His clothes were his armour. Buttoning up his shirt, he tied his cravat into a simple knot. Only a fresh, ironed cravat could be transformed into the mathematical tie. It was something he did himself, unlike most dandies whose valets arranged their neckcloths.

'Thank the heavens that you buttoned your shirt,' Becca said in a prim voice, brimming with laughter. 'You were practically *naked*, Phineas. Being a delicately raised debutante, I nearly swooned at the sight of your chest. Oh, wait, we are playing pretentious. I was nearly rendered unconscious.'

'That I do not believe,' he replied, slowly getting to his feet. 'I have heard that the Stringham children were raised like wild beasts with lions and bears.'

He offered her a hand and she took it. Standing up, she was barely shorter than him and even more generously curved than he'd first imagined. Phineas did not believe in love at first sight. What a ridiculous concept! But he was definitely attracted to her more than he recalled being to any other woman in his life. He was also intrigued by her wit, but mostly by her effervescent sense of joy. Her smile melted all the barriers around his cold heart. Becca leaned over to pick up her muddy glove and he enjoyed the view of her backside.

'And don't forget our largest pet, Sadie the Indian elephant,' Becca said. 'She is more enjoyable to ride than a horse.'

Phineas's lips twitched upwards again. 'I've been thrown by one animal already today. I do not wish to repeat the experience with an elephant.' Though truthfully, despite the terrible pain in his head, he would have happily allowed his horse to toss him off again just for the opportunity of meeting Lady Rebecca Stringham. 'Oh, there is my said horse and my groom, Ned. No doubt coming to my gallant rescue.'

He watched her face turn towards the two horses galloping their direction. 'Then you are in good hands. I should go and find Alonzo. Goodbye, Phineas.'

Turning, she started to walk away from him and instinctively he stretched out a hand and grabbed her arm. He felt a jolt of awareness throughout his entire body. Her neck swivelled to meet his gaze. 'Is something wrong, Phineas?'

Everything.

Nothing.

All he knew was that he didn't want her to leave. No one had called him Phineas since his nurse left for a new charge and he'd been sent to school at Eton. His parents had always called him by his honorary title, Viscount Biddestone. His schoolmates had nicknamed him 'Stone'. And after the carriage accident that had caused his parents' deaths, he'd become 'Lord Norwich' to his rivals and 'Norwich' to his fashionable London friends. Even his ward called him Norwich. He missed being plain old Phineas. And he particularly liked how Becca said his name. He didn't know who this Alonzo person was, but he knew that he didn't like him. The fellow should never have left Becca alone in a public park.

'I cannot leave you unattended,' he said in an undertone. 'Where is this Alonzo fellow? Is he your groom? And where is your maid, for propriety's sake?'

'Phineas, you're being a bit pretentious again,' she said, appearing amused. 'Alonzo—Mr Lawes—isn't my groom, he is my tutor. I have difficulty—difficulty reading, you see. And he left me alone because he had a romantic assignation with his secret fiancée. We left the footman and maid before we even got to the park. They are also courting. I only came along with Alonzo as a decoy and very dull it has been until the mouse spooked your horse.'

He shouldn't have felt so relieved that Alonzo was engaged to someone else. He'd only met Becca this very morning and he had no intention of marrying. His title could go to any of his second cousins after he died. He wouldn't be alive to care. Maybe he had hit his head harder than he'd suspected. His obstinance, however, was still very much intact. 'Rat. And I can assure you that I am never wrong.'

'Mouse,' she repeated, pulling out of his reach and hailing a man dressed in sober colours probably twenty yards away. 'There's Alonzo. You needn't be worried for my safety or reputation any longer. Ride home and have your servants fetch you a doctor or a physician to examine your head, Phineas.'

Becca walked a few more steps away from him. He forced himself not to follow her. He didn't want to spook her by being too forward. He was only seeking the lightest of dalliances to alleviate the oppressing boredom of late.

'Will you be assisting in a romantic assignation tomorrow morning?' he called after her.

She turned around again to meet his eyes, a lovely blush in her cheeks. 'No. My presentation to Queen Charlotte is tonight and I intend to have a nice long sleep tomorrow. What about the day after?'

Phineas found himself smiling again and was a little surprised at the young woman's daring. He supposed it was the result of her untraditional rearing—the Stringhams were known to be eccentric. Still, he'd smiled more in the last ten minutes than he had in the last ten years. 'Very well. I shall be here. Do watch out for rats, Becca.'

'Do they wear twelve-caped riding coats, Phineas?'

He threw back his aching head and laughed. He should have known she would have the last word. Phineas watched her confident stride until she reached the gentleman and he offered his arm. He groaned—he didn't like Becca touching another man. His head pounded harder than ever. As did his heartbeat.

'Are you all right, My Lord?' Ned, his groom, asked.

Stooping down, Phineas picked up his squashed beaver hat. 'Never better.'

Chapter Two

'Who was that gentleman you were walking with?' Alonzo asked.

Becca blinked her eyes and played dumb. 'What gentleman?'

Snorting, her tutor pointed at Phineas and his groom as they rode away. She couldn't help but glance one more time at Phineas's handsome frame. She wished that she knew his surname and title. He had a good seat and his riding coat looked rather magnificent with all the capes. Pinks of the *ton* were certainly delightful subjects to study.

Alonzo covered his face with his hands and groaned. 'Did he recognise you, Becca? If your mother finds out that you were alone in the public park, she will kill me. And if she doesn't, your father will. They might even dismiss me from my position.'

She tucked her arm into the crook of his elbow and patted it reassuringly. 'Nonsense. Mama will not dismiss you. How many other people do you know who earn two hundred pounds a year to be someone's friend?'

Poor Alonzo's ears turned red. They read together most mornings, but aside from that, her tutor's duties were simply to be companionable. Her parents had sensed that she needed a friend of her own age after her sister Helen's marriage and kept him on after Becca had become competent enough at reading and writing.

She couldn't blame him for being embarrassed, for he had received a double first at Oxford and was a very intelligent young man. He deserved employment more suited for his many skills and Becca believed that she had made all the progress she was going to make with her reading studies.

Alonzo shook underneath her touch. 'Your presentation to the Queen is tonight and you will no longer need a tutor for your reading. Being your friend is the best position in the world—I would do it without pay. But I shall have to look for a new position in another household. And I will miss spending time with you.'

She squeezed his arm gently. She was not ready to lose him as a friend and companion just yet. Even if she didn't quite believe Alonzo would have remained her friend without a wage.

'You're right. There is nothing to be done but to find you another position—a better one. And you'll need at least twice as much income per annum to marry your Cassandra. I shall talk to Mama about it this very afternoon. She mentioned just the other day how she needed a secretary to assist her with both her business and social duties. Would you mind working for a duchess?'

He stopped and turned to gaze at her in wonderment. 'I should be most honoured. But are you sure Her Grace would consider me appropriate for the position? I have no experience being a secretary.'

Becca started to walk again, tugging him along beside her. 'Of course she will not only consider you, she will select you. Alonzo, you've lived with my family for over a year. Don't you realise how much we all like you? And you've taught me how to read, slowly but proficiently. My parents will never forget that. You are guaranteed a position of your choice. And if you'd rather be a clergyman, a foreign diplomat, or a politician, I can assure you that Mama will make it happen.'

She observed that Alonzo's neck was now red, too. 'I am honoured by your esteem and I should like nothing better than to learn more about business from the Duchess of Hampford. She is a savant.'

They followed the path to the edge of Hyde Park where they met Miss Shepherd, Becca's lady's maid, and Jim, one of the grooms. Shepherd was slight in build with blonde hair and blue eyes. Her hair and clothing were always neat and dainty. Becca thought that Shepherd looked more like a debutante than she did. It had come as quite a shock to both of them when Shepherd became smitten with the tall and muscular Jim. He stood at least a head taller than her and was twice as broad in the shoulders. He had a shock of red hair and a smile that made all the kitchen maids giggle.

Yet her lady's maid scowled at her. 'Why is your glove dirty, my lady? And why is your dress covered in mud?'

Becca's ears felt warm and she wished she hadn't enjoyed Alonzo's discomfort quite so much. Still, she had no intention of divulging the entire truth. Certainly not about Phineas. It was rather delightful to possess a secret from her many servants and large family. 'There was a mouse.'

Sighing, Shepherd shook her head.

Becca glanced down at the walking gown and muddy glove. She wondered if they were ruined. Even if they weren't, she had given her maid more work with all the mud. 'I am sorry, Shepherd. I shall be more careful of my clothing in future. Do any of you mind if I stop in and say hello to the Duke of Glastonbury? I shan't stay for more than ten minutes.'

'Of course not,' Alonzo said.

'Anything you wish, my lady,' Jim said.

Shepherd sniffed. The mud stains were not yet forgiven. Jim nudged Shepherd with his elbow and gave her a sappy smile. 'Very well.'

The prim lady's maid would not have given in to Becca so easily without his encouragement. Love was truly a fascinating phenomenon to observe and probably even better to experience.

Becca wanted a great love like her sisters Frederica and Helen had found with their husbands. Even a forbidden love like her dear friend Alexander and Cressida's. Their attachment to each other had existed for over thirty years and it had been doomed from the very start, for Cressy was already married to the lecherous Lord Dutton. Alexander had fallen hard for her and their affair lasted over twenty years, before he fulfilled his duty as a duke and wed a younger woman to provide an heir to the Glastonbury dukedom.

Unfortunately, he had married Becca's eldest sister Mantheria and it had been nothing but unhappiness for both of them from the very first day. Her sister had loved another man and Alexander had adored another woman. Mantheria gave birth to a son and heir, Andrew. But after a few years of being married in name only, they formally separated. For the sake of their shared son, they were civil—friendly, even.

When Alexander's health had begun to deteriorate a few years before, Mantheria and Andrew had accompanied him and Lady Dutton to the sunnier climates of Italy and then the Mediterranean. Becca and Helen had been lucky enough to go with them to Greece. She'd learned so much about the animals there and become dear friends with her brother-in-law, who was thirty years her senior. He doted on her and Helen like a favourite uncle and never once told them no. A rare thing for outspoken Stringham girls.

His mistress also treated them like gold. It had been impossible not to like Cressy.

Becca held on to Alonzo's arm as their party of four walked to Lady Dutton's London town house. Jim lifted the knocker and the butler answered the door. Becca went upstairs to the family apartments and her three companions descended to the kitchen for tea and gossip with the servants of the house. She had not yet reached the top stair when she heard Cressy say, 'Oh, Becca, I am so glad that you stopped by!'

Becca climbed the last stair and was swept into a warm embrace. 'Cressy, you shouldn't hug me. I'm all muddy.'

Her older friend didn't seem to care and squeezed her even tighter. Cressy's grey and brown curls tickled her cheeks. There were dark circles under her brown eyes like bruises. 'You are just the sunlight that we needed this morning. Alexander had a difficult night.'

Wiping a tear from her own cheek, Becca asked, 'Can I see him? Is he feeling well enough for visitors?'

Cressy took Becca's hand. 'He's always well enough to see you, dear girl.'

They walked together to the master's chambers and Cressy opened the door for her, but didn't follow Becca inside. She saw that Alexander was still in his bed, not in his invalid chair, which made her fear for the worst. She walked haltingly towards the canopy bed. If he were sleeping, she did not wish to wake him up. Alexander's eyelids fluttered open. His countenance was pale, his hair now salt and pepper grey, but she could still see traces of his youthful handsomeness.

He held out a frail hand to her. 'Becca, how kind of you to come. What have you been up to, my dear friend?'

She rushed to take it in both of her hands and sat down on the chair beside the bed. 'I met a secret suitor.'

Alexander gave her a tired smile. 'Do tell.'

'Then he wouldn't be a secret any more.' And she didn't know his surname or title!

Her friend gave a short laugh. 'I promise that I won't tell anyone. Not even Cressy. Word of a duke.'

Alexander had kept her confidences before and he only gave advice when she requested it. He seemed intuitively to know when she merely wanted to be heard and when she needed help. Still, she wasn't sure that she was ready to share her secret assignation. Nor the one planned for the day after tomorrow. It was too delightful and if he thought Becca was in an unsafe situation, he might see that Mantheria or her mother stopped them. 'I don't think you'll approve, my friend, and I should hate to quarrel with you.'

'Have you told your older sisters?'

Becca shook her head. There had not been time or opportunity. Not that she would. Mantheria and Frederica treated her like a child who was unable to make her own decisions.

'What about Helen?'

'No. She doesn't arrive in London until later today. The trip from Scotland has taken nearly twice as long as they anticipated because she's expecting a baby,' Becca explained. 'Mark sent a short note to reassure us that all is well and that his wife is in a delicate state. Helen added six pages, front and back, where she catalogued her vomiting and other bodily symptoms in great detail and the measurement of her stomach. She wrote that there isn't nearly enough scientific writing on the subject of human pregnancies and she intends to rectify that.'

Alexander gave her another tired smile. 'If anyone could do that, it is our Helen. But I feel as if you are trying to divert me from our original topic. Would I know this mysterious suitor of yours?'

Phineas had to be in his late twenties, possibly as old as thirty. Alexander had been a very popular Corinthian before his health began to fail six years before and he was a duke. She was certain that their paths must have crossed.

'Probably.'

'Is he a member of the *ton*?'

Raising her eyebrows, she nodded.

Alexander released a long sigh. 'Well, at least you aren't having an assignation with a handsome footman or a lusty young groom. There is some relief in that knowledge.'

Becca couldn't help but giggle.

He shook his head against the pillow. 'Let me see. Is he a peer?'

'Yes.'

'Ring the bell for Cressy,' he said, pointing to the golden one on the bedside table.

Rushing to her feet, she released his hand. 'Has there been a change? Are you feeling unwell? Should I leave?'

'No, my dear. I am simply going to ask her to bring me a copy of *Debrett's* to help me narrow down who your mysterious suitor is. There aren't too many unmarried peers. I am certain that I will discover your amour.'

Laughing, Becca sat back down. 'You had me worried sick and I shan't let you guess who my secret admirer is. At least not yet. But I will tell you another confidence, if I may.'

'I suppose I shall accept the lesser confidence.'

Becca leaned forward, her heart beating quickly for quite another reason. 'Dear friend, how do I convince my family to treat me like a grown woman instead of a little girl who needs protecting from every gust of wind? Do you think it is because of my reading difficulties?'

Alexander closed his eyes and exhaled, shaking his head back and forth. 'No. I believe it is because you are the youngest in your family, Becca, and they are not quite ready to lose you.'

Swallowing, she tilted her head to the side. 'They won't lose me if I marry.'

One of his lips quirked up into a half-smile. 'But it will not be the same.'

She giggled again. 'I should hope not!'

He laughed, too, but closed his eyes again. Her visit must have tired him. She got to her feet and dropped a kiss on his brow. 'I shall try to stop by tomorrow, if I can.'

'I appreciate your visits, Becca. But your first Season should be all about you. Don't waste your time on a sick old man. Find a good husband and become the mistress of your own house. Then don't let anyone boss you around ever again.'

'You're my dear friend, Alexander. And I only have a few precious friends.'

'Then make more. Anyone would be blessed to call you their friend.'

If only it were so easy. As a daughter of a duke, people usually were interested in Becca's position and not in herself. And since she was bullied at school because of her plumpness and inability to read, she found it difficult to be friends with girls her age.

Despite longing for a true companion to confide in, she had always doubted the sincerity of any friendship that had been offered to her, or feared they were making fun of her behind her back. Nor did she wish for other debutantes to discover her difficulty reading and spelling. And it didn't help that her main interest was Animalia, which was not considered a suitable subject for ladies to study, as her sister Mantheria reminded her all too often.

Phineas had not seemed shocked, but rather intrigued by her knowledge about Muridae. He'd treated her as an equal and he'd been so easy to talk to. As if they were already friends. Had she met him at a ball she might have been tongue-tied, but how does one stand on ceremony with a man whose head has already rested on your lap?

Becca bid Alexander farewell and took her leave of Cressy with another hug. Alonzo, Jim and Shepherd escorted her home. She was fond of all three of them, but they were not truly her friends, for they received wages. Despite what Alexander said, Becca found it nigh impossible to talk to members from her own class of a similar age to herself.

She smiled. Except for arrogant asses named Phineas.

Shepherd stabbed another pin into Becca's tall coiffure. 'I'm finally finished. As I would have been ten minutes ago if you would have stayed still, my lady.'

Becca tried to appear chagrined and not to smirk at the reproof from her servant. 'Thank you, Shepherd.'

Her lady's maid left the room. Bouncing her knee, Becca examined her appearance. Three long pigeon feathers graced the back of her hair and made her appear taller. Her white presentation gown was worth the three hundred guineas her mother had paid for it. It was trimmed with black ribbon which brought out the blue in Becca's eyes. Unlike the prevailing fashion, the gown had a lower waist and a hooped skirt. The sleeves were three-quarter length with delicate blonde lace, the same lace that was tucked around the square neck of her bodice. The skirt was wide and intricately detailed with flounces and furbelows.

She looked at herself in the mirror as she spun around. Court style was far more flattering to Becca's fuller figure than the current fashion for empire waists. Still the black and white of the gown reminded her of a dairy cow. She mooed at her reflection and then tilted her chin up. If she could stare down a dandy, surely she shouldn't be afraid of a queen?

'You look nothing like a heifer,' Helen said from behind her.

Becca twirled to look at her sister whom she hadn't seen in nearly three months. It felt like three lifetimes. She ran to Helen and threw her arms around her. Helen was two years older than Becca and six inches shorter. Her hair was blonde and her figure was willowy. The body type that Becca wished she had, for Helen had never had to worry about eating too many sweets or fitting into her stays. Helen squeezed her tighter than a bear and Becca could feel the small bump of her sister's belly.

Helen put Becca's hand on to her stomach. 'Isn't it amazing? I'm growing a human being inside me.'

'You have always been amazing. I have missed you so much!'

Her sister gave her a sneaky smile. 'Do not worry. I have kept a very detailed journal since Christmas that you can read. It includes all of my sicknesses and I mean to publish it one day. I am beginning to find the human species nearly as interesting as reptiles. At least the small life forms.'

Grinning, Becca raised a gloved hand to her lips and feigned shock. 'No!'

Helen elbowed her in the stomach. She was the best elbower in the family and Becca yelped. 'Yes. And there is no need to moo at yourself. You look simply gorgeous and don't worry—if anyone is mean to you, I'll stick a snake down the back of their dress.'

'Even at St James's Palace?'

Her elder sister was undaunted. 'I'll shove one down Queen Charlotte's bodice if she even raises an eyebrow at you.'

Helen put her arm around Becca's waist and they left the room together. Becca didn't fear anyone or anything with her sister at her side.

'Shall we have something to eat before we go?' Helen asked. Her appetite had increased since she'd become pregnant.

Becca's stomach rumbled in nervous agreement.

They were on the way to the front parlour to call for tea when their older sisters Mantheria and Frederica caught up with them. Mantheria looked gorgeous in a champagne-coloured gown that accentuated her tiny waist and slender frame.

Frederica's dress was made of celestial blue silk with a large hooped skirt and a delicately embroidered peacock bodice. It fit her curvy frame beautifully, but her lovely sister did not look at all well. Like Helen, she was expecting a child and Frederica's countenance was pale, tinged with green. Her eyes were shadowed and her brown hair dull. She looked as if she might cast up her accounts at any moment.

'What are you two doing?' Mantheria demanded like the Duchess she was. 'Mama has already called for the carriages.'

'Ordering a small repast before we go,' Helen said, holding her belly. 'One rarely eats well at such events. We need to keep up our strength if we are to stand in line for hours at

St James's Palace for Becca to spend only a couple of minutes in front of Queen Charlotte and have her brow kissed.'

Covering her mouth with one gloved hand, Frederica nodded. 'An excellent idea.'

Touching her own far from flat stomach, Becca doubted that Frederica would be able to eat a bite, or keep it down if she did. Helen took Frederica's arm and escorted their queasy sister down the hall to the parlour. Becca was about to follow them when Mantheria touched her shoulder.

'Are you sure that you are hungry?' she asked. 'I would not eat if I were you. You don't want to need a *bordaloue* at your presentation.'

It was true that Becca did not wish to relieve herself in a small dish that was inserted underneath her large hooped skirt in the retiring room. But Mantheria had not been concerned about Helen or Frederica having to use a *bordaloue* in the retiring rooms. Just Becca. The plump sister.

Her stomach churned. Both her appetite and her anticipation for the presentation were gone. 'I shan't partake of even a bite.'

Mantheria beamed at her. 'How wise of you. And you might also want to try one of Lord Byron's methods for slimming.'

'I thought the poet was not at all the thing,' Becca retorted. Lord Byron had fled England after the failure of his marriage and rumours of an affair with his half-sister, Augusta Leigh, had circulated among society. It was even said that Mrs Leigh's daughter Medora was his child. Even in the animal world, mating with immediate family members was not acceptable.

Her eldest sister wrinkled her nose. 'I am not suggesting that you emulate his personal life, but he was very successful at slimming. Sometimes he ate only biscuits and drank soda water. Other times, he subsisted on a diet of boiled potatoes in vinegar.'

Becca would rather have died than subsist on soda water and vinegar potatoes. She disliked them both. She licked her lips ironically. 'Delicious.'

Her elder sister missed the sarcasm in Becca's tone. 'That's the spirit. You could try either method of slimming, or perhaps both. And you will fit in better with the other debutantes—so much of one's position in society is based upon one's appearance. Shall I speak to the cook for you? I am certain that she would be more than happy to provide you with those specific foods.'

Becca could have sworn that her mouth tasted like vinegar at this very moment. She forced herself to smile painfully. 'I can speak to her myself.'

But she wouldn't. She'd already limited her sweets at Mantheria's behest and she was careful not to overeat. Besides, Becca had no intention of following the advice of an inbreeding poet.

Chapter Three

Lord Phineas Adolphus Robert Howard de Courcy, Baron Goulding, Viscount Biddestone and the Earl of Norwich had never danced to the tune of a woman's bidding. Or anyone's for that matter. Since his parents' death, he'd answered to no one for his choices or his actions. Even before their death, he'd not seen much of his parents.

He'd been left home at Ridley Hall in Norwich while his parents participated in both the London Season and the little autumn one. They would usually stop for a few weeks in the summer to check on his progress, before attending parties at other grand estates. Long enough to tell him that he was too short. Too skinny. Too slow. Too stubborn. Too unsocial to make friends. Or too stupid to amount to much.

He was a disappointment to his father, a great, big fellow with a jaw like a hammer and figure like a bull. Phineas was too pretty for him. He took after his mother. The resemblance between them had been marked. Instead of endearing Phineas to her, his mother could barely endure looking at him. He was a physical reminder that she was growing older and that with every minute her great beauty was fading. He never saw her looking anything but her best. Nor without cosmetics on her face. From the perfectly arranged golden curls on her head, to her stylish gown, her jewellery, accessories, and slippers, his mother always appeared stunning.

Phineas had hated them both. Despised them as much as he wished for their elusive approval. He'd originally become a dandy to try to please his mother. Clothing and jewels were the only languages she understood. The last time he saw her alive, before he left to go to Cambridge, she'd said, 'You look rather well, Biddestone. I should not be ashamed to be seen abroad with you.' And then patted his shoulder—a rare showing of affection.

His father had merely grunted and muttered, 'Try to pass your examinations.'

He received a first at only nineteen, but his parents never saw the certificate. Or his graduation. They had died in a carriage accident only a month before. After university, he'd gone to London and joined a wild set that was always getting into trouble and kicking up a breeze. He'd even been taken under the wing of the Duke of York and nearly gamed away his entire fortune. Then Kitty had been dumped on his doorstep and Phineas had come to his senses before his 'windmill dwindled to a nutshell' as the phrase went.

He'd stopped drinking to excess, gambling beyond his budget, duelling with other bucks and behaving recklessly, but his reputation had remained tarnished. And housing a bastard child on his Winfield Park estate didn't help either. Not that he minded at the time. It had kept the matchmaking mamas away. And Phineas meant to do right by his ward and make her feel loved and wanted. Unlike his own unhappy upbringing.

In a matter of months, he'd lost his new 'friends'. Despite his parents' belief in him being stupid, he wasn't dumb enough not to realise that those young men had never been his friends in the first place. He spent nearly a year getting his affairs in order and had decided to remedy his financial distress with an heiress. After that plan did not work out, he'd focused on making his own fortune on the stock exchange. And with it, he'd tried to do some good in the world to prove to himself and to his late parents that he was not worthless.

Phineas was the sole patron of a foundling hospital and he laboured in Parliament to improve conditions for the poor. He could never forget the dirty and starving state that he'd discovered Kitty in. No child deserved to grow up like that. He didn't care that there were rumours among the *ton* that he only donated money to support his own illegitimate children. And the less Phineas cared, the more society seemed to admire him. His clothes and demeanour did the rest—no one came near enough to hurt him again.

Certainly no one told him what to do.

No one except Lady Rebecca Stringham, who made him laugh and spoke Latin.

She'd insisted that he see a doctor and he was quite certain that she would quiz him about it the next time they met. Somehow he knew that Becca would be upset if he didn't follow her express orders. And for some inexplicable reason, he didn't wish to disappoint her. Which was silly, for a duke's daughter couldn't be more than the lightest of dalliances or Phineas would find himself leg-shackled for life. And he'd seen enough of marital misery to wish to avoid it. Yet he wanted to see her again. Happiness was such a fleeting feeling in his life that he wished to experience it for a little longer.

Head pounding and a slight sneer on his lips, Phineas rang the bell for his secretary and he moved the ice pack on his head.

Mr Walkley came into the parlour a few minutes later.

The man was the same age as Phineas, but he looked older. He also dressed soberly like a country curate. Walkley wore a plain black coat and tied his cravat in a simple knot. He was, however, unfailingly honest and, for that reason, Phineas forgave the man his lack of fashion.

His secretary bowed. 'My Lord.'

Gesturing with one hand to a chair, Phineas said, 'Thank you for coming, Walkley. I had a fall and would like to consult a doctor or surgeon. Do you have someone in mind?'

'Mr Gordon is known for his studies of the brain and injuries to the head. Shall I have him call on you this afternoon?'

Phineas breathed in deeply, his nostrils flaring. Of course his secretary was aware that he had hit his head. There were no secrets in large houses. The servants knew everything. 'Please.'

The secretary cleared his throat. An ominous sign. He wished to discuss something more with Phineas.

'What else needs addressing, Walkley?' Phineas asked, trying to keep his impatience out of the tone of his voice. His head ached and he was in no mood to be polite.

Mr Walkley cleared his throat a second time. 'I have received another letter from Miss Eves, my lord. It appears that Kitty ran away again.'

Phineas touched his pounding skull. His ward, Kitty, gave him a headache on a good day and, besides meeting Becca, today was not a good day. Kitty was only eleven years old, but she was already uncontrollable. If she was dismissed from Miss Eves's school, he didn't know where he would send her. She'd already attended three other similar institutions in Bath in the last year and had been asked to leave all of them.

He cared for her deeply, but Phineas had no idea what

to do with the headstrong girl. His own parents had been awful and he was certain if he tried to play the father to his ward that it would be an unmitigated disaster. She would probably end up hating him as much as Phineas had loathed his own parents. And their true familial connection did neither of them any favours. That was why he'd instructed Kitty to never mention the name of her guardian and all of the arrangements and funds passed through his secretary and under Mr Walkley's name. He didn't want Kitty to be tarnished by the title of bastard her entire life.

'Offer Miss Eves more money,' Phineas said, massaging his temples. 'And the promise of a one hundred guineas' bonus if Kitty completes an entire term at her school.'

His secretary rose to his feet and bowed. 'I will, My Lord.'

'Thank you, Walkley.'

The man bowed awkwardly and then left the room.

Phineas flinched when the door closed. What was he going to do with his ward if Miss Eves didn't take the bribe? Kitty was running out of options of schools in Bath near his Winfield Park estate, where she had grown up. He was trying to do his best by her, but his best was obviously lacking. Phineas couldn't help but believe that his parents' estimation of him was more accurate than he'd like—he was worthless. A handsome shell with nothing inside.

Tonight would be Becca's presentation to Queen Charlotte. Despite his miserable head and aching body, Phineas was more than half tempted to show up at St James's Palace and see Becca in her presentation gown. He was certain she would look magnificent in it.

But no. If they were formally introduced, then she would know his name, title, and her family would tell her about his terrible reputation—that he mostly deserved. Phineas would keep his assignation with her the day after tomorrow. He didn't want to make even one wrong step with her. Which was the reason he would even allow himself to be quacked by Mr Gordon.

It wasn't until he had left his third gaming hell of the evening that Phineas admitted to himself how very dull his life had become. Every card game, every room, every person seemed exactly the same. Of course, their features varied as did the stakes. But gambling no longer thrilled him the way it once did.

Since he'd recovered his fortunes after nearly losing his shirt, Phineas had given himself a strict gambling budget of one thousand pounds. He kept his winnings in a separate bank account with the promise to himself that if he ever lost it all, he would stop wagering. In nine years, he'd won and lost that thousand pounds dozens of times. At the moment, his gaming account had over seven thousand pounds in it. A few years ago he'd had an amazing run of luck.

There used to be a thrill in winning.

A stab of disappointment in losing.

And now there was nothing.

At least, he had secured two more Parliamentary votes for his increased funding bill for foundling hospitals. Unsurprisingly, most gentlemen and lords did not want their name attached to a building that housed illegitimate children. Society seemed to think that a man would only contribute to the welfare of a babe if they were of his own blood, instead of having an innate decency to provide for those who couldn't care for themselves and a realisation that every life had worth.

He had not yet reached the age of thirty and found himself discontented and bored with his privileged life. He would order a new coat tomorrow from Weston, but he wasn't sure that would help either. He could find female companionship, but such a thought paled when compared to Lady Rebecca Stringham.

She had been so very much alive.

And she had so many delightful curves that could keep him well occupied for hours, days, possibly even weeks before he grew tired of her. Not that he would get to explore them. He was a gambler and not a fool. Lady Rebecca Stringham would be a peer's wife and Phineas was not looking for a wife. He was already a disappointment to his ward. He did not wish to fail another woman in his life.

He gave his hat and his gloves to the maître d' and entered Watier's club. Only dandies of the highest calibre were allowed inside its hallowed walls. They also played cards for high stakes at Watier's—it was a good thing that Phineas had been lucky of late or he would not have been able to join the table. He doubted that number would be as high after this visit.

'By Jove, Norwich,' St Albyn said, hailing him. 'That new quizzing glass is a work of art.'

Phineas fumbled with the diamond-studded glass and brought it up to his left eye and examined his old acquaintance with it. St Albyn's own raiment was nothing to sneeze at. His collar points were so high that he could not turn his chin from side to side. His crimson coat and striped waistcoat in the same colour were truly stunning. He held a matching pink snuffbox with a little silver shovel—his new affectation.

'Yet you still eclipse me. Unfair.'

St Albyn's cheeks flushed slightly, but he didn't smile. Dandies never did. They only smirked. He pointed a fashionable leg with a polished crimson shoe and a pink diamond belt buckle. 'The latest style from France. Are you burning with jealousy?'

Boredom was more accurate. But Phineas smirked, nodded his head and joined the next game of cards. He didn't leave the club until he was two thousand pounds poorer and three additional lords had pledged to vote for his foundling bill. Sighing, he calculated that he needed at least two dozen more peers for it to pass.

Chapter Four

Alonzo kept gazing around the park like a hunter looking for his prey.

'I am sure Miss Betrump is coming,' Becca assured him, patting his arm. 'She has probably only been delayed by a few minutes. And you can tell her the wonderful news about your position and the salary which enables you to finally marry.'

He stopped mid-path and looked both ways. 'What if she has been caught?'

Becca did not think this very likely. Miss Betrump was the fifth child of seven daughters. Her father was a baronet in financial difficulties and, as far as Becca could tell, he was not the brightest coin in the treasure box. Otherwise, he would have learned about his daughter's five-year secret engagement before now. As the son of a vicar, even the second, Alonzo was not a bad match for Miss Betrump. Even if she was the daughter of a baronet, she possessed no dowry. It was unlikely that she would receive another more advantageous offer when all her father owned were debts.

The young woman in question stepped out of the trees with her ever-present maid—a dour woman of uncertain age.

Becca pointed in her direction. 'There she is with her maid, Alonzo.'

The look of concern on his face vanished into the most adorable sappy smile. 'Isn't she the very picture of beauty?'

'She is,' Becca lied. Miss Betrump had dark blonde hair and her facial features were sharp like a ferret's. She also seemed to think very highly of herself and her manners were haughty rather than friendly.

He dropped her hand and took a few long steps in the direction of his beloved. 'Are you sure that you do not wish to join us? Your parents think that I have accompanied you to the park as well as Jim and Miss Shepherd. What if a stranger should approach you?'

She was sincerely hoping that a stranger *would* approach her. One who dressed like a dandy and had the face of a golden Greek god. 'Do not worry, my dear friend. I shall be perfectly safe. My sister-in-law, Lady Trentham, taught me how to wield a dagger. If I am overtaken by brigands, I shall put up a good fight.'

Becca walked away from the star-crossed lovers. And if her own step increased in speed, it had nothing to do with a handsome and elusive lord whose title she didn't know. It was important for all animals, including humans, to get proper exercise. She enjoyed riding, but poor Alonzo did not have a very good seat on a horse. Hence, he preferred to travel by foot. And walking was her second favourite type of exercise. She loved being outside at Hampford Castle. Her family's main estate was very large and she enjoyed roaming around the woods, finding mice and squirrels and observing the order of nature.

Every animal seemed to understand its place and purpose. She only wished that she was as certain about hers. As the youngest daughter of a duke, she was expected to marry a man of rank and fortune. Then provide the peer with heirs. It all felt rather too similar to the life of a breeding mare.

But Becca was no horse.

She would not wed simply to meet societal expectations.

Time passed and she did not see Phineas. Becca was silly to think that he'd actually intended to meet with her in the park this morning. The dandy was probably still asleep in his bed and when he finally woke up at noon, or another decadently late hour of the day, he would laugh at the mousy young debutante's foolishness.

Becca had risen early and had her maid arrange her curls becomingly with her white chip hat. When she'd met him the first time, Becca hadn't bothered to do more than pull her hair into a loose chignon at the back of her head. But there was nothing loose in Phineas's appearance. Even after he'd been thrown from a horse, his hair and clothing were perfect. Blushing, she remembered running her hands through his curls, feeling for a bump. She had mussed his hair, but he'd still looked as handsome as sin.

Much too beautiful for the likes of herself.

Clutching her bag closer to her navy pelisse, Becca turned to walk back to where she had left Alonzo, Miss Betrump and her maid. She hoped that Miss Betrump would finally agree to let Alonzo ask her father for permission to set a wedding date.

She'd taken only three steps when she heard a voice call out, 'Watch out for rats, Lady Rebecca.'

Pivoting on one boot, she twirled back to see Phineas striding towards her at a steady pace. He didn't run to meet her, but she supposed that dandies never ran. It might mess up their intricate cravats and windswept curls. Phineas certainly looked perfect and even more handsome than he had before. He was wearing a close-fitting lavender coat that must have taken two servants to squeeze him into. His snowy white cravat was in a different style today, one just as complicated as the style she'd untied when they first met. His yellow pantaloons were also contoured to his slight and muscular frame and his Hessian boots shone as they had the day before.

He took out his quizzing glass from his pocket and peered at her through it. An ornate little piece encircled with diamonds. His beautiful thin lips turned upwards, sneering slightly.

Becca was ready to sink into the mud with her glove from two days before. Why had the gentleman come to meet her, if he only wanted to mock her? Why had she awoken early to meet with such a man? How young and foolish she had been.

Swallowing, Becca tried not to be a mouse. 'Don't be a rat. Either smile at me, Phineas, or I am going home. It's much too early in the morning for sneers.'

He dropped his quizzing glass. The edges of his lips quirked upwards in a reluctant smile that warmed her heart. He took her hand into his own and kissed the top of her glove before releasing it. Becca felt the blood rush to her face as she remembered his head lying in her lap and touching his hair with her fingers. She experienced similar symptoms to the day before last: her body felt overheated, her breath quickened and her pulse would have won any race.

'You look beautiful this morning, Lady Rebecca.'

She liked how her full name sounded on his lips. Silly girl that she was, she liked everything about the stranger. 'I'm sorry if I was snappish, My Lord. I thought perhaps that you had come to mock me and I couldn't endure it.'

His eyes widened slightly and she could have lost herself in their pale blueness. 'Why did you think I would mock you?'

Lowering her head, Becca could no longer meet his eyes. 'You were sneering at me, my lord. And I will not put up with any unkindness.'

'Call me Phineas. And I did not mean to be unkind. I sneer at everyone. It isn't personal.'

She shook her head, her gaze still on her kid leather boots. 'It is to me. I had a rather terrible time at school years ago. I was bullied so badly that my brother Wick came and rescued me. I learned more at home anyway. My governess was very supportive of my naturalist studies.'

'Of mice?'

'They are much nicer than rats and less prone to carry diseases,' Becca admitted.

Phineas didn't answer immediately. Instead, he took her hand and tucked it under his arm. Becca liked touching him. The sinuous strength of his forearm. As she stood close to him, he smelled of musk, leather and spice. She wondered if he was wearing one of her mother's colognes. The Duchess of Hampford owned the most exclusive perfume shop on Bond Street: Duchess and Co. It was the sort of shop she thought a dandy would be a patron of.

'I was bullied at school, too,' he admitted in an attractively low voice, with no hint of superciliousness. 'I was small and the other boys said that I looked like a girl. They would trip me in the halls, push me on the stairs and punch me in the dormitories. I had never been more miserable in my life and I wanted to go home badly. But I had no elder brother to rescue me. I wrote a pleading letter to my father and his reply was only two words: *Toughen up*. He thought sending me to school would make a man out of me.'

Becca scoffed, shaking her head. 'Being bullied does not make one tough, it makes you miserable.'

He stopped and turned his body slightly so that he could look her in the eye. 'A few months later, a new student arrived and the bullying stopped.'

'Who?'

'Lord Charles Stringham. Being silly boys, we called him "Stringy" because he was so thin and tall. He made it clear that he was my friend and no one wanted to fight with his older brothers.'

Wick and Matthew.

Becca barely remembered her late brother Charles. Her eyes filled with water and a tear slid down her cheek. He had died of scarlet fever when she was only three years old. And she didn't know if the few memories she had of him were from the stories her siblings told or if she truly did remember her brother.

She wiped the second tear away with her free gloved hand. 'I was so little when Charles died. One of the only memories that I can picture is him putting me on top of our elephant Sadie. He loved her so much and he taught Sadie how to do tricks, such as putting on her own cloak and how to wash her house.'

Another tear escaped her eyes and, before she could wipe it away with her glove, Phineas was gently dabbing her cheeks with his handkerchief. It was white, lacy and fancy enough for any dandy. There was also a very decorative N embroidered in the corner of it. He was all sartorial splendour and she was the sort of girl who was constantly dishevelled with her hem covered in mud.

'Charles was a good friend to me. He used to tell the funniest stories of his nemesis—a mean swan that he called Satan. It chased him around and tried to bite him.

He would have all the boys in the dormitory laughing. He made friends easily, but I have never been one to let down my guard. I suppose that is one of the reasons I don a sneer in public. It keeps people away from me.'

A sneer was certainly an effective social shield. No one wished to be a figure of fun. Nor did Phineas's sardonic gaze inspire one to share their confidences.

'Isn't it lonely?'

He lightly brushed the handkerchief against her opposite cheek. 'I like being by myself, which is fortunate, because after Charles died, I did not make a new friend, although I was not bullied any more. It was not until I left school that I found companionship among the dandy set. But while their clothes are sharp, so are their tongues. One has to be careful not to expose oneself to ridicule.'

Her father had once said that London was a den of vipers. A statement that her snake-obsessed sister Helen had found fascinating. She loved snakes and poisonous ones even more. Her slithering pets often ate Becca's mice. Becca wondered how society could function when everyone was trying to bite each other—or swallow each other whole and digest their prey slowly.

'I do not think I could be a dandy,' Becca whispered. 'So if you wish to be my friend, you cannot raise your quizzing glass at me and you must smile. Not sneer. And I will not shrink like a lady from a social cut, I will probably swear like a man and my mama will not be best pleased.'

Phineas gave a breathy laugh. 'I can promise you not to sneer, but I am not much for smiles—you made me laugh more the other morning than I have in my entire life.'

'It could have been your head injury.'

'Per your instructions, I saw a physician. A Mr Gordon, who is a brain specialist, and he said that I am as fit as a fiddle.'

'And twice as handsome.' Those words escaped her lips before she could stop them. She felt her cheeks grow hot. Her eyes fell to his mouth. His lips were the perfect shade of pink—not feminine, but not so pale that they were lost in his complexion. She wondered how they would feel against hers. Would they feel soft or rough? Dry or wet?

'Becca, you flatter me.'

'I dare say that I am not the first person to do so. You are a very fine specimen.'

Phineas chuckled again. 'You make me sound like a four-legged beast.'

'Four-legged beasts can be fearsome. But I have discovered that two-legged beasts are twice as dangerous, for they use their tongues as well as their claws to injure.'

'Are you thinking about my tongue, Becca?'

She found herself blushing furiously. She was *now*. Phineas was clearly much better at flirting than herself. 'It is certainly a wicked one!'

'I would be more than happy to give you a demonstration.'

'I dare say it would be quite the education,' Becca parried, although she was more than half tempted to allow him to. 'No doubt you are a notorious rake. The sort that matchmaking mamas warn their daughters against.'

Her words must have hit close to the mark, for Phineas blanched and was quiet for several moments. 'My reputation is perhaps worse than I deserve. Although, like any human I have made many mistakes.'

'I would happily be the judge of your past sins if you gave me your name.'

Phineas shook his head with another smile. 'I am not ready for our little game to be over yet.'

'Neither am I,' Becca admitted easily. 'You did give me a clue earlier and I am tempted to go home and look up the titles of lords that start with the letter N, since you had such a lovely embroidered letter N on your handkerchief.'

'Have you thought of any N titles yet?'

'Nincompoop.'

He barked out a loud laugh. 'I am afraid not.'

'Notorious.'

'That one is slightly better.'

'Nonesuch.'

'I like that one.'

'Shall I call you Lord Nonesuch?'

He stopped and turned to her, forcing Becca to look at his full handsomeness. 'I prefer Phineas from your lovely lips.'

She let go of her hold on his arm. 'And my *tongue*?'

Phineas threw back his head and laughed. It was no longer breathy, but deep and full. Becca saw Alonzo walking towards them from a distance. She didn't want him to identify her secret suitor. The mystery was as tantalising as their secret meetings.

'I must go. My mother's new secretary awaits. Shall I see you tomorrow morning in the park?'

He took her hand and lifted it slowly to his lips, his eyes never leaving hers. There was a vulnerability in his expression that she had not seen before. Not even when he'd awoken in a strange woman's lap. 'Do you want to see me again, Lady Rebecca?'

Becca found her neck growing quite hot. She didn't wish to appear too eager, but she did want to meet him again.

'My eyes do desire to see you, but my tongue is entirely indifferent.'

'Because I have yet to give it an education.'

'Or a reputation. Adieu, Phineas.'

She hurried past him, content with her last repartee. She was slightly out of breath by the time she reached Alonzo. He fidgeted his hands and appeared to be quite agitated. 'We are going to be home late and your mother will suspect something.'

Becca scrunched her nose. 'She will not. If I appear guilty, Mama will think that I am simply covering for you, or Jim and Miss Shepherd. That's the good thing about being the obedient daughter, no one expects you to behave badly.'

She put her hand through his arm and they began to walk home at a quick pace.

'I shall lose my new position if the Duchess discovers that you are secretly meeting a stranger.'

Patting his arm comfortingly, Becca changed the subject, 'We are not in trouble yet. How did your own assignation go?'

'Miss Betrump has given me permission to ask her father for his consent to our engagement.'

'You have my congratulations, Alonzo. You are about to become a tenant for life!'

Alonzo smiled, but Becca's mind was on quite a different man. A stranger who was so handsome and witty that he made her heart palpitate. One who she very much hoped would be walking the park tomorrow morning.

Becca was almost as excited for their family dinner this evening as she had been to meet with her secret suitor. She was the youngest of six living children and so she had watched one by one as her dear brothers and sisters left to make homes of their own.

Mantheria had been the first to leave with Alexander, Duke of Glastonbury. They separated three years later, around the same time that Wick married Louisa. Then Matthew fell for Nancy. Frederica married her childhood enemy Samuel. And last year, her dearest and closest sister Helen had fallen for Mark, a Scottish earl. And despite promising to live near Becca always, she'd moved to Scotland.

From six children at home to only one in the castle had been a lonely change for Becca. Her parents were loving and wonderful. Papa showered even more praise and attention on her. As did her mama. But it wasn't the same. Her siblings had flown the nest and Becca longed to as well. Not that she didn't love Hampford Castle, but she wished for a home of her very own where no one would treat her like a little sister. Where she would be the mistress and everyone would take orders from her, rather than tell her what to do.

Frederica and Samuel were staying with them at Hampford House for the Season, but Becca didn't see her sister as often as she'd like to. Frederica was a mother and spent a great deal of her time with her son Arthur. And when she wasn't with her son, she was working with Mama at her perfume business which she would one day inherit.

Her eldest brother Wick and his wife Louisa were the first family members to arrive. Wick had the same shade of brown hair as Becca and had always been her champion. He'd saved her from the bullies at school and found her the perfect governess. His wife, Louisa, was a lovely redhead. Her skin was covered in a dusting of red freckles that reminded Becca of a speckled egg. Becca eagerly hugged them both. Wick had always been her favourite brother because he spoiled her with kittens and presents.

Wick stepped back from her. 'No jewels this evening?'

Shaking her head, Becca laughed. 'It's an informal family dinner.'

'But you are a debutante now,' her brother said, pulling a double string of pearls out of his pocket and handing it to her. 'You should always wear jewels.'

She gasped as she touched the beautiful pearls with her fingers. They were exquisite and expensive. 'I love them.'

'Allow me,' Louisa said, taking the necklace back and then clasping it around Becca's neck. They lay perfectly above her gown, but not too high and tight so that she felt as if she were choking. 'And here are the matching earrings.'

Becca was grateful that her sister-in-law helped her put those on, too. They both matched her blue-and-white-striped gown perfectly.

'There,' Louisa said when she was finished. 'Doesn't she look beautiful?'

Wick smiled at both his sister and his wife. 'Becca has always been beautiful.'

The sincerity of his words touched her heart. Her brother had never once suggested that she try 'slimming'. Or that there was anything deficient with her intelligence despite her difficulty reading. Wick was a dear.

Wiping a single tear from her eye with her glove, Becca sniffed. 'Thank you both so very much. You didn't have to give me anything. It isn't my birthday.'

Louisa put her arm around Becca's shoulders for a half-hug. 'We wanted to celebrate your first Season with you.'

Wick's hands formed into fists. 'And frighten off any man who is unworthy of you.'

Becca laughed, but she knew that her brother was not joking. Wick tended to be a bit overprotective. If he had his way, no gentleman would come within five feet of Becca.

Which would make dancing very difficult and discussion impossible.

Helen and her husband Mark arrived next. Her sister immediately noticed the beautiful new pearls. 'How lovely.'

Becca couldn't resist touching them with her fingertips. 'Wick and Louisa gave them to me.'

'And what did you bring for Becca, Helen?' Wick teased from behind her.

Her sister shrugged her shoulders. 'My presence is present enough.'

And everyone laughed.

Once Mantheria, Matthew and Nancy arrived, they all sat down to dinner. Her family had barely started their first course when Mantheria began offering unsolicited advice. 'If I were you, Becca, I would not tell a gentleman about your difficulties reading. Not until you are certain of his suit. You would not wish for him to spread unflattering rumours about you.'

Becca had already told Phineas, but felt instinctively that he would keep her confidences. Her very own Lord Nonesuch. 'Yes, Mantheria.'

'And perhaps don't talk about mice either,' Frederica chimed in. 'Especially at your coming-out ball. Reserve such exciting titbits for the eighth or ninth encounter with a gentleman. Once he already knows and adores you the way we do, I am certain that he would not be put off by your rodent obsession.'

'He still might,' Helen said with her typical brutal honesty. 'But if he is, then he was not worthy of you anyway.'

Mantheria gave their sister a quelling look. 'We are only suggesting that Becca does not scare off her suitors.'

Unperturbed, Helen lifted up her glass as if to toast.

'I scared off all of my suitors and I still married the right man. I am certain that there is another such man and that our dear youngest sister does not need any help attracting him. Becca is beautiful and wonderful. She will be beset with suitors.'

Becca's heart warmed at Helen's defence—she only wished that *she* had stood up for herself.

Matthew hit his knife against his goblet. 'Here! Here! Becca will be the most sought-after debutante of the Season and Papa will have to scare the suitors off with one of his many pets. I suggest the caracal.'

Her eldest brother Wick tapped the table as if to silence the rest of his wild siblings. 'Mama, who are the catches of the Season?'

Her mother dabbed her napkin at the sides of her lips. 'Lord Talbot as a marquess is perhaps the most eligible, but there is also Baron Whitehurst, who has the larger fortune.'

'Terrence?' Becca said. 'I hope that he doesn't still pick his nose.'

Helen snorted and her husband Mark laughed before covering his mouth with his napkin.

Becca set down her fork. 'He followed Frederica around like a puppy with his tongue sticking out.'

Frederica giggled this time.

'That was nearly ten years ago,' their mother said with the dignity of a duchess. '*Lord Talbot* is of a proper age with an excellent reputation, he is good looking, in possession of several fine estates and a healthy yearly income that no mother would sneeze at.'

'A father might,' Papa added, winking at Becca. She couldn't help but think that Phineas had a bad reputation. Her family would not like that at all.

'Theophilus, do not start,' Mama said, a touch of exasperation in her tone. 'We all know that you don't want Becca to get married, but she has turned twenty and is ready to try her wings.'

'She can try her wings without a husband,' Papa continued obstinately. 'I dare say she would fly faster, higher and further without one.'

Becca was certain that her father would be in trouble later. Mama signalled for the butler to refill the drinks and for the second course to be brought round. She loved all of her family so dearly, but she wished that they would stop giving her unsolicited advice. And it appeared that her mother unfortunately favoured Terrence's suit. Becca wondered what she would think of Phineas.

If Phineas wished to court her, that was. Becca didn't know what his intentions were, or if he had any at all. With that melancholy thought she chewed the piece of broccoli until it was mush in her mouth.

Chapter Five

Phineas hadn't intended on being late the morning before. He'd underestimated how much time it would take to walk from his London house to the park. He almost always rode or drove his phaeton. His fashionable clothes were best seen from a height. Nor did he wish to appear sweaty or windswept in public. He had a reputation as a dandy of the first consequence to maintain. A social distance to protect.

However, he hadn't wished to be burdened with a horse or a groom when he met Becca, but now he worried that Becca would already be gone by the time that he arrived on foot. In the past, Phineas would have considered missing an appointment with a beautiful woman to increase her interest in him. Flirting was a game of chess after all. But she wasn't a widow or a lightskirt and he feared that she might withdraw and not keep on playing.

He didn't want their little game to stop. Becca surprised him. He couldn't recall being so smitten with a woman since he was a young man, new to London. She made him laugh with her witty words and he enjoyed gazing at her lovely figure. He wouldn't mind doing a bit more than simply looking, but she was a duke's daughter and anything more would require him to make an offer. And if his parents had taught him anything, it was that marriage was misery once the initial lust had passed.

Yet there was something about her that made him want to confide in her. Becca's boldness? Her honesty? And he hadn't confided in anyone since her brother Charles had died nearly seventeen years ago. He'd certainly never told another soul that he'd been bullied at school.

Phineas wondered if the feeling of comfort he felt in her presence was because of her connection to Charles. But he knew the rest of the Stringham family and he had no such similar experience with the other members. Lord Cheswick despised him for courting his wife for her money. He did business with Lord Trentham, but they were not friends. He had danced with all of Becca's sisters and none of them had inspired anything in him besides alleviating the boredom of a ball.

He'd never shared his past with any of his mistresses either. Their connections had always been merely on the physical level. To be enjoyed and quickly forgotten. And not even the most beautiful widow or expensive *incognita* had ever made him feel the way Becca did. Certainly not this warmth that spread through his chest at just the sight of her.

Becca looked exceptionally lovely this morning in a chip bonnet and pale pink spencer. Phineas's lips twitched and he gave her a full smile. Her cheeks turned rosy as he approached her and made her appear even more beautiful.

Phineas took one of her gloved hands and bowed over it. 'Lady Rebecca.'

'Lord Nonesuch.'

He couldn't help but grin at her again. He could get used to smiling. And Phineas was more aware than ever of her luscious curves and recently bitten lips. 'We had better start walking, for if we don't, I will push you against that tree and kiss you senseless.'

'I dare say that I should like that very much—if only I knew your surname.'

Shaking his head, he laughed and offered his arm. He was enjoying their little game and he didn't want her to know that he had proposed marriage to her sister-in-law. 'Oh, Becca. So should I. But I am not yet ready to tell you my name and I have at least fifty questions to ask you about yourself.'

'Only fifty,' she said, attempting to scowl at him and failing miserably. 'I should think I was a fascinating enough individual to warrant at least twice as many questions.'

Phineas unconsciously moved closer to her and bumped into something large in her reticule. 'What did you bring with you?'

She opened it up to reveal a book.

'I thought that reading was difficult for you.'

Swallowing, Becca nodded. 'It is. But this book had two purposes. One, to hit anyone if they approach me. I wasn't entirely sure that you would come this morning and I'm quite far from where I left Alonzo.' He frowned at her words. She opened the book and pulled out a loose sheet of paper tucked into the first page. 'And two, I brought a sketch for you. A little present. Not that you have to take it, or like it. Or—'

He pressed a gloved finger to her lips and Becca stopped her disjointed speech. 'I would treasure any gift from you.'

Breathing in deeply, she turned over the caricature and handed it to him. Phineas touched the edges of the paper as if it were a delicate document that should be handled with care. He gasped as he recognised himself.

'You drew me as a lion.'

She raised her eyebrows. 'But a very well-dressed one.'

Phineas laughed softly, more air than sound. 'I confess, I have never seen a handsomer lion. I am flattered. Do you often turn people into animals in your drawings?'

Becca glanced down at the ground as if embarrassed. 'Usually. My pencil seems to prefer caricatures to more detailed and serious sketches. The first day that I met you, you reminded me of a lion basking in the sun... As I have already confided in you, I had great difficulty learning how to read. The only way I could communicate with my family was by my drawings.

'When I begged Wick to take me out of the girls' school, I wrote only four words, three of them misspelled: *Plees tak me hom.* But it wasn't my words that brought him the next morning to Bath in a chaise and four, but the sketches that I sent him. I heard it said once that every painting tells a story.'

'Your sketches certainly do,' he said, more than a little amused that she'd drawn him as a lion. Still, it was very recognisably himself: his eyebrow raised, his quizzing glass and a sardonic look on his face.

Becca's neck turned pink and Phineas thought how much he'd like to kiss her there. 'I drew myself as well. Between your feet. I am the mouse. And if you look closely, you can see a snake and a spider in the grass. I always draw my sisters in every sketch that I make.'

He took out his quizzing glass to study her sketch closer. 'Ah, I can see both Lady Inverness and Lady Pelford, but not, I fancy, Lady Glastonbury.'

'Oh, no. I never draw Mantheria. She married when I was just a girl. Besides, she wouldn't appreciate or approve being included in my drawings. She's terribly top-lofty and a stickler for the rules of society. And she does not like mice. Especially the naughty kind that get into places and things that they are not supposed to.'

'The Duchess is not alone in her lack of preference for the Muridae family of species,' he said drolly, causing her to giggle charmingly.

Becca scrunched her nose. 'Do you not like mice?'

He touched the tip of her nose with his gloved finger. 'I like one mouse very much.'

'Maybe I shall push *you* against a tree and kiss *you* senseless.'

Her words surprised him so much that he laughed loudly. Phineas had known many women, some of them exceptionally clever, but none who made him laugh the way Becca did. She was pure joy. Again, he was more than half tempted to let her try. But even in an empty park, there was always someone watching and the Duke of Hampford would not stand idly by if his daughter was compromised. Nor would her large brothers.

It was time for safer subjects. 'Now to those fifty questions. What is your favourite colour?'

'Violet. And yours?'

'Seafoam.'

Becca shook her curls. 'You're being pretentious again, Phineas. You should have simply said green.'

Another laugh escaped his lips. 'Green it is. And your favourite game?'

'Whist. So only play me for small stakes or be prepared to lose heavily.'

'I believe that I have already lost something to you.'

'And what is that?'

'My heart.'

Phineas had expected her to blush prettily at his exaggerated compliment, not to chuckle loudly.

'I suppose that I shall accept your heart, but I was hoping for your wicked tongue. You shameless flirt!'

It was his turn to laugh. He wasn't sure that a hardened rake like himself even had a heart. Becca was right to call him on his overly flirtatious words. 'Perhaps we should stay away from speech about anatomy. What is your favourite dance?'

'The Roger de Coverley,' she said with a glowing look at him that made Phineas feel rather overheated in his coat. 'I shall not ask yours for I am certain that it is the waltz.'

It was.

'Am I a fribble that is so easily seen through?'

'You're a flirt and possibly a rake. The most scandalous dance is the waltz and therefore it would be your favourite.'

She was not wrong. Yet her honest words grated on him. Phineas truly did wish to know her better. Not merely as a passing dalliance, but perhaps as a friend. He would not tempt fate with something more. He felt at ease in her company and confidences, if only he didn't wish to kiss her so much.

'And you are a scandalous Stringham,' he parried. 'Which sibling are you the closest to?'

'My sister Helen, Lady Inverness. We are two peas in a pod. We both love the natural sciences. And you? Do you have many siblings, Phineas?'

As far as he knew, Phineas had seven half-siblings that he'd paid off after his father's death. The brothers emigrated to America. The sisters, save the youngest, were all married. But it wouldn't surprise him if another one turned up demanding money. His father had been all too free with his favours among the lower classes and he had taken no precautions to prevent baseborn children.

'Alas, I am an only child.'

'Poor Phineas,' she said, patting his arm. 'How lonely your childhood must have been.'

She had no idea just *how* lonely and Phineas wasn't about to enlighten her about his horrible experiences growing up with his narcissistic and critical parents.

'Your favourite ice?'

'I adore them all, except for parmesan. The texture is not quite right and it's rather savoury. And you?'

The only thing Phineas was interested in licking at the moment was Becca. Her hand tightened on his arm and his body ached for her touch. He'd never been more tempted to test fate. Phineas needed to cool down. He forced his eyes to focus on the Serpentine and not the beautiful woman beside him. 'Do you like to swim?'

'Yes, we have a lovely river by our castle,' she said, sticking her nose up in the air a little. 'And you?'

Picturing Becca swimming had not cooled his ardour and Phineas regretted asking her the question and tried to change the subject. 'Occasionally. Who is your favourite artist?'

Becca glanced down, away from his amorous gaze. 'I know that I am supposed to say Gainsborough or perhaps an Italian classical artist like Leonardo da Vinci or Michelangelo, but truthfully, I adore the satirical sketches of the late Mr James Gillray. They are rude, funny, often naughty and always sharp. The images say so much and they are only accompanied with a few choice words which are easy to read and understand, even for someone like myself who has difficulty reading.'

He felt his own colour rise. By her embarrassed manner, he assumed that Becca felt insecure about her learning difficulties which made her appreciate the caricaturist's works that didn't need words. He felt privileged to receive her confidences. With his pointer finger, he tipped her lovely chin up so that her eyes met his. 'Never underestimate how brilliant you are, Becca. I wish the entire world was more like you.'

'Phineas—'

His name on her lips was almost more than his self-control could handle. He imagined angling his mouth to her red lips and gathering her closely into his arms. Her soft form would meld like hot candle wax to his as he pressed her magnificent breasts closer to him and deepened the kiss.

He was so lost in his fantasy that he didn't hear her next words. All he could do was ask another question. 'Who is your favourite composer?'

Becca blinked at him.

'Someone who writes music,' he explained.

Swallowing, Becca gave him a little scowl. 'I am not an ignoramus. I know what a composer is. I was just thinking, which is very hard to do with you being so close to me.'

'Would you like me to let go?'

Her grip on his arm tightened. 'No. But you already know that.'

Phineas grinned. He would have been loath to let her go. He'd only been jesting with her a little. Presumably he would be living without her very soon, since he did not plan to offer her marriage. When he grew bored of her, Phineas would leave her slightly wiser, but her reputation unharmed. Becca would give her hand to another man. A worthier one.

Her lady's maid had arranged Becca's hair beautifully, but Phineas wished to see it down in all its shiny glory. A view only a lover would have. 'Still thinking of a composer?'

She shook her head slightly and said pertly, 'I do not think that my brain has had anything to do with our conversation this morning.'

'I would kiss your brain if I could.'

'I don't think that would help it work any better,' Becca

said, pressing her cheek briefly against his shoulder. 'Your proximity is the problem. Are all rakes as distracting as you?'

'Not at all. I am a special case.'

Licking her lips, Becca said in a rather breathless voice, 'Mozart. Particularly his opera *The Magic Flute*. I adore the Queen of the Night in all her dark majesty and her aria is one of the most transcendent pieces of music that I have ever heard.'

Phineas loved music, particularly Mozart. However, Becca's choice of the villain's aria was a fascinating thing to understand about her. He would have assumed she preferred the hero, Tamino, or the heroine, Pamina. But no. She liked the powerful dark Queen whose song was one of the most difficult pieces of music for sopranos to sing. Not even the most talented female voices could always hit the keys in the highest register. It was a song written for the angels.

'Do you sing?'

'A little,' Becca said, her voice not quite as breathless as before. Nor was her delicious chest rising up and down as quickly.

'Do you play the pianoforte?'

She twisted her hands together. 'I couldn't read words when I was a child, let alone musical notes. Do you play?'

'I enjoy playing the pianoforte,' Phineas said, his own voice not quite as deep as he'd like it to be. 'I even like to compose a little. That's not something I typically share with others. I thought you deserved one of my secrets since you shared one of yours.'

Her hands stilled. 'Thank you for trusting it with me. Your confidences are always safe.'

'As are yours in my care.'

The air was charged like a summer sky after a lightning storm. He could feel the electricity between them. If Phineas wasn't careful they would both be singed. He took another step back from her, breaking their connection. 'Shall we check on Mr Lawes?'

She gave a jerky nod and walked past him. Phineas followed behind her, but didn't attempt to offer his arm again. They both needed to calm down.

Becca and Phineas had nearly reached where she'd left Alonzo and his betrothed, but she was not ready to part with him yet. Becca touched his muscular arm and she felt a tingle of electricity move from her fingers up her arm. 'My sister Helen is hosting a soirée tonight for naturalists to discuss the fossils purchased by Lieutenant Colonel Thomas Birch from the Anning family in Lyme Regis. You should come. All of my family will be there.'

The expression on his face went from one of tender amusement to alarm. His eyes widened and his nostrils flared. It was rather nice to see Phineas off balance for once. Becca couldn't help but giggle. 'There is no reason to be afraid. My family won't eat you. Cannibalism is frowned on in nearly all cultures and there will be at least fifty other people in attendance.'

He placed his opposite hand over hers on his arm. 'I don't have an invitation, Becca.'

'But you're an earl. Earls don't need invitations. They are welcome at any social event.'

He inhaled sharply, his blue eyes paler than before. 'Good manners suggest that they should.'

'And you still have forty questions to ask me,' she pointed out. 'Are you going to be a lion or a mouse?'

Phineas sighed. 'Must I remind you, Becca, that I am a rat and if I were to attend tonight you would know my name and our little game would be over.' He took her hand in his and intertwined their fingers. It felt more intimate than merely a touch on his arm. 'Adieu, my lady.'

He released her hand and strode away before Alonzo could get a good view of his face. Becca watched him go breathlessly.

Phineas hadn't agreed to go to Lady Inverness's scientific soirée.

He never attended an event that he did not wish to—or stayed at any place longer than he wanted to. He would be entirely out of place at a bluestocking party, like a false coin. Or out of fashion like a pale coat in the autumn season.

Picking up Becca's sketch from his desk, Phineas couldn't stop grinning when he looked at it. Becca had drawn him with a tail. A furry tail! She'd managed to include every cape on his riding coat and the tassels on his Hessian boots. It was very recognisably both a lion and himself. Even her little mouse had her eyes. He could see her in the lines of its mouth as well.

Underneath the drawing was written three beautifully formed letters: *Fin*. She had spelled his name wrong, but it didn't matter. He wasn't interested in her abilities to spell, or the speed of her reading. Becca was clever, kind and talented. He'd already received an invitation to her coming-out ball. She would be formally introduced to him then and their little game in the park would be over. He would miss her conversation and her curves.

Phineas rang the bell for his valet. He would go to his club so that he wasn't tempted to appear uninvited at a naturalist soirée to discuss ancient bones. Or give his blackened heart to a woman who was sure to crush it between her beautiful fingers when she realised who and what he truly was.

Chapter Six

'Why do you keep glancing at the door, Becca?' Helen asked loudly.

'I'm not,' Becca lied, wincing at the volume of her beloved sister's question in the middle of her naturalist soirée.

'Yes, you are.'

Helen never saw social cues and even if you pointed them out to her, she didn't care what others thought of her. She would no sooner stop asking why Becca kept watching the entrance than she would fly. The only hope that Becca had was to distract her.

'I can finally see your tummy growing.'

Helen beamed when Becca mentioned her pregnancy and cast a glance at her handsome husband. The poor man was stuck in deep conversation with an avid avian expert. Mark drew birds, but clearly there were many details that he was unaware of that the expert was kindly explaining to him in great detail.

Oh, no! She saw Papa join the conversation and turn it to bird faeces. Her father thought that almost everything about an animal could be learned through its waste.

Her sister touched the slight bulge of her abdomen and grinned. 'And my breasts have grown, too! They are unfortunately rather sensitive to the touch and they'll never be as large and impressive as your set, of course. But when I asked Mark if he'd noticed them—we were in the library at the time—he said, I looked "booksum" instead of buxom.'

Becca had to press her lips together to keep in her laugh. Only Helen would consider speaking about the size of her chest as an appropriate topic of conversation at a naturalist soirée. Becca wasn't sure which embarrassed her more—being caught looking for Phineas or speaking about the comparative sizes of their décolletages.

Helen was incorrigible. Indomitable. And infinitely unconcerned about societal rules. Becca was none of those things. She was as shy as a mouse and as sly as a rat. She preferred to be tucked into a dark corner of the room where she could enjoy the party in her own way. She liked watching people like Mark enjoyed watching birds.

Unnoticed.

Unseen.

And she didn't see Phineas all night, despite watching the door for most of the evening and ignoring the lively discussion about Miss Mary Anning's many large fossil discoveries.

On the way home, she'd been more than a little disappointed that Phineas hadn't come. Maybe her delightful flirtation with the notorious Phineas was over.

Her very own Lord Nonesuch.

Becca shouldn't have been glancing over her shoulder this morning either. Phineas was probably not going to come. She was wasting her time on a rake who would flirt, dally, compromise her reputation and leave her for his next victim. Becca turned around and nearly bumped into him.

'You came,' Becca said breathlessly and rather stupidly. It was quite obvious that he'd arrived at the park. He was standing before her looking devastatingly handsome in an olive-green coat and an embroidered waistcoat.

Phineas lifted his hat to her before he took her hand, brought it to his lips and brushed the back of her glove. She wished that he had been able to kiss her skin and not simply the lace of her glove. He must have guessed something of her thoughts, for Phineas glanced left and then right, before turning her hand over and pressing a burning kiss against her bare wrist. Becca gasped in surprise and pleasure. Heat spread through her chest and belly.

He released her hand, as was proper, but continued to stand close to her. His scent filled her senses and she wanted nothing more than to kiss him. Her eyes kept darting to his lips. Did Phineas think she was too plump? Too eager? Too young? If he kissed her, would he find Becca wanting?

Unlike her sister Frederica, she hadn't embraced every handsome groom within a ten-mile radius of Hampford Castle. In fact, she'd never been kissed by a man. Becca had always been well protected by her parents, her brothers, and her sisters. Yet she wasn't now and, despite his flirtatious words, Phineas had not attempted to take advantage of her. Something that surely spoke in his favour.

Or signified his lack of interest.

She had teased him like a brother or a close friend. Perhaps he only saw her as an amusing acquaintance.

One side of his mouth tilted up into a half-smile. 'Becca, I can see the thoughts turning behind your eyes this morning. I can't wait to hear them all, but first we ought to start walking.'

Phineas offered his arm and Becca was not shy in taking it. 'What did I miss last night at the naturalist soirée?'

'A very heated discussion over Miss Mary Anning's fossil bones and whether dragons really exist.'

'And which side did you take?'

The side without cake. For her sister Mantheria had said, *'You'll regret that chocolate cake when you try on your gown tomorrow night.'*

Feeling her colour rise, Becca did not tell him about that. 'Not a dragon in my humble opinion. There was no indication of wings among the bones and the sheer weight of the beast would make flight impossible. I am more inclined to believe that the fossil belonged to a prehistorically large sort of lizard.'

'Extinct, I hope?'

'Definitely, for it would have been the size of a carriage.'

Phineas let out a low whistle. 'Oh, Becca, every minute in your company I adore you more. I have only known you for less than a week and I am already besotted. Bewitched. And bedazzled.'

Becca was not a great reader, but her sister Frederica had read aloud many a romance. None of them, however, had prepared her for flirting with a gorgeous man who captivated her both body and soul. But the beautiful line seemed too studied to be sincere.

'Imagine what I could do to you if you'd known me for an entire week, a fortnight, even a month.' She tried to make a jest of his words. Humour was always her friend when she felt uncomfortable or unsure of herself.

'I only hope to know you that long after you learn my surname and title.'

'Is your reputation so very terrible?'

'I am the spoiled product of a loveless, faithless marriage. I suppose that I turned out exactly as my parents expected: worthless.'

His icy blue eyes never left her face. She could see the slight lines around them. He had to be nearly thirty years old and it seemed as if he'd never felt loved or valued. She couldn't imagine anything sadder. Her body cooled and her heart ached for him. Forgetting all the rules that Mantheria had drilled into her head, Becca said, 'Phineas, I am so terribly sorry. Why did your parents not care for you?'

Phineas sneered, but she knew this time that it wasn't directed at her. 'I was too small and pretty for my father and too much of a reminder of my mother's ageing. She was a great beauty and every day she feared a little of it was slipping away from her.'

'How ridiculous,' Becca said and then wanted to hide behind a hedge. What a stupid thing to say about his parents. She released her hold on his arm, knowing that he would not wish to be touching her any longer.

He took her hand and held it tightly. 'My parents were ridiculous, weren't they? How much easier my life would have been if someone had explained that to me earlier.'

She glanced down at their joined hands. 'My words were thoughtless and cruel. I am ashamed of myself.'

'You have nothing to be ashamed of. My parents were thoughtless and cruel,' he said in a low tone. 'It took me far too long to realise that.'

'Then have you realised that their estimation of you is entirely wrong?' Becca said, her voice shaking a little.

His gaze met hers for only a moment and she saw that same raw vulnerability in them. The pain of years of rejection. Becca had her own troubles, but she had never been in doubt of her parents' love or belief in her abilities.

'If you knew who I truly am, you might agree with them.'

'I wouldn't,' Becca said, shaking her head. 'They sound

as if they were awful people and I am not an awful person. And your worth, Phineas, does not change with what you have done or haven't done. Every person has innate value and every human being deserves love and respect.'

'I think my nurse might have loved me. She was the only person besides yourself to call me Phineas. My parents called me by my honorary Viscount title.'

No longer able to meet his gaze, Becca lowered her head. 'It is no wonder that you did not love them when they only loved themselves.'

'They were tedious people and hardly worth wasting our time over. I was rather hoping that you would have focused on the first part of my speech where I mentioned several B words.'

'That B word would be *Bedlam*. Or F for *flirtation*.'

Phineas grinned at her, which always made Becca feel as if she'd accomplished a great feat. She could make this sardonic, gorgeous man smile. Not her beautiful sister Mantheria. Not her talented sister Frederica. Or her bookish sister Helen.

She.

Herself.

Becca.

They had been so wrapped up in their conversation that Becca didn't realise how close they were to Alonzo. There was no avoiding the meeting between the two men. Phineas bowed elegantly and Alonzo jerkily nodded his head. After Phineas was out of earshot, Alonzo groaned, rubbing his eyes and shaking his head. 'I'm dished. You're dished. We're all dished.'

She touched his shoulder lightly. 'What do you mean?'

'You were alone with the notorious Earl of Norwich,' he

said, between gritted teeth. 'His bad reputation precedes him. The Duchess of Hampford will be furious. When I tell her, I will not be surprised if she no longer wishes for me to be her secretary. And Cassandra will be so disappointed in me. Without a secure position, we will have to wait even longer to marry.'

Phineas was Lord Norwich. Becca had heard of *him*. Norwich was infamous for being handsome, fashionable, a hardened gambler and a heartless rake. 'Then I suggest that you don't tell my mother.'

Alonzo's eyes widened. 'You want me to lie?'

Becca shrugged her shoulders. 'It isn't lying if she doesn't ask and why would she enquire about our morning walks? Particularly when we are accompanied by both Shepherd and Jim.'

He gave her a look of dismay. 'But we aren't walking with Shepherd and Jim.'

She tucked her hand in his arm. 'Yes, but *Mama* doesn't know that.'

Glancing once more at Phineas's retreating figure, Becca pulled her overly honest friend out of the park.

Chapter Seven

Phineas had dropped another thousand pounds at Watier's the night before and couldn't even assuage his conscience that he'd persuaded more lords to vote for his foundling bill. His gambling account was down to four thousand pounds, the lowest amount in years. Lords Champman and Tooting refused to have their names associated with better conditions for illegitimate children—or, in their words, 'base-born brats'. As if it were the babes' fault that their parents were not married.

At this rate, Phineas's bill would not pass and his gambling days would soon be over. His mind had not been on the game, but on a pair of sparkling blue eyes. Becca's beauty and body filled his every thought, making it impossible to concentrate on anything else. He wanted Lady Rebecca Stringham more than he'd ever wanted anything else in his entire life.

And not just her body.

Although it would have been temptation enough.

It had been her words that had kept him up all night. She believed that he had intrinsic worth as a human being and that he deserved love and respect. He'd received neither from his parents, nor from the other boys at Eton, except for Charles.

Phineas couldn't help but wonder what his life might have been like if he'd grown up in a loving family with parents who cared. He did not see Lord Cheswick at gaming hells, or Lord Trentham. They were not members of Watier's, but White's, and he did not often run into them there. It seemed that the Stringhams actually liked spending time with their own families.

That they loved them.

Everything about Becca was well cared for, from her fashionable clothes to her paid tutor to her travels and to her studies. She deserved a husband who would love her as well. One that had more to offer that Phineas did. For despite her words, he still feared that she would find him shallow when at last she saw beneath his handsome exterior.

If she had been a mistress, he would have instructed Walkley to send a parting gift of jewels to signify that the relationship was over. Phineas always bolted when someone got close enough to see the real him. The one he tried so hard to hide behind his beautiful clothes. His sluggish heart could not take another beating.

He almost stayed home that morning. He'd been up half of the night, tossing and turning. There would be black circles underneath his eyes and his countenance would be pale. He was no Lord Nonesuch today. But the thought of Becca wandering alone in the park waiting for him was too much to bear. No, he had to meet her and put an end to their dalliance face to face.

Phineas allowed his valet to do his best to make him presentable before he hailed a hack to the park. He only hoped that Becca had not given up on him coming. When the carriage stopped, he hopped out of the stuffy vehicle and flicked the driver a coin. He straightened his hat, before striding on to the walking paths.

He looked around. Becca was not on the gravel path, but sitting on a tree stump reading a book. How Phineas wished that he was someone else. Or that she was!

Slowly, he made his way towards her, trying to catch his breath.

Becca didn't look up at him, but continued to stare at an illustration of what appeared to be the insides of a mouse. 'So you decided to come after all? I thought our flirtation must be over. A note would have been nice, Phineas. I can read, you know.'

It was over. But he didn't want it to be. Phineas felt closer to her than he had to anyone else. 'You think I was flirting with you?'

She glanced up. 'Or T for *trifling* with me. The gossip around town is that Lord Norwich is not interested in a wife.'

'You discovered my title.'

'I did. Not from *Debrett's*, but from Alonzo. He recognised you yesterday morning.'

'And warned you against me?'

'Of course.'

This was the moment. She finally saw him for what he was: a worthless fribble. Phineas could bid her adieu and go back to his boring, fashionable life where the most scintillating discussion was of the latest boot buckle design from Paris.

'And yet you are here with me alone this morning.'

Becca sighed, her breasts lifting and falling in a most distracting manner. 'I am indeed. I am a Stringham. I am not afraid of anything or anyone. Even handsome and heartless rakes.'

Without thinking, he opened his mouth. 'I can assure

you that I am not entirely heartless. If you would care to feel my chest, you will feel a steady beat there.'

Becca got to her feet and set down the book on the stump. She reached towards his chest as if about to touch his lovely coat, but then grabbed his wrist and felt for his pulse there. 'A steady beat, my lord. I was never in doubt of you possessing a heart, but in your knowledge of how to use it.'

'A scientist like yourself would know that the heart is merely an organ and has no sense of feeling.'

She stepped closer, her eyes searching his face. 'Why are you so afraid of people seeing the real you? The one underneath the fancy clothes and handsome exterior?'

Phineas wanted to flee from her scrutiny that saw all of his faults, but his feet would not move. He tried to make a joke of it. 'Are you trying to get me to take off my clothes, Lady Rebecca? For I am more than willing to give you a private viewing.'

'Are you trying to shock me or to deflect from answering truthfully?'

Sweat formed on Phineas's brow and he blushed like a debutante at her first ball. 'You do not know me, Becca, or you would not ask to see what is beneath the mask I wear to the world... Besides, it is not much. I am a shallow and worthless man after all, who only cares for his clothing.'

'I know you better than you realise,' Becca said, sticking out her chin defiantly. 'I know that you like the colour green in all of its most pretentious shades. That you never faint or pass out, you're merely rendered unconscious. I know that your parents were awful and that your childhood was unhappy. That they made you feel worthless. I know that you have a reputation as a rake, but you still love to waltz. I know that you think that you are a rat, but that you do not have a tail.

'I know the sound of your laugh and the curve of your smile. I know that you are not shallow, but there is darkness in your depths. Perhaps even darkness that scares you. I know that you do care a little for me. For despite your shockingly flirtatious words, you have not tried to compromise me or take advantage of me in any way. And you did not leave me alone today waiting in the park. You came even though it was painful. I see you, Phineas. The real you. And now you must decide if you wish to stay and be my friend or run away.'

He took a deep breath. 'And if I were to stay?'

Becca licked her red lips. 'You would have to be honest with me.'

'I do not know how much more I will be able to confide in you,' he whispered, stepping closer so that their toes met in their boots. 'I have already told you more than I have shared with anyone else.'

She stared at him unblinkingly in the eyes. 'Then I shall have to discover the rest on my own.'

'I should like to stay and be your friend, but I fear that I will eventually disappoint you.'

As he had his parents. And Kitty. Phineas could not offer her more than friendship.

Becca smiled at him and Phineas's face grew even hotter. 'You have already disappointed me by being late, my *friend*. Now you shall have to make it up to me by going on our walk and asking me a great many questions.'

He offered her his arm and she didn't hesitate to move closer to him again. He led her to the stump where she retrieved her book and reticule. 'Do you prefer walking or riding?'

They had returned to the footpath. 'There is no polite way for me to answer that question without our conversation becoming naughty again.'

He paused and then guffawed loudly, shaking his head. He understood her innuendo. 'Since you are so fond of horses, do you drive your own team?'

'Yes, of course. I am a Stringham. I can handle a pair of horses without great difficulty. I have even tried driving unicorn-style before, with three horses, but it is a great deal harder. My father taught me how.'

'Am I to take it that you are closest to your father?'

Becca nodded and her cheek brushed against his beautiful soft coat. 'Yes. I have followed my father around since I could walk. He always took time to teach me about his animals and share his observations. But I love my mother dearly, too.'

Phineas felt a pang of envy as sharp as a knife to know that sort of love and to speak of it so easily. How much Becca took for granted, having parents who were patient and taught her things, rather than pointing out her faults and criticising her weaknesses.

The discussion of families was perhaps too painful, so Phineas changed the subject. 'Where did you learn Greek?'

'In Greece, of course.'

A reluctant laugh escaped his pinched lips. 'Do you enjoy travelling?'

'Yes. It is always wonderful to observe new habitats and to see how species learn how to survive in such different climates. If they grow thicker hair, longer tails, or if they camouflage their skin to match their surroundings. It is fascinating, but I must stop talking. I can be a regular gabster about my favourite topics.'

'I find *you* fascinating.'

And it was true.

'Perhaps I should seek a position at Astley's Amphitheatre, then? A real duke's daughter. No doubt I would become a main attraction.'

Phineas led her off the path and underneath the shade of a yew tree, where he stopped and turned to look her eye to eye. 'Why do you not accept compliments, instead of turning them into a jest?'

'I feel as though my faults are being examined underneath a magnifying glass. I suppose that I use humour the way you wear your fine clothes and jewels. As armour to keep the rest of the world from coming too close. If I am laughing, too, society cannot laugh at me.'

'Why would anyone laugh at you?'

'I could give you a litany of my faults, but the most glaringly obvious is that I read like a small child and my spelling is atrocious.'

'But you said that every human being has worth and deserves love and respect—presumably that would include duke's daughters with reading difficulties.'

She elbowed him slightly. 'Using my own words as weapons against me. Unfair. I suppose that you are right, though. It is much easier to give advice than it is to receive it. And it is much simpler to believe that other people's problems are not as difficult as your own. I suppose we are all our own harshest critics.'

Phineas could only hope so. When he was with Becca he could almost believe that he was more than a shallow dandy or a disappointment of a son.

'And I hate turnips,' Becca said, deftly changing the subject and continuing their walk. 'Is there a food that you dislike?'

'Liquorice.'

'But it is a sweet!'

Phineas wrinkled his nose as if he was smelling something most unpleasant. 'Chocolates are a sweet. Liquorice is nasty.'

'I love chocolates, too,' Becca agreed. 'We always have them at Christmas. My favourite holiday. Which one is your favourite?'

'You.'

The word came out instinctively.

'Your favourite *holiday*, my shameless flirt.'

He exhaled slowly. 'I am not overly fond of holidays, but I do like jewels. Diamonds to be precise. And yourself?'

'Sapphires in all of their shades.'

'They shine like your eyes.'

She rubbed her chest and he wished that she wouldn't. He was already having a devil of a time not staring at her glorious breasts. 'And I like your rings.'

Phineas wiggled one hand and the diamond ring on it sparkled and shone. 'Do you prefer rings or necklaces?'

'Rings. Necklaces feel as if they are trying to choke me and earrings pull at my earlobes after wearing them for a few hours.'

He wouldn't mind nuzzling and kissing her neck or her ears. 'I have been tempted to pierce one of my ears, but now I shall not.'

'I dare say you would look quite dashing with an earring. But you always do look dashing.'

Phineas took her hand from his arm and twirled her around. A giggle escaped her clenched teeth as he twirled her a second time. 'Do you prefer boots or dancing slippers?'

Becca curtsied to him as if they had just finished a set. 'Boots. For I am a scientist and one can hardly observe the world in dancing slippers.'

'But you are able to observe me in my dinner clothes. A fine consolation for any lady.'

She bit down on her lower lip again, not out of consternation, but to keep in her mirth. Becca failed miserably and laughed until Mr Lawes arrived to take her back home. He was as stiff as a board when he bowed to Phineas, his disapproval apparent on his face. Phineas merely smiled and watched her walk away from him. Her figure grew smaller and smaller, until he could no longer see Becca or her shadow.

Despite his brave words about hearts not having feelings, his own felt as if it had shrunk when she left him.

'I discovered my secret suitor's identity,' Becca said, later that afternoon at Lady Dutton's town house. She had stopped by to visit with Alexander. She did not know how many days he would have left.

Despite his impending death, there was a slight smile on Alexander's face as his head lay on the pillow. 'What is the lucky fellow's name?'

Taking a deep breath, Becca thought about Phineas and how happy she'd been in his company. 'You must promise not to tell a soul. Especially not my mother or sisters.'

'I promise.'

'The Earl of Norwich.'

Alexander no longer smiled. His brow furrowed in concern. 'You're playing with fire. He is a dangerous man. I wouldn't trust him within ten feet of you. I have seen Norwich drop five thousand pounds in one night gambling and, for all his fancy clothes, the Earl's fought more than one duel. And winged his man every time.'

Becca took his thin hand and patted it. 'Now, now, Alexander, your reputation is *much* worse and yet I am alone with you in your bedchamber. Perhaps I shall faint. No, I need my smelling salts! Ring the bell. I must have Cressy call me a physician immediately!'

Alexander closed his eyes and shook his head against the pillow. 'You'll be the death of me.'

The smile slipped from her face. He looked paler and thinner than he had only a few days before. 'I certainly hope not.'

'I shouldn't have said that,' Alexander admitted, groaning. 'And it's not true, my dear friend. I only want what is best for you. For you are deserving of the very best... I have finally allowed myself to realise that I am going to die. The pain gets worse every day. It is difficult to breathe. And oddly enough, you are the reason I am holding on.'

Her chest tightened and she leaned over his bed. 'To stop me from making a fool of myself over my secret suitor?'

'To not ruin your coming-out ball with my funeral. Cressy received an invitation nearly three weeks ago. Your mother's new secretary—Mr Lawes, is it?—must be very busy with all the preparations. The Duchess likes everything to be just so. Mantheria is afraid that if I die before your ball, your parents might make you wait another year. And I should hate that. You've waited long enough to shine, my little friend.'

Despite the pain in her heart, Becca's lips twitched. 'Or explode. Like a comet hitting the earth's atmosphere and bursting into flames.'

'Memorable though.'

Shaking her head, Becca said, 'But not for the right reasons.'

'You're a very clever, dear young woman. You are not a comet, but a beautiful debutante. And even that rogue Lord Norwich seems to see your worth. More suitors will, too. Ones who are worthier of your regard. And don't let Mantheria's slights about your waistline dim your light. A man likes a woman with generous curves.'

She squeezed his hand tighter. Alexander was dying and he held on simply for her, despite the great pain. She wished that her coming-out ball was this very evening and that her friend could finally find peace and rest.

And light.

Chapter Eight

Phineas did not admit weaknesses. Nor did he ever show others his vulnerability. He'd learned at an early age that it could be exploited and used against him. Even by his so-called friends. But he knew that Becca would never treat him like that.

Her sincerity had made him feel off-kilter.

Unsure of himself for the first time since university.

And then she'd challenged him to stay. To be her friend.

Phineas rubbed his cheeks, his face hurting from all the smiling he had done the previous day. He hadn't realised how difficult it was to be near Becca without constantly touching her and kissing her. They had been fully clothed but he'd never felt more exposed.

He wanted Becca to stay, but if she knew the truth of his past—about the existence of Kitty—she would run away. Phineas was too broken, old and cynical for someone as young and as perfect as Becca. Meeting her this morning, being her friend in secret, was only putting off the inevitable end. Becca would eventually see there was not much in his murky depths and move on to a better man. A better lord.

Unless she truly did see him, flaws and all. But she came from a large and happy family. She would want a loving marriage. He was more than willing to make love to her, but he didn't know how to love her. Or how to prevent them from growing apart the way his parents had. At least if they had children, Becca would love them and not merely endure their presence the way his mother had. And he would not be unfaithful like his father. Phineas had seen first-hand the misery that it caused for all members of the family.

Still, it would be a gamble.

With the highest stakes of his life.

Phineas would be risking his blackened heart.

'Not riding again this morning, my lord?' Ned asked, holding the reins to his saddled horse.

Startled, Phineas shook his head. 'You'll have to exercise Chesapeake for me.'

The groom winked at him. 'Fair smitten you are, sir. And a fine-looking lady, if I do say so myself. And it's about time you thought about settling down and providing a few heirs.'

It was unlike his servants to be so familiar and he was tempted to give Ned a sharp set-down. However, something inside Phineas told him that Becca would not have. She treated even her servants with respect. 'Is it that obvious?'

The groom doffed his hat. 'Happens to every man eventually, my lord. You meet the one woman that you can't live without.'

'And don't forget to pick your lass a posy, my lord.' Phineas turned to see one of the scullery maids was dumping dirty water. She couldn't be older than sixteen or seventeen. 'Ladies love flowers.'

He could not recall any of the maids speaking to him before. It caught him entirely off guard. He touched his hat. 'Thank you. I will.'

Phineas chewed over his servants' comments the entire walk to the park. He stopped and purchased a single rose.

A pretty pink one that reminded him of Becca. He didn't need a dozen to know which bud was the best. Only one.

Was that how love felt?

Not wanting to be with anyone else?

Always wishing for the other person to be near you?

Never having them far from your mind?

He'd never fancied himself in love before with his past mistresses. Any feelings he felt for them had always faded into indifference and he'd paid the women off with gifts. And he'd always been careful to keep them from falling in love with him. The parting on both sides had been amicable. But he didn't want to part with Becca. In friendship or otherwise.

There were not many people in the park. It was cold and early in the morning. That's why he usually rode at this time. Otherwise, it was not considered good *ton* to gallop in the park and Phineas preferred to ride hard. It was the only appropriate gentlemanly pursuit that he enjoyed. He cared nothing for fencing, boxing or any blood sport. He enjoyed driving his horses, but did not race them. Horses, like dandies, did not like to be covered in sweat.

He was a member of the Four Horse Club and drove his team at a strict trot with the other members from London to Salt Hill. His mother would have been horrified if any part of his person had been disarrayed. He always kept the persona of perfection up in public.

As a child, he'd taught himself to play the pianoforte. His father had boxed his ears and told Phineas that music was for women and the lower classes. Becca was right—his father had been *ridiculous*.

Nearly twenty yards away, he saw Becca and she was accompanied by Mr Lawes. Phineas saw when she first noticed him, for her step became almost a skip and she smiled widely. Becca looked even more beautiful this morning. His refined eye believed it was the addition of colour. Her knee-length spencer was a dark shade of pink and set off her rosy complexion to admiration. Her straw bonnet had matching flowers and ribbons. The skirt of her gown was white, the colour of a debutante, but had a pattern of small dark pink rose vines.

The gentleman at her side increased his pace to keep up with hers. When she was only feet away from him, Becca outstretched her hand. Phineas took it and bent over her wrist, not kissing it in front of the disapproving Mr Lawes.

'Lord Norwich, what an unexpected surprise it is to see you this morning in the park!' Becca said with a giggle that warmed his entire person. 'I had no idea you enjoyed walking.'

Phineas handed her the rose. 'Lady Rebecca, it is always a pleasure to see you. Allow me to give you this small token of my esteem.'

Accepting it, she brought it to her nose and sniffed. 'It smells as lovely as it looks. Thank you, Phineas.'

The other man tutted.

She beamed at both men and used the single rose to point. 'Lord Norwich, may I formally present my former-tutor-now-secretary, Mr Alonzo Lawes? Mr Lawes, this is my friend, Lord Norwich.'

Phineas inclined his head politely. 'Mr Lawes, good morning to you.'

He examined Becca's former tutor more closely. Mr Lawes did not look to be much older than her. His hair was a dull brown, his cheeks were rather round and there were two red spots on his chin. His dark blue coat was simple and his cravat tied in a basic knot. His appearance was pleasing without being handsome.

Mr Lawes bowed stiffly. 'Lord Norwich.'

Becca took Phineas's arm and said over her shoulder, 'I do not think the path is wide enough for three. Perhaps you might go and find Miss Betrump, Alonzo?'

Then she tugged Phineas along at a pace that was practically a jog.

He had to hold on to his top hat with his free hand. 'What's your hurry, dear one?'

'If we get far enough ahead, Alonzo will not be able to hear our entire conversation.'

'Or we could speak really quietly.'

Becca stopped abruptly and nearly tripped him. 'You're right.' And then she threw back her head and laughed loudly as if they were the only two people in the park. Ned had been right—he was *'fair smitten'* with everything about her. 'And Alonzo is no longer trailing behind me like my little nephew Arthur. Do you like children?'

Her question caught him off guard. He'd never thought about liking children—most men saw them as a necessary part of life to continue on the title. Another duty of his position like the care of his tenants and estates. One that he had intended to ignore, the way his father had him. Although the late Earl had had no trouble fathering children. But if he were to court Becca and eventually marry her, he would become a father. And he could tell that Becca loved children—of course, she did. She loved her family. Her friends. Her father's animals. Even the little rodents that no one else liked.

He wanted to please her, to answer in the affirmative, but she had been honest with him. She had seen the true him underneath the surface and she hadn't looked away. Phineas could not lie to her now. 'I have not had much to do with children.'

Except for his ward. He'd stayed with her in the summers, but she'd been mostly in the care of her late nurse. Phineas had no idea how to be a parent. Or even how to be a member of a family.

'Oh,' she said, her smile faltering a little.

'I am an only child. My mother only had me and then she said that her figure was never quite the same afterwards. The thought of having a second child was entirely out of the question.'

Becca squeezed his arm that she was holding. 'How sad for you. I adore my brothers and sisters, even if they are all obnoxious busybodies who all still treat me as though I am a little girl instead of a woman grown. Even my friend the Duke of Glastonbury doesn't trust me to make my own decisions about my future.'

Phineas didn't have a reputation for being shrewd for nothing. It was obvious that the dying Duke did not approve of her secret meetings with him in the park. 'Has my character been sunk below reproach?'

'I knew that you were a rake, Phineas,' she said, her tone less playful and her expression serious. 'But you forgot to mention that you are a hardened gamester and duellist. I can't help but wonder what makes me different from the other ladies you've befriended. Or if there is no difference at all and I am merely deceiving myself.'

Phineas licked his teeth. 'And I am not a hardened gamester any more. After my parents' deaths, I fell in with a bad set and nearly diced away my fortune. I also fought several duels. Happily, I was not yet one and twenty, so I was unable to touch the principal or the estates themselves. Once the money ran out, so did my new friends.'

She pressed her body against his side. 'Oh, Phineas. People can be so cruel.'

He tried to focus on her sweet words and not the effect of her sweeter curves. 'Being young and rather foolish, I decided to recover my lost funds by marrying an heiress. I proposed to the former Lady Louisa Bracken who is now the Marchioness of Cheswick—your sister-in-law. I will not attempt to deny that I had an eye on her fortune, but I also found her to be agreeable company.'

And he'd thought that Lady Louisa would be a good mother to his young ward, but Phineas wouldn't mention Kitty now. Her very existence brought up awkward questions and embarrassing confessions that he was not yet ready to make.

'I put myself on a strict gambling budget of only one thousand pounds and I swore if I lost it all that I would never gamble again. Because I was no longer desperate, I had the devil's own luck at the tables. Then I began to study the stock exchange. Your brother Trentham and your grandfather Stubbs's speculations always turn a fair profit.

'One hates to boast, but I am a very wealthy man now and no one has taken a shot at me from ten paces for several years. I also have three estates. Ridley Hall in Norwich is my principal one. But I have two smaller ones in Bath and near Brighton.'

'And don't forget you're an earl,' Becca added with her ready smile.

'And an ass.'

A small gurgle of laughter escaped her lips and he wished that he could kiss her on the spot. A glance behind told him that Mr Lawes was still there and watching them closely. They continued to walk, more slowly than before. Becca's side pressed against his, her attention on his words. 'That, too... Unbelievably, I like you even more now than I did a moment ago, you arrogant man.'

Phineas knew that he was well past liking. 'What number question are we on now?'

'Around five and twenty, I believe.'

'Are you afraid of any animals?'

'Wolves.' Growling, she bared her teeth at him like a wolf. Phineas couldn't help but laugh. He could get used to such joy.

'And you, Phineas?'

He took a deep, cleansing breath. His first thought was that he didn't fear animals, but a future without her. 'I am the one asking the questions, sweetheart. What makes you angry?'

'When people don't answer my questions.'

Phineas was enchanted. He wanted nothing more than to kiss her on the spot. His brain function was at half-capacity at best. But he managed to say, 'Do you like hats?'

'I don't dislike them. I suppose on the whole I am indifferent to headwear.'

He was very fond of hats himself, but he preferred to look at Becca's glorious brown locks. 'What is your favourite season?'

'Autumn,' she said, dazzling him with another smile. 'I love it when the leaves turn different colours and fall. Change can be such a beautiful thing.'

He gazed into her sparkling blue eyes. 'I wouldn't change one single thing about you.'

And it was the truth.

Chapter Nine

Phineas never arrived on time to a ball. The hostesses were lucky if he came at all and even then, he was always fashionably late. Yet here he was arriving in Berkeley Square nearly a half an hour early. He'd seen other men make fools of themselves over women and he'd scorned them. How humbling it was to join their number—at least his golden tailcoat and breeches were beautiful. A work of art by Weston, as were the matching pair of shoes with golden buckles in the new Parisian style.

He'd planned to wear them for the first time at a more exquisite affair than a coming-out ball. But that was before he'd met Becca. He'd paired his golden outfit with ruby rings and a new stickpin. Phineas had gone through six neckerchiefs before he'd arranged his cravat in a perfectly pointed Oriental tie.

He knew that he looked his best and *his* best was incomparable. Still, his stomach felt as if he'd drunk an entire bottle of champagne. It bubbled most uncomfortably.

A footman opened the door to his carriage and Phineas took a deep breath before exiting and walking up to the Stringhams' door. He was met by a butler who ushered him inside. The entry was lit with hundreds of candles, but neither the Duke nor the Duchess of Hampford were there to greet their guests. He was embarrassingly early. A social faux pas that he would never repeat.

Spinning on the heel of his golden shoes, Phineas decided to go and then come back. He had nearly reached the butler and the door when he heard *her* voice. 'Oh, Phineas, don't leave!'

He glanced over his shoulder and the vision of loveliness that met him made Phineas catch his breath. Becca's gown was the predictable white of a debutante and deceptively simple. Not a flounce or flourish to be seen. White silk tulip sleeves, a low square neck, empire waist and only small tucks beneath her impressive décolletage. Stepping closer to her, he saw the silk had a faint pattern that caused the material to reflect the light. Often a woman's gown was more beautiful than she, but Becca's highlighted her glorious figure and burnished curls. Around her neck was a priceless set of amethysts that looked as if they were antique. Fragile and perfect gems encircled by diamonds. She also wore a matching pair of amethyst earrings.

Becca and jewels.

His two favourite things.

She gave him a blissful smile. 'You look very handsome, Phineas. Like King Midas.'

Phineas took her hand. She was not yet wearing gloves and he was able to brush a kiss, or two, against her warm skin. She tasted sweet and he wanted nothing more than to devour her on the spot.

'If I were King Midas, you would have turned to gold.'

'How do you know for certain that I haven't?' she countered with a smile. 'You can't see my insides.'

Heat pooled in his belly. He would love to see every inch of her.

The butler made a disapproving sound behind them.

Becca left him speechless for the second time that evening when she grabbed his hand and dragged him to the back of the house and into a dimly lit conservatory full of plants.

'We won't be disturbed here and I wish to speak to you privately.'

'Must we speak?' he asked in a droll voice.

Becca grinned. She must have caught his joke about kissing. She stepped closer to him. Barely two inches away. The air between them felt charged with electricity. Whatever was between them was more than friendship. More than any other feeling he'd ever experienced with another human being.

She held out her left wrist where his flowers were attached. A spray of gardenias that he'd selected himself. 'Thank you for the bouquet, Phineas. They are beautiful.'

Unable to resist any longer, Phineas moved the two inches until their bodies were touching, hip to hip, chest to chest, and his hands pressed against her waist. He'd been longing to hold her in his arms since waking up in her lap. 'But not as beautiful as you or the amethysts around your lovely throat.'

He said the words flippantly, but they were true.

Becca took a breath before meeting his eyes. 'Alexander—Glastonbury gave me these. He bought them for me in Greece. I only wish that he could be here tonight to see me wear them, but he is too ill. The doctors do not think that he will last the week.'

A tear slipped down her cheek. Phineas took off his golden gloves and let them fall thoughtlessly to the floor. He wanted to wipe away her tears with his fingers—to feel his skin against hers. With a gentle thumb, he brushed them away.

Becca blinked at him. Her eyes were full of unshed tears.

'You must think me a dreadful watering pot. I promise I do not cry this much always.'

Phineas cupped her satin cheek with his hand. 'You can cry as much as you please.'

'But not on your cravat,' she said with a sniff. 'It is another work of art.'

He opened his mouth to assure her that not even his beloved clothes were as important as her to him—but he realised that she was smiling. Teasing him. Even crying, she had a wicked sense of humour.

His eyes fell down to her necklace. As a connoisseur of jewels, he knew that the delicate set of amethysts appeared to be from the sixteenth century. He would have guessed they were originally created in Italy. Amethysts were not particularly expensive themselves, but the perfectly cut diamonds around them, paired with the pure gold of the necklace made it a very pricey piece of jewellery.

Another tear fell down her cheek and Phineas did not know how to comfort her. Instinctively, he ran his thumb over her bottom lip and then pressed his mouth to hers. Becca stiffened for only a moment, before throwing her arms around his neck and tightening her hold.

It was a rather wet kiss—she was crying after all—but he could not think of a better one. Her lush lips were open and supple against his. She met the pressure of his mouth with an eagerness that he found very pleasing. When his tongue touched hers, she moaned and he deepened the kiss.

Phineas could tell that she had never kissed anyone before him and it inflamed him. He didn't want anyone else to touch her. To feel her lips smile as she returned his kisses. To tangle with her wicked tongue. Possessiveness was a wholly new feeling that he'd never experienced before.

She was *his*. Becca's fingers moved through his hair

and Phineas couldn't hold in his own moan of pleasure. He thought that his valet would probably be indignant to have his hard work ruined, but Phineas didn't care. If playing with his curls made Becca happy, she could do whatever she pleased with him. He was hers to do with what she liked.

Phineas took a quick breath before bringing her mouth back to his. Kissing Becca was like sipping wine for the first time. Heady and marvellous. He gentled the kiss to savour the taste of her mouth. The feel of her body pressed tightly against his. To enjoy the way she clung to him. He pressed one last kiss to her lips and then buried his head into her beautiful neck. He couldn't resist kissing it as well.

'Thank you, Phineas.'

He lifted his head, for he could not smile and kiss her at the same time. 'You are most welcome.'

She gave a watery chuckle that stole another piece of his blackened heart. 'I had no idea that kissing could help one stop crying. But for it to be a proven scientific theory, one would need to test it multiple times to ensure the same results.'

Phineas smiled at her tenderly. 'You're very scientific, Becca. But saying *Kiss me again* would work just as well.'

'Kiss me again,' she repeated, her face flushed from his previous kisses.

His hand still cupping her cheek, he angled her mouth against his. With his other hand, Phineas made a slow burn from her waist up her curved back. Everywhere he touched was soft, luscious and entirely womanly. Her body was the only scientific expedition that he wished to embark on and he would take his time to discover everything that pleased her.

With one last sweet kiss, he said, 'We must stop, Becca. Or we will get caught.'

Becca nodded. 'You're right. My siblings will soon be descending upon the house like a swarm of locusts and I do not wish for them to know about our secret friendship yet. They would pick it apart like a group of naturalists.'

Phineas had never thought of what it might be like to be a member of a large family. To have them be involved in his choices. His few memories with his parents were painful. His principal estate, Ridley Hall, had never felt like a home, which is why he preferred the London house. He'd sold his father's London mansion and bought his own smaller, but more fashionably located, town house. Phineas had decorated it himself. He supposed that his private world was also small, but he wanted her to be a part of it.

'I would like to encourage your scientific endeavours,' he promised, his lips curling up on the sides. 'Particularly in the science of kissing.'

Giggling, she smiled at him. 'A very important field of study.'

'I would even say that is *the most* important field of study.'

She leaned up on her tiptoes and kissed the tip of his chin. Phineas had never been kissed in that specific location before and he found that he quite liked it.

Becca released her hold on his neck and stepped back from him. He missed her warmth immediately. 'We have a coming-out ball to go to,' she said, stooping down to pick up his gloves. She handed them to him. 'Once you go inside, there is a retiring room through the first door to your left. I am going to run up the servants' staircase and have my maid ensure that I am presentable for the party.'

Phineas squeezed her hands and gave her the slightest of smiles. 'May I have your first waltz?'

'I don't think that is a good idea, Phineas.'

He could not imagine a better one. 'Why not?'

'Because we will not be formally introduced until tonight and, if we wish to keep our friendship a secret, we cannot appear to be too familiar.'

Sighing, Phineas wanted to point out that they had been very familiar only moments before. And that he was starting to dislike the word *friendship*, but he'd given her no indication that he wished to form a serious attachment with her. He just didn't want to lose her and he feared that they were the same thing.

'May I ask you for a country set in the middle of the ball?'

Smiling, she came back to him and brushed a kiss against his cheek. 'Yes, King Midas.'

'I'll take Midas over an ass.'

'Or a rat,' she reminded him with a wink and then left him alone in the dark conservatory with only the plants to keep him company.

After such a welcome, Phineas thought he would be delighted to arrive early to any party with Becca in attendance. Still, he was a dandy and did indeed follow her thoughtful advice to go to the retiring room and fix not only his golden gloves, but his hair. King Midas needed to be golden perfection. Especially if he was seriously considering courtship.

And courtship usually ended in marriage.

The state of wedlock had never appealed to him before. Was he even capable of being a good husband? He had no such examples from his own family. And marriage would require complete honestly, but how could he properly explain about Kitty without causing Becca to run away? She was a living scandal that he would never abandon. Not for anyone. Not even for Becca. Kitty had been discarded once by her mother and he'd promised her that she would always have a home with him. Phineas had felt emotionally abandoned by his own parents.

But he wanted Becca badly.

And he always got what he wanted.

Phineas consoled himself with the thought that Becca's kisses would be worth a lifetime of misery.

Chapter Ten

Papa held out his arms to her at the bottom of the grand staircase and Becca jumped into them. 'My darling girl. You look like a glorious chrysalis just emerging from a cocoon. But I wish that you had remained a caterpillar a little longer.'

'What your father means to say is that you are beautiful, Becca,' Mama said from behind him. 'Both inside and out. And that we are both exceedingly proud of the woman you have become.'

Becca released Papa and hugged her mother tightly. 'Thank you for everything, Mama. This is going to be the most wonderful ball of the Season.'

Her mother had spared no expense on the golden decorations in the ballroom and on the dinner menu for Becca's coming-out ball. There was even edible gold adorning the fruit. She knew that both her mother and Alonzo had worked very hard to make her ball memorable. Mama had even written a personal invitation to the Prince Regent and he'd sent Becca a royal gift, the golden butterfly pin that she wore on the bodice of her gown. Prinny, as her brother Matthew called him, promised to drop into the party, thereby ensuring its success.

But in Becca's mind it was already a success. Phineas

had come and *early*. Something that fashionable dandies did not do. They never wished to appear eager. They wore a sneer or an expression of boredom the way other men wore hats. Phineas did not act bored around her, although, how could he when they were kissing? His lips had better things to do. Indeed, she could almost fancy herself flying like a butterfly in those beautiful moments when their bodies and mouths were joined together.

Becca now understood why Frederica was always kissing Samuel and Helen's hands were constantly touching Mark. It had felt marvellous! As if every cell in her body was aware of his. And despite her lack of experience, Phineas hadn't seemed displeased with her abilities. Would she improve? Could Phineas teach her more? Unlike most debutantes, her mother had explained to her several years ago how babies were made. Kissing was only the beginning. Mama said that making love was for pleasure and to bring a married couple closer to each other.

Becca tried not to think about his reputation as a rake. Or that she was not the only person who found him irresistible and that he might be toying with her. Perhaps her naivety amused him—a depressing thought.

Phineas had kissed her, but he hadn't given her any indication that he wished to court her. Their stolen embraces might have only been pleasurable distractions to him. Yet his touches had meant the world to her. Becca was starting to care for him—all sides of him. The witty and wicked one. The shy and vulnerable one. Even the sneering and serious one.

But she would not ruin her ball obsessing over Phineas. She'd waited her entire life for this moment and she meant to enjoy herself fully. Becca opened the ball by dancing with her brother-in-law Samuel. He was an excellent dancer and partner, even if he kept glancing at her sister. Poor Frederica's morning sickness seemed to last all day long and into the nighttime. Her complexion was rather green and Becca sincerely hoped that her sister wouldn't retch on the ballroom floor. It would make her ball memorable for all of the wrong reasons.

For the next set, Alonzo was her partner. They flew through the steps with the ease of old friends. She had never seen him happier since Miss Bertrump's father had allowed them to set a wedding date. She didn't even mind that all he could talk about during the dance was another woman. It helped keep her mind off Alexander's impending death.

No.

She would not think of him either. Her dear friend had held on for weeks in great suffering so that she could enjoy this night. She had to honour that sacrifice and all of her mother's work to make her coming-out ball a success. She only wished that Lady Julia was not enjoying her dance with Phineas quite so much and that Miss Kate Simpson would stop batting her eyelashes at him.

Instinctively, Becca blinked.

'Is something in your eye?' Alonzo asked.

Blushing and giggling, she shook her head. 'No. Thank you for the dance, dear friend. I am so delighted for both you and Miss Betrump. And I believe you should go and ask her to dance.'

Her former tutor grinned and bowed, before seeking the company of his betrothed.

After a few more dances, Becca felt less like an elegant butterfly and more like an earwig. After many years of dancing the man's part with her sisters, she made several silly mistakes during both the quadrille and two country sets. And she had wished to appear perfect in front of society. She was breathless, blushing and wishing that she had not asked Phineas *not* to waltz with her. Since it was her coming-out ball, everyone was watching her anyway. She might have at least enjoyed the set with him. Not that Lord Philip wasn't a good partner and Lord Talbot was light on his feet. But they were also both lacking in humour.

Unfortunately, there were many other ladies in attendance who were accomplished dancers. It grated on her nerves every time she saw Phineas dance with another woman. Which was ridiculous, since she was dancing with other men. Still, she longed to stand in the middle of the dance floor and say in a really loud voice, 'I have kissed the Earl of Norwich.' Phineas might be amused by such behaviour, but her mother most certainly would not be. Mama had clearly worked hard to find her multiple partners, despite still having a bit of a head cold. And, unfortunately, she had not included Phineas on her list of acceptable suitors.

After kissing him, Becca could well believe that Phineas had been a rake. But she thought he could change. How sad it would be if people were not allowed to transform like the autumn leaves. Or Papa's metaphor with the caterpillar: the crawling creature becomes something new and then is able to fly. Humans might be animals, but unlike their furry, four-legged friends, they could change and become more than they ever believed was possible.

Lord Whitehurst led Becca back to her mother who beamed at the young man. Mama's nose was a trifle red around the edges, but otherwise she looked elegant and predatory, like a hawk. Whitehurst was closer to Becca in age than Phineas and he did not have a sullied reputation either. Nor was he as handsome. The young lord was gaunt, with a long nose, and his dark hair was in need of a washing. But what was worse, he hadn't spoken to her once during their dance.

'Is that the Roger de Coverley I hear?' Mama said, clapping her hands as if she hadn't chosen every piece of music that the quartet would play that evening. 'Lord Whitehurst, do you enjoy dancing?'

Becca groaned inwardly. Mama was trying to force the Baron to dance with her again when he obviously had no interest and wasn't a good partner.

His Adam's apple bobbed up and down. 'Well—it—is, I should be honoured to—to dance with Lady Rebecca again.'

'Alas,' a cold voice cut in, 'this set is already taken.'

Phineas.

The organ in her chest did something odd. She would have described it as her heart leaping, but hearts could not leap. They were connected by valves to other organs and tissues. Phineas had been handsome in the darkness of the conservatory, but his golden apparel was glorious in the well-lit ballroom. His mouth did not smile at her, yet his eyes did. No, that was ridiculous. Eyes could not smile either. They did not have the correct muscles.

She put her hand in his. 'Our set, Lord Norwich.'

His fingers tightened slightly over hers as they left her mother and Lord Whitehurst with their mouths gaping open like fish. Phineas led her to the dance floor and then spun her into his arms. Becca discovered that it was nearly impossible to think when dancing with a gorgeous man who looked at you as if you were the most beautiful person in the world. It wasn't true, but she would be the last person to disabuse him of his false notion.

'I hope you don't mind that I stole you for this set,' he said in an undertone as their hands joined in the circle. 'I was not certain if you or Lord Whitehurst appeared more miserable at the prospect of the dance.'

Mantheria had told her countless times that a proper debutante does *not* show her emotions in public. It was considered vulgar. However, it would have been scientifically impossible for Becca not to grin back at Phineas. She loved the way the edges of his lips quirked upwards when he was determined not to smile.

'I was the most miserable,' she admitted, squeezing his hand a little tighter, thinking of Miss Simpson and Miss Bergstrom. 'I didn't wish to see you dance it with another woman.'

'Jealous?'

'Yes,' Becca said, another social faux pas. A young lady was never supposed to be forward, but she supposed it was much too late for that. 'In some animal groups, the females fight each other for the attention of the male. I grew up with Frederica and Helen and I believe that I could hold my own against any debutante here.'

Phineas pressed his lips into a thin line, but he could not keep back his smile, then his chuckle as their hands met again in the figure. 'Becca, you are going to ruin my reputation.'

'As a rake?'

She felt his hand gently caress her fingers when they next touched. 'As a serious and fashionable dandy who never smiles.'

'Your smirk is very handsome. And even your sneer is attractive, but neither hold a candle to your smile. And I love your laugh.'

He obliged her by giving another chuckle. Becca's grin widened. How could it not? 'Everyone in this room will think me a great wit. I have made the Earl of Norwich laugh.'

The musicians played the last note. Phineas didn't release her hand, but brought it up to his lips and kissed it in front of everyone. 'And you are a great beauty who has awakened his black heart.'

Breathless and blushing, he returned her to Mama who had another young suitor waiting to dance with her. Becca didn't mind one whit. Nor was she jealous when Phineas danced with other women. Her friend didn't smile at them and he certainly never laughed.

After the last guest had left, it was nearly four o'clock in the morning. Becca could hardly wait to go to bed. Yawning widely, she found that it took nearly all her energy to climb up the first stair. She held on to the banister, for she was more than half asleep. And her feet were very sore. Dancing slippers did not provide a great deal of support.

A sharp rapping on the door caused her to jump. Her eyes widened and she wondered who in the world would be calling on her family at this hour? Mr Harper, the butler, went to the door with his candle and opened it a crack.

'Is the Duchess of Glastonbury here?' the messenger asked.

'She has gone home.'

'I shall go there next.'

Before Harper could close the door, Becca called, 'Wait!'

She went down the few steps much faster than she had climbed them. With the last of her energy, she dashed to the door. 'How is the Duke of Glastonbury?'

It was dark outside, but she could see the grief on the man's face. 'His Grace is fading fast, my lady. He asked to see his son one last time.'

She heard footsteps behind them and then she saw her mother. 'Sir, please tell Lady Dutton and the Duke of Glastonbury that we will bring my grandson over immediately. Harper, please call for the carriage. Come, Becca, let us fetch our wraps. It would not do to wake the servants. They have already had a long night.'

Still wearing her ballgown and jewels, Becca put on her velvet cloak. She tried to focus her thoughts on her nephew and not the fact his father was dying. She breathed in slowly and steadily. Alexander had endured more pain so that his death wouldn't interrupt her coming-out ball. He was a dear. The only person not of her blood that she had ever confided in.

Except for Phineas.

Mama did not say a word as she put on her own cloak. Becca followed her out the front door, Harper held a lantern for them. Papa was already in the carriage, his cravat untied and his blond and grey hair mussed. He didn't like wearing dinner clothes. Especially fashionable ones. Becca took the seat next to him and Papa put his arm around her and dropped a kiss on her forehead. He was the physically affectionate parent.

Mama sat on her other side and patted her knee. She was bracing, rather than loving. Particularly in a crisis. 'At least the horrible Duke had the decency to die after your debut.'

A lump formed in Becca's throat and her eyes pricked with unshed tears. She didn't blame her parents for hating Alexander. He'd betrayed their daughter and the Stringhams were a very tight-knit family. Her mother did not forgive someone who had caused her child such anguish. Still, she hurt for Alexander and grieved for herself.

Papa squeezed her shoulder and Becca leaned more against his chest. When the carriage arrived at Mantheria's house in Mayfair, he got out first. 'Becca, why don't you stay? I'll go and fetch Andrew and your mama can remain with Mantheria.'

'Very well, Papa.'

He took her mother's hand and led her into the house. A few minutes later, her father came out with Andrew. They were holding hands, something that her eleven-year-old nephew usually refused to do. He thought himself too grown up. Andrew was nearly as tall as herself, but his red-rimmed eyes were those of a child. Becca couldn't help but think that, today, her nephew would leave his childhood behind.

The trio of them were silent during the drive to the house where Alexander and Cressida lived. When they arrived, they did not even need to lift the knocker. The front door opened and the main floor was all alight. An unusual sight at half past four in the morning. Alexander's butler led them up the staircase and to the master's rooms. There were a great many candles burning in his chamber, illuminating his four-poster bed where Cressida sat holding his hand. She was in her early fifties and, although she was not married to Alexander, their relationship had lasted more years than Becca had been alive.

A painful smile lit her face. 'Andrew, thank you for coming. And you, too, Becca and Your Grace.'

Papa nodded and gave Andrew a little push towards his father. Her nephew's eyes were wide and Becca could see the fear in them. At the age of twenty, she also feared death. Taking his hand gently, she brought Andrew to the other side of the bed. She sat down on the edge of it and her nephew sat close to her. Alexander's eyes were closed and his breathing shallow. Becca didn't know if he would speak again. Inhaling deeply, she took his other hand in her own and put Andrew's on top.

Alexander's hand was still warm. When he'd first married Mantheria, he'd been a hale and hearty man in his late thirties. Active and adventurous. It was hard to believe that twelve years later, he would be a bedridden and frail version of himself.

His eyelids opened slowly as if they took a great deal of strength. 'My son. My son. I love you, Andrew.'

Becca's eyes welled with tears as Andrew began to sob. He moved to hug his father's body, wrapping his thin arms around him. She tried to hold in her own weeping, but she couldn't. Despite her beliefs in a Great Creator, there was a finality in death. An end.

She released Alexander's fingers, not wishing to intrude in his final moments with his family. The woman he loved and his only child. She stood up, but he said her name.

'Becca, please forgive her.'

Another sob escaped Becca's lips. She knew exactly who the 'her' was, even though no one else in the room did. It was his estranged wife: her eldest sister Mantheria. Someone she both loved and hated. Perhaps Alexander had cared for Mantheria after all. Human beings were the messiest of animals when it came to emotions. And Becca had confided in him about how Mantheria's constant criticisms of her behaviour and remarks about her weight made her feel small. As far as she knew, he'd never broken his word not to tell another soul. How could she deny his last request?

'I will,' she blubbered.

He moved his head ever so slightly on his pillow. 'I'm a luck-lucky man to be dying sur-surrounded by the people I—I love.'

Becca cried so hard that she could no longer see. It wasn't

until she heard Cressy's wails a few minutes later that she realised Alexander was gone. Papa pulled her into a tight hug and held her for several minutes, before gently detaching Andrew from his father's body and holding him as he sobbed.

Sometimes there were no words.

And this was one of those times.

Chapter Eleven

Phineas hadn't expected Becca to be in the park the morning after her coming-out ball. It had only ended a few hours before. But when she wasn't there the second day either, he went on a long hard ride. Somehow, in only a matter of weeks, her presence had become essential to his happiness.

He remembered Ned's words: *'Happens to every man eventually, my lord. You meet the one woman that you can't live without.'*

He felt impatient. Dissatisfied. Furious at the smallest things. A wrinkle in his coat. Mr Walkley bringing him another letter from Kitty's school complaining about her wild behaviour. A change in the dinner menu. The only thing that seemed to help was to ride until he felt exhausted, but then he still missed her. Becca was like the sunlight after weeks of rain. She carried an inner glow that could not be diminished, even by a miserable sot like himself. He didn't deserve her, but no other man of the *beau monde* did either, so it might as well be him.

Phineas had never denied himself something that he desired before and he wasn't about to now. He wanted Becca like an ache. Thoughts of her consumed his every waking moment. He decided that he would woo her, wed her and bed her. And if their marriage was miserable, at least they would be miserable together.

But Becca wasn't the type to wallow. No matter the circumstances, she would find a way to see the positive. To make a jest of it. Her wit and humour would make any day better. Surely a marriage to her would not be complete misery. Phineas didn't want to be like his father, so he would be a better husband. Becca's parents appeared to be quite happy together. Surely a happy marriage was possible and, with Becca, even probable.

Dismounting from his horse, he found Ned waiting for him. Phineas handed the groom his reins and began to walk away.

'Excuse me, milord,' he said with a strong Norfolk accent. 'But my missus wanted me to give ye a message.'

Phineas did not know his groom's surname, let alone who his wife might be. Such a request was impertinent and he was already irate. But his late father had taken out his anger on the servants and Phineas swore that he never would. He did not wish to be like his father in any way.

'I dare say it is of great importance.' Before meeting Becca, he had rarely spoken to the man. Phineas's behaviour had changed since meeting her. He was kinder and more grateful.

'Indeed, milord,' Ned continued eagerly. His groom was apparently fonder of Phineas than he'd previous realised. 'I was telling me missus about your lady and she said that every woman deserves to be properly courted at least once in her life.'

'And what does "properly courted" mean?'

The groom grinned. 'I asked her the same question, milord. My missus said that you need to buy your lady baubles and write her pretty letters. Ask for her company formal, like. She suggested an afternoon drive on Rotten Row during the promenade. To let t'other society folks know you's serious in your courtship.'

His words grated, but Phineas couldn't help but feel that his groom was right. Or at least, his missus. He adored walking and talking with Becca, but he needed to make her feel special. Wanted. Courted. Heaven knew he'd been pursued by enough young ladies and their matchmaking mamas to understand the importance of a well-appointed gift. Or a surprise meeting when he'd least expected it. Phineas had disliked being on the receiving end of such ambushes, but he flattered himself that Becca would be happy to see him.

He exhaled. 'What is your surname, Ned?'

The groom bowed. 'Jenks, milord.'

'Mrs Jenks is a very wise woman. Please thank her for the excellent advice.'

Ned grinned at him. 'That she is. I'm a lucky git.'

'That you are,' Phineas said and gave the man a brief nod before entering his house. The best part of Mrs Jenks's plan was that it included shopping—his favourite pastime.

An hour and half later, Phineas was bathed and dressed to perfection to go 'on the strut' of Bond Street. That particular phrase had always amused him. No doubt Becca would find it ridiculous, as she did most nonsensical societal behaviours. Still, his salmon coat and striped waistcoat were works of art.

He only took a few steps when he saw his friend Lord St Albyn walking towards him. St Albyn was the leader of the dandy set after Beau Brummel's fall from grace—the once arbiter of fashion had been unable to pay his gaming debts and fled to cheaper living on the Continent. Not that

Phineas had missed that conceited tulip. Brummel preferred dark, plainer garments and often mocked dandies who preferred colours and embellishment to their coats, fobs and boots. Flamboyant colours gave him joy.

St Albyn was a man after his own heart. His sparkly blue coat fit like a second skin to his frame, cinched in at the waist. The shirt points of his collar were pointy and reached his chin and his cravat was tied in the scholar. His tanned gloves were the same shade as his Hessian boots and he carried a jewelled walking stick. It looked very well on the dandy and Phineas was half tempted to buy one or two of his own. Merely for decoration, of course.

Tipping his hat, he greeted his acquaintance, 'Good day to you, St Albyn.'

'And to you, Norwich,' St Albyn said, using his cane instead of his finger to touch his beaver hat. No doubt in a few weeks every peer would be doing the same. Dandies always set fashion. They never followed it. 'I'm off to purchase blacks.'

Phineas blinked. He loved wearing colours. Black reminded him of Brummel and, even worse, his late father.

Something of his confusion must have shown on his face for St Albyn's eyes narrowed.

'The Duke of Glastonbury died yesterday. He was an old friend. The funeral is tomorrow at St Sebastian's Chapel.'

'My sincerest condolences.'

'Thank you, Norwich,' he said, tapping his hat with his cane once more.

The serious dandy walked on. Phineas stood for a few moments considering his options. He could not hope for bespoke clothing in only a day. Perhaps Weston had some mourning clothes ready-made that could be altered in time to fit his frame. He would need to go there first and then he could purchase new cravats, black handkerchiefs and a matching ring.

He could not attend the funeral with Becca without causing the sort of gossip she wished to avoid. But he knew how much Glastonbury had meant to her as a friend. Becca would be devastated. She would be inconsolable—in need of several handkerchiefs. He would purchase her a half a dozen new ones as well as a mourning ring.

Phineas smiled wryly when he thought about Mrs Jenks's excellent advice. He was certain the good woman had not meant surprising his lady with gifts at a funeral, but he missed Becca. He needed to see her and if that meant attending a dead philanderer's funeral, then so be it.

Chapter Twelve

The bottom of Becca's black gown was wet from the rain and the bodice from her tears. Her handkerchief was sopping and the funeral service had yet to start. She stood in the chapel near her family, but she felt alone.

Wick held hands with Louisa. Nancy was leaning her head on Matthew's shoulder. Samuel was rubbing circles on Frederica's back as she breathed slowly—probably trying not to cast up her accounts on her shoes again. They'd had to wait for her to change her first pair for that very reason. Helen stood next to her, holding her small belly—no doubt Becca would hear its measurement later today. Mark's hand was on top of it, too. Even in front of her, Mantheria had her son Andrew. Grandfather and Grandmother Stubbs stood close together. And Papa's arm was snugly around Mama's shoulders.

She was truly happy that her siblings had found the perfect partners. That they had a person to stand next to and mourn with them at this difficult time. It was only since Helen had married Mark last year that Becca had felt out of place in her own family. Her former tutor had become her companion instead of Helen but, as wonderful as Alonzo was, it hadn't been the same. And it never would be again. Alonzo was marrying Miss Betrump in less than a month.

Change was the only constant of life.

And death.

Alexander's casket was in the front of the church, covered with a spray of dark purple carnations. More tears welled up in her eyes. She'd made him a promise to forgive Mantheria, but she had no idea how to fulfil it. And she couldn't ask her mother. Mama treated Mantheria as though she was an expensive glass figurine. As her saddest child, Mantheria garnered the majority of their mother's attention and support. Seeing her eldest sister's head bent forward in her black bonnet covered with a black veil, Becca could not resent either her mother's preference or her sister's needs.

If she told Frederica, her queasy and fearless sister would try to fight the battle for her. And it would become a bitter exchange, which was the last thing that Becca wanted. She truly wished to forgive Mantheria, but she could not if her eldest sister continued to belittle her. Glancing at Helen next to her, Becca knew she couldn't ask her for help either. Helen could not comprehend how Becca could both resent and care for her eldest sister at the same time. Such a nuanced relationship her snake-obsessed sister could never understand. She either loved people or hated them. There was no in between. No painfully mixed feelings.

Raising her soaked handkerchief to her eyes, Becca knew that she had to find a way to forgive Mantheria. To fulfil the last promise that she made to Alexander. She allowed her own head to hang low. Her eyes focused on her dark shoes.

'Might I offer you my handkerchief?' a soft and utterly marvellous male voice uttered. 'Yours appears to have already fulfilled its purpose most admirably.'

Becca looked up with her puffy red eyes and saw that Phineas was standing next to her dressed in glorious black.

He held out a fresh black handkerchief trimmed with black lace. It matched his all-black tailcoat and trousers and the lace on his shirt cuffs. Even his cravat was black and tied in an intricate knot that probably had a fancy name. Her lips quirked up a little: Phineas could make even mourning stylish.

She took the black handkerchief. 'Thank you, Phineas.'

His pale blue eyes met hers. 'I brought several spares. Just in case.'

If she hadn't been in a church, she would have laughed. Instead, she smiled through a new set of tears as he handed her no less than five black handkerchiefs. Becca pressed one of her handkerchiefs against her puffy cheeks. She probably looked a fright. She'd spent most of the last three days crying, but Phineas's gaze was soft and tender. His friendship was even more dear to her than before.

She watched him reach into the little pocket that usually held his quizzing glass, but instead of pulling it out, he held in his fingers a ring. The jewel was a black diamond and it was cut in a circle. The dark silver band was braided and intricate. Before she knew what he was about, he took off her right glove and slid it on her ring finger. It fit perfectly.

'I thought you might need a mourning ring. I know how dear His Grace was to you and I am so sorry for the loss of your friend. I hope that when you look at the ring, you can remember all of the good memories of him.'

She glanced down at her hand. It was beautiful and costly. She could almost hear Mantheria's voice in her head saying, *'A lady cannot accept such an expensive gift. You must return it.'* But Becca didn't want to.

Phineas had given her something to wear against her skin. Every time she saw it, she would think of both him and Alexander. Two different men who had both believed in her. Each time she felt it on her finger, she would remember that Phineas had come to the memorial service and brought her a fresh stack of black handkerchiefs.

Half-heartedly, she went to remove it. 'It is too dear. I cannot accept it.'

Phineas took off his right glove and sure enough there was a similar black ring. The diamond was square-cut and the band thicker and more masculine. Silver rings adorned all four of his other fingers. His hand was as impossibly beautiful as the rest of him.

He wiggled his ring finger. 'You see I already have a mourning ring, so you cannot return yours. If you did, I might cry and I cannot be certain that there are enough handkerchiefs for the two of us.'

Sniffling, Becca smiled again. 'I love it, but you needn't buy me expensive gifts. I like you well enough without them.'

Phineas shook his head. 'That is where you are wrong, my dear one. My groom's wife informed me that I needed to court you properly which includes the purchasing of baubles. Mrs Jenks was most insistent.'

His endearment warmed her heart even more than the ring. Butterflies seemed to fly in her stomach and chest. A lovely sensation that could not be defined by a scientific explanation. Her torso only held her heart, organs, bones, blood, muscles and tissues. There could not possibly be small insects darting around her ribcage. 'Are you courting me, Phineas?'

'Not properly according to Mrs Jenks, but, yes, I do wish to court you, Becca.'

She almost didn't believe what her ears were hearing. Her beautiful and flirtatious friend, who had taught her how to kiss, wanted to court Becca. The least pretty of the Stringham sisters. 'And Mrs Jenks reprimanded you?'

'Not to my face, but through her husband,' Phineas explained in a whisper, his breath warm on her ear, which sent a shiver of pleasure down her spine. 'Ned gave me quite a talking to yesterday morning after my ride.'

'I'm very sorry that I've missed our walks,' she whispered.

'And I am very sorry every second of the day that I am not with you.'

Becca's chest rose and fell. Her heart felt battered by the death of her friend and dizzy with the warm feelings of attraction. She did not know what to say. She would usually attempt humour, but his words had been so wonderful that she did not wish to cheapen them with mirth. Or for Phineas to suppose that she did not revel in them.

She was saved from having to respond by the Archbishop of Canterbury beginning the service. Her mother gestured for her to come forward and join their family. They walked to the front of the chapel and filled the first several pews.

It was not a very long meeting, but Becca managed to soak through all six of Phineas's handkerchiefs.

Later that night by candlelight, Becca picked up her charcoal pencil and began sketching Phineas again as a lion. She drew him holding an umbrella, like the one he had given her after Alexander's funeral to protect her from the rain during the graveside prayers. She sketched the six black handkerchiefs on the ground beside the lion. Behind the gravestone, she added a snake slithering for Helen. Then a spider crawled up the side as Frederica. Lastly she placed the mouse that represented herself, wrapped securely in his furry tail. She had felt Phineas's warmth that day. His thoughtfulness. But she supposed that all rakes were thoughtful. Why else would women fall in love with them in droves?

And he'd said that he wished to court her.

Was she just another foolish woman who had fallen prey to a rake's wiles? Or did he really mean it? He'd bought her a beautiful mourning ring and a half-dozen black handkerchiefs—just what she needed, when she needed it the most.

Becca wrote at the bottom of the sketch: *Thanks, Fin*.

Covering her sketch with an envelope, she decided she would ask Alonzo to deliver it to Phineas's house tomorrow.

Chapter Thirteen

The morning after the funeral, Phineas's lips tightened into a flat line as he saw two new gentlemen accompanying Becca on her morning walk. The tall one he easily recognised as the Duke of Hampford, Becca's father. Her favourite person. Her hand was on his arm. He was a famous naturalist and keeper of exotic animals. The Duke dressed rather shabbily and his riding boots were scuffed. He was well known for despising London society and dandies. Which was unfortunate.

The other man he was unable to identify until they were mere yards apart on the path. He had a strong figure of middling height. His dark green walking coat was refined, but not memorable. Phineas thought the same of the man's face and dark hair. Terrence Burman, the Marquess of Talbot, was no dandy, but he was a well-looking gentleman. He was also only four and twenty. Five years younger than Phineas. Talbot was in possession of a large fortune, well-managed estates and a title higher than an earl. Worst of all, the lord's reputation was so spotless that it'd earned him the nickname 'altar boy'.

Phineas's eyes met Becca's. She was dressed very prettily in a pink pelisse with rosettes and a matching bonnet. Her sparkle was a little dimmed by the loss of her friend, but she gave him a small smile as if expecting Phineas to find the humour in their situation. He did not. Talbot was serious in his suit and would probably make her a fine husband. He was not a bad bet like Phineas.

Talbot bowed to Phineas. 'Lady Rebecca, may I introduce you to Lord Norwich?'

'Thank you, Terrence, but we danced a set at my coming-out ball,' she said brightly. 'And, Norwich, you are acquainted with my father, the Duke?'

Phineas executed a perfect bow.

The Duke made an impatient sound and dipped his head briefly.

'Norwich, I didn't take you for an early morning man,' Lord Talbot said in a drawl. 'Unless it was to go to your tailor.'

Phineas executed another bow worthy of a court presentation. 'I did not know you were in town, Talbot.'

The Marquess puffed out his chest a bit. 'My mother says it's high time I married and secured our family's line.'

Since Lord Talbot possessed no fewer than three sisters and four younger brothers, Phineas did not believe the Burman line was in any fear of becoming extinct. His own family name, however, was not so fortunate. Phineas was an only son of an only son. If he'd died from the fall on his horse, his name would have ended with him.

The only person who might mourn his death was Kitty. He'd left her well provided for, but he was her only family and he didn't want her to be alone ever again. She needed much more than an inheritance. Kitty deserved a proper home with loving parents. He'd always done his best, but he'd wanted Kitty to have more than just him. He wanted her to have everything that he hadn't. His death was a sobering thought. That Talbot sought to wed Becca was equally unpleasant.

Phineas should have known that Becca would be the belle of the Season. As the only daughter of a duke debuting that year and with a healthy dowry, she would be beset by suitors, fortune-hunters and annoying worthies like Talbot. He despised them all.

'If it is high time you married,' Becca quipped, her face prim as her blue eyes sparkled, 'then poor Lord Norwich must be past his last prayer at nearly thirty.'

The Duke of Hampford snorted, but Phineas could see that her father found Becca's wit humorous.

Talbot's brow furrowed. 'Why would Norwich be praying? I never took him as a religious fellow.'

Such statements about being on their 'last prayer' were for spinsters, not bachelors. The blockhead Marquess didn't even understand how clever Becca was.

'One only hopes that he is not too old to beget children,' Becca continued.

Talbot leaned towards Becca, wrinkling his nose. 'What do children have to do with church? I don't quite follow.'

'Perhaps Papa could explain about the birds and bees to you,' Becca said in a falsely sweet voice. She dropped her father's arm and took Phineas's. 'Lord Norwich, shall we walk ahead for a little while? The path is growing narrow here.'

He was nearly as blockheaded as Talbot, for his mind all but stopped when she placed her hand on his body. His pulse raced and his temperature heightened. He wanted to kiss her so badly that his jaw ached. Recalling himself, he walked beside her for a few steps until there was a little space between their pair and Talbot and her father.

'I swear that I didn't invite Terrence,' she said in an undertone. 'Nor Papa for that matter.'

'Then they are well paired.'

Becca awarded his feeble wit with a glittering smile. 'Oh, no. Terrence will bore Papa to tears, but I suppose he deserves a little punishment for allowing Mama to foist the Marquess upon me.'

Phineas heartily approved of her appraisal of Lord Talbot, but the fact that she used his given name worried him a little. 'How long have you known *Terrence*?'

'For ever,' she said flippantly. 'Although not well. One of his minor estates is near Hampford Castle and we played a few times together as children. He was covered in red spots and smitten with Frederica then. But since I am the last Stringham sister unwed, I suppose that I will have to do.'

There was something in the tone of her voice, a sort of self-effacement that he didn't like. 'You are very similar to Lady Pelford in appearance, but in my elderly opinion, you are more beautiful.'

Disbelieving, she shook her head. 'Maybe you need spectacles, old man.'

'Or you need a new looking glass, young lady.'

Phineas did not have any brothers. Nor did he have any close cousins to compare himself to. Becca's sisters were all pretty, but none of them held a candle to her in his opinion.

'I shan't buy a new looking glass, I will borrow one from you. I dare say a dandy like yourself will have plenty to spare.'

She was teasing him and trying to change the subject of conversation from herself to him. Usually, he was more than happy to talk about himself. But not today. During these precious moments with Becca he wanted to learn more about her.

'By my reckoning, you owe me twenty-four more answers.'

'Will any answers suffice, or should you like to ask the questions first?'

He grinned. Becca's needle wit had stabbed him again.

'I should like to ask the questions first, my saucy minx,' he said. 'How many children should you like to beget?'

Becca's cheeks turned the same pink as her gown. It was a personal question, but she'd begun it by insinuating about his age and virility. 'At least a half a dozen. I love babies.'

The number didn't surprise him, neither did her answer. He only hoped that the children were more winsome than Kitty had been and that they scratched less. 'Do you have names already chosen?'

'Of course and they all start with the letter B. Besotted. Bewitched. And bedazzled.'

A laugh broke from his throat. She'd rattled off the flirtatious words he'd spoken to her a few mornings before. She'd remembered them. He hoped she'd thought about him half as much as he had about her. 'Excellent names for the girls, but what about the boys?'

'Bewildered, Bespoke and Bepuzzled.'

He gave a false sigh. 'No Bedlam?'

'Perhaps as a middle name.'

Phineas found himself grinning like a fool. She was so quick witted. 'What was your favourite toy as a child?'

Becca raised her eyebrows. 'Do pets count?'

He shook his head. 'That is another question entirely.'

She released a long breath. 'My stuffed bear, whose name is Burt.'

'Another excellent B name,' he agreed. 'Now you may tell me what your favourite pet's name is.'

'Kieran the camel leopard. I saw him the first day he was

born and he was already taller than me. He is eight years old now and quite the impressive fellow. The most beautiful spots. Do you like animals, Phineas?'

'I am the one asking the questions.'

Becca beamed up at him. 'Fair is fair.'

For her smiles, Phineas would answer some of her questions. He'd already decided that he wanted to marry Becca, but he was still trying to warm himself to the idea of having children. 'My favourite childhood toy was a rocking horse and my favourite animal is undoubtedly a lion. Particularly one in a tailcoat and trousers with a furry tail, who poses for artists.'

Her curved hip pressed against his. 'Then you will be pleased to see that your lion is the subject of yet another such drawing.'

Phineas raised his brows. 'Indeed? And when shall I get to gaze upon this artistic masterpiece that I inspired?'

'It is rather larger than the last drawing, so I put it in an envelope and I shall ask Alonzo to bring it over this afternoon or early evening. Whenever he can get away. He's become Mama's new secretary.'

He hoped that the tutor-turned-secretary would bring it promptly. He adored Becca's art for it highlighted her sharp wit. 'Did your family receive an invitation to Lady Astley's ball tonight?'

'Yes.'

'And shall you be dancing?'

Becca's bright eyes left his face and went to the black gloves on her hands—a sign of her mourning. Typically, one did not dance in black gloves. But the Stringhams were anything but typical.

'Yes. Since I have waited three years past most young

ladies, Mama does not intend to make us sit out for the rest of it...she hopes that I will find a husband.'

Phineas loved watching how Becca's blush grew from her plump bosom to her neck, to her cheeks. 'May I ask why the Duchess put off your presentation?'

Becca shook her head slightly, biting her lower lip in the way that inflamed him. 'Papa did not wish to part with us.'

'All of his children?'

Phineas cared deeply for Kitty. But he also looked forward to marrying her off and allowing the practicalities to be another man's problem.

'Only Helen and myself. We are his favourites. The last of his daughters. And we were not raised like debutantes, but as little naturalists. We trailed behind him to take care of the animals in the menagerie from the time that we could walk. And when the opportunity to travel was given to us, neither Helen nor myself could refuse it. A woman's world is often small. I discovered that mine is, but it is also wonderful. I have enjoyed freedoms that few could boast of.'

Unlike his father, Phineas did not intend to be a dictator, but a partner to his wife. To Becca. 'I would never wish to take away your freedoms and I would love to boast that I had the first two dances with Lady Rebecca Stringham at Lady Astley's Ball.'

'Very well. Boast away, my dear braggart.'

She blushed so adorably then that Phineas longed to pull her into his arms and follow the trail of her blush to its natural destination. But he reminded himself that her father and Talbot were walking behind them. He would not get to hold her until his set tonight.

'I assured Lord Talbot after the funeral that you would only be too pleased to reserve your first two dances with him for Lady Astley's ball,' Mama said in the carriage that afternoon.

Despite Alexander's memorial service being two days before, the only change Becca wore to signify her friend's death were black gloves. At home, Miss Shepherd was sewing black ribbons on her ball gowns. Shepherd's beau, Jim, rode on the back of the carriage. He took Mama's calling cards and brought them to the doors of her many acquaintances. Her mother wanted to make sure society knew that Becca was still participating in the London Season. And while she sincerely mourned Alexander, she'd spent the last three days weeping and she needed a change of scenery.

Becca wished that Papa was with them. Her mother was always softer when he was near. But her father hated *ton* morning calls—which took place in the afternoon—and was probably at his club, hiding in an old coat and reading the latest naturalist paper. In his place sat Mantheria. She wore a sombre grey gown, but she did not intend to follow society's dictates that would have her remain home for over a year in mourning. Mantheria had been separated from her legal husband for over eight years. It would have been a mockery to do more.

'How unfortunate,' Becca said, fiddling with her black lace gloves. 'My first two dances are already taken. But I will happily give Lord Talbot the third.'

Both Mama and Mantheria smiled at her.

'Did Lord Whitehurst already reserve the quadrille?' Mama asked eagerly. 'I saw him speak briefly to you after the funeral.'

She shook her head. 'No. Lord Norwich kindly asked for the quadrille and the second set this morning in the park. Papa, Terrence and myself met him on the path.'

Mantheria and Mama wore identical frowns. In features

Mantheria did not resemble their mother, but took after Papa. She was blonde and slender. Mama had rich brown hair that was beginning to show streaks of grey and a curvaceous figure, but unlike Becca, no one would ever have considered her mother plump.

'He is a handsome man and a fine dancer, but I wouldn't encourage him if I were you,' Mantheria said, tutting. 'Norwich is a rake and a hardened gamester.'

'One quadrille is hardly a courtship, my dear,' Mama said, touching her daughter's knee. 'But, Becca, your sister is not wrong. Although the Earl of Norwich is considered a matrimonial catch, he has not been caught in a decade and I would not waste your time on him. Every year he attends a few balls and breaks a few hearts before returning to the country.'

A shudder shook Becca to the very core. 'I will not allow him to break my heart, Mama, but I cannot refuse to dance with him tonight at Lady Astley's ball without making a scene.'

'She's right,' Mantheria said, wrapping her arms around herself.

Becca could only humbly nod.

'We should return home, Mama,' Mantheria continued. 'Becca could use some rest before going to the ball tonight.'

'Alas, she will not get it today,' Mama said. 'Becca, you are to go driving with Lord Whitehurst at three o'clock this afternoon.'

'Excuse me?' Becca scoffed, blinking. 'But he never asked me to.'

Mama inhaled slowly. 'His mother arranged it with me. We are both eager for you two to expand your acquaintance. Lady Whitehurst has confided to me that she is most desirous to have you for a daughter-in-law. And I will not deny that Lord Whitehurst also has my approval. He is a serious gentleman with a fine estate, deep pockets and a steady character.'

Since Becca was not entirely certain who the matron was, the compliment was not to her. If Lady Whitehurst wished for her son to marry Becca, it was because she was the daughter of a duke. Lord Whitehurst had appeared miserable at the prospect of waltzing with Becca at her coming-out ball. How much more he must loathe taking Becca on a drive.

'I do hope Lady Whitehurst has confided her dearest wishes to her son. He did not appear at all interested in me at my coming-out ball.'

Harrumphing, Mama shook her head. 'Lady Whitehurst assured me that her son was merely feeling shy. It is also his first London Season.'

Becca could only harrumph as well. If she spoke, she would say something cutting.

Chapter Fourteen

Lord Whitehurst was over a half an hour late to pick Becca up for their drive. If she was in any doubt of his lack of interest in her, she was certain of it now. Her lovely light blue pelisse and matching bonnet with feathers were entirely wasted on this trip.

The Baron did not even bother to come up to the door, but sent his groom instead. Becca was half tempted to refuse to leave the parlour until Whitehurst gave her a modicum of courtesy. But Mama had arranged this *charming* outing and she would be upset if Becca did not go driving with the uninterested Baron.

Harper, unlike the Baron, offered Becca his arm and escorted her to the phaeton and handed her in. Lord Whitehurst made no effort to assist her and only acknowledged her existence by touching the brim of his hat. She'd barely sat down when he let his horses go. Her gloved hands gripped the side of the carriage and Becca closed her eyes as they passed close enough to a wagon to scratch the wheels of the phaeton. The sound grated on her ears.

Clearly the Baron was ham-fisted with the reins.

They had nearly made their precarious way to the park when a feral cat ran in front of the horses and caused them to bolt. Whitehurst blanched, but he obviously had no idea how to control his steeds. Becca grabbed the reins from him and forced the spirited pair of horses to go around another carriage and to avoid a fruit cart. She was certain that if she hadn't taken charge she would have been in an accident with either or both wheeled carts and they would be covered in fruit.

'There now, it was just a cat,' she crooned to the horses as she pulled hard against the reins, forcing them to slow to a more respectable city pace. 'What lovely fast horses you are. But you must listen to me and calm down. Galloping in town is *not at all the thing*.'

Once they were under control, she led them through a tight turn and back to Rotten Row in Hyde Park. She'd calmed the horses and they were walking at a respectable pace in the park before she handed the ribbons back to Whitehurst.

He gulped as he took the reins back from her. 'They're new. I got them from Tattersall's last week and I have yet to learn their paces.'

'A small animal can spook the finest of drivers or riders,' she offered, but she wasn't thinking about the boring Baron. She was remembering her meeting with Phineas and the mouse.

Whitehurst managed to control the horses at a slow walk. His acquaintance in London appeared to be even smaller than her own, for he did not touch his hat or speak to anyone.

She waved to her sister Frederica who was in an open curricle with Samuel. Her brother-in-law pulled his horses to a stop, but Whitehurst did not do the same. He drove past without even acknowledging them.

Becca glanced over her shoulder and Frederica made a funny face at her and Samuel merely smiled. It would have been nice to speak with them in the park, but since they were staying in the same London house, they had ample opportunity for conversation. And perhaps Whitehurst didn't know that he was supposed to stop and chat with the occupants of the other carriages.

At this rate, their drive would be the dullest and the fastest ever known on the fashionable promenade of Rotten Row.

It became clear after at least a quarter of an hour that Whitehurst was not going to initiate any conversation. Unless she wished for another half-hour of silence, she would have to draw him out. Her first thought was to speak about the weather—the safest topic of all. But she was already aware that it had rained that very morning and most of the afternoon. The ground was a little muddy and discussing it at length would be more tedious than silence.

What would Phineas do? He certainly wouldn't speak about the weather unless he could turn it into something flirtatious or scandalous. Or he would ask her more of the fifty questions that he'd promised to.

'Perhaps I can ask you some questions so that we may become better acquainted?'

The Baron was silent for over a minute before he said, 'I suppose so, Lady Rebecca. If you wish to.'

It was hardly an encouraging response, but Becca persevered anyway. 'Is this your first London Season?'

'It is.'

Succinct.

She took a deep breath and asked a second question. 'And are you enjoying your time in town?'

'I suppose so.'

'Have you made many new friends and acquaintances?'

Whitehurst straightened his top hat. 'I suppose so.'

The Baron clearly 'supposed so' often and he was not keeping up his side of the conversation. Her questions had been common, but Phineas's had not been. 'What is your favourite colour?'

'Excuse me?'

'Your favourite *colour*. Mine is violet.'

He blinked at her twice. 'I suppose blue.'

Of course he *supposed*. 'And what is your favourite season?'

'Definitely not the London one.'

Becca giggled and the gaunt young Baron's face turned the same red as his spots. He appeared very young and ill at ease.

'I meant no offence, Lady Rebecca.'

She forced herself to sober, but she couldn't keep her lips from smiling. 'I am not at all offended, but I was thinking more along the lines of spring, summer, autumn, or winter.'

Whitehurst sucked his teeth. 'Summer.'

Becca fanned herself. It was hot. 'We are going to find speech between us a great difficulty if you keep giving such short answers.'

Sighing, the Baron replied, 'I suppose so.'

Shepherd arranged yellow feathers in the back of Becca's hair. They were not quite as tall as her white presentation ones, but they definitely added height to her appearance. Their particular shade of yellow matched Becca's evening gown to perfection with its flower pattern. The waist was very high, just underneath her bust. The tops of her shoulders were bare and her elegant sheer sleeves went all the way to her wrists. Where her short sleeves usually ended were furbelows of yellow flowers and green vines. The same furbelow was repeated at the bottom of her skirt just above the flounce.

Her lady's maid handed her a pair of delicate lace gloves and a little fan to wear around her wrist. Becca had always enjoyed pretty clothes, but she had not appreciated all of the little details until she met Phineas.

The two most important details of Lady Astley's party were that the first two dances were already promised to Phineas. And after the painfully silent drive with the boring Baron, Becca was fairly certain that Whitehurst would never ask her to dance or drive again. If only her mother would stop accepting on her behalf from *his mother*. The entire situation was ridiculous. Becca would have preferred that Whitehurst denied his own mother's matchmaking machinations, but she could imagine him saying, *'I suppose so.'* She would have to put an end to them herself.

Glancing about the house, Becca thought that Lady Astley's decorations for her ball were rather garish. London hostesses tried to outdo one another and Lady Astley's choice of stuffed animals around the hall was enough to put any person off their supper. Except for Lord Astley, who was an avid hunter and liked trophy kills. It appeared that he had also been to Africa like her parents, but instead of studying the animals, he had shot them.

Becca was not opposed to killing animals for food, but the idea of taking a life only to display—and not to eat— was abhorrent to her. She did, however, manage to curtsy correctly to both Lord and Lady Astley and even smile when they compared her to a swan unfurling her feathers.

'I am glad that I am no goose, or I might have been nailed to one of your boards.'

Mama grabbed Becca by the elbow. 'We are so happy to be here. Thank you again for your invitation.'

Her mother pulled her from the reception area and to the ballroom which had even more trophy heads. Unlike Mantheria, Mama did not lecture Becca on her less than grateful words to their hosts.

Mama wrinkled her nose in distaste. 'They would be more appropriate in a hunting lodge.'

'Or still attached to the animals who belonged to them.'

Turning her back to the largest framed trophy head of a bear, Mama said in an undertone, 'Remind me not to accept an invitation from Lady Astley next Season. Trophy heads are in terrible taste. Your father would be horrified.'

Becca shuddered. 'I dare say there will be even more decorations by then.'

'We don't have to stay.'

Her mother's words had double meaning, for she saw Phineas striding towards them in a zebra-striped waistcoat, navy knee breeches and tailcoat with golden buttons. As always, he was handsomer than a peacock with its fancy feathers unfurled.

He bowed lowly before them. 'Lady Rebecca, my set, I believe?'

She placed her hand in his. 'I will allow you the set, if I may win the match.'

Phineas smiled at her as he led her to the dance floor for the quadrille. 'Are we speaking of tennis or trophies or ballrooms?'

'All of the above.'

Becca was sad to let his hand go, but the quadrille was a very old dance and one didn't touch their partner as much as in a modern one, like the waltz. Still, it was fashionable to have the first dance of a ball be the quadrille. And she got to see his face clearly as they circled one another and then promenaded down the centre. It was a lively, happy dance and Phineas was light on his feet. Lord Tooting was not and did the wrong figure and bumped his backside into Becca. He turned to apologise, but she continued to dance as if nothing had happened.

She was sad when the string quartet played the final notes. She bowed formally to Phineas and was glad that he had secured the second dance. It was still a country reel, but they were able to speak more.

'I asked Lord Whitehurst several of your questions,' she said archly.

He raised one eyebrow. 'Were his answers satisfactory?'

'*I suppose so*—or rather, that was his answer to every question including his favourite colour.'

Phineas laughed and there was more sound to it than before. It was no longer breathy, but deep and full throated. '*I suppose* that I should ask you some questions before our set is over all too soon. And they are thoughtful ones.'

She spun around and then returned to him. 'I shall prepare myself accordingly.'

'What is your idea of a full life?'

It was a deeper question and much more difficult to answer than her favourite colour or season. Luckily, the dance parted them for several moments and Becca was allowed to think of her answer before she returned to Phineas. 'It is not unique: my idea of a full life is a husband and children. A home of my own. Visiting my family. Perhaps seeing more of the world and studying the many incredible animals of God's creation. There is so much yet to be discovered from fossils to—'

'*Rattus.*'

Becca laughed this time, for *rattus* was the Latin word for the genus of rats. 'I only like one particular rat.'

Phineas smiled back at her and happiness transformed

his already handsome features to something almost godlike. 'Thank you, my dear one. I am more than happy to be your rat... Next question: what does happiness mean to you?'

His questions this evening were certainly causing Becca to scramble for more than flirtatious words. They were seeking to the very centre of her soul. Yet her answer was only a few syllables like the boring Baron's. 'Family.'

'Your future or current family?'

'Both,' Becca said, twirling around him. 'Happiness is time spent with the people that I love. And what does it mean to you?'

Phineas didn't smile this time, but appeared to be in deep thought. It was clear that he wasn't asking her questions to hear the sound of his voice, but that he truly wished to know her answers and to understand them. And to share himself with her.

'You. Lady Rebecca Stringham. You are my happiness.'

She lost a little more of her heart to him in that moment. 'Whether that is true or not, it is the best answer you could have given.'

He gave a short laugh before asking, 'What lessons has life taught you?'

Another soul-searching one. 'Did Ned come up with these new questions?'

Touching his chest, Phineas feigned offence. 'No. I thought of them myself. I did not ask my groom for help. Nor his wife.'

Their hands met again. 'The imitable Mrs Jenks.'

'You are stalling.'

'And you are handsome.'

Phineas laughed. 'You are charming and beautiful, but you are still stalling.'

Becca took a deep breath. She was a little winded from

all the dancing and from the personal nature of the question. 'That people aren't defined by their mistakes... What has life taught you?'

His brow furrowed. 'That you cannot change the past.'

She wondered what mistakes that he had made that were still plaguing him now. She wished that he could forget them or forgive them. 'You cannot change the past, but you can let it go.'

'You are wise beyond your years.'

She raised her eyebrows. 'A lady never admits her age.'

Phineas's lips twitched. 'Does a lady admit if she is afraid of anything?'

'She does. I worry that society will judge me harshly for my difficulties with reading, despite how hard I have tried to overcome them.'

'Society can be swayed by the wind,' Phineas said, his lips curling into a sneer. 'Its opinion does not matter.'

They broke apart again and Becca was eager to get back to him in the figure. 'Then whose opinion does matter?'

'Yours.'

She'd expected Phineas to say his own. He was a leader of the dandy set and raising his quizzing glass was known to overset duchesses. He also was an earl and held power in Parliament, unlike her father who avoided the House of Lords. On the other hand, Becca was the daughter of a duke, which gave her social status, but nothing beyond that. As the youngest in her family, she was rarely asked for her opinions or suggestions. No one deferred to her judgement.

Becca tugged up her slipping glove. 'Why mine?'

'Because your own opinion is the only one that you can control.'

For the first time at the ball, Becca was glad for their parting in the dance. It gave her a few moments to collect her thoughts before they met again for the end of the song. Phineas took her hand one last time and they bowed to each other as the fiddlers played the last note.

After curtsying, she allowed him to escort her back to Mama and the third dance with Terrence. When they reached her mother, Phineas bowed over her hand one last time. He held it to his lips and brushed a kiss against her glove. Another piece of her heart was lost.

'You are wise, too, Phineas. But exactly in proportion to your years.'

Phineas dropped her hand, presumably in surprise, and laughed loudly.

Chapter Fifteen

Phineas wore a seafoam-green coat that few men could wear to admiration. He'd wanted Becca to admire him in it, but he hadn't seen her this morning at the park. He'd lingered for over an hour before returning home for his horse and going on a long hard ride. It didn't dispel his disappointment, but it helped his temper.

Pulling his horse to a stop, Phineas dismounted and handed the reins to Ned who stood waiting for them. A smile on the gruff man's face. Oh, dear. Phineas was certain he was about to receive more well-intended courting advice.

'Thank you, Ned.'

'My lord,' the groom said, holding out a large envelope in his free hand. 'This arrived for you this morning from the Duchess of Hampford's secretary. A Mr Lawes, I believe.'

Phineas took it and could hardly wait to open it. He'd waited for it to arrive all yesterday afternoon and it never had. The next best thing to being with Becca was seeing one of her caricatures.

Ned clucked his tongue.

Sighing, Phineas asked, 'Is there anything else, Ned?'

'I shouldn't wish for Your Lordship to think I was a gossip, but I exchanged a few words with the Duchess of Hampford's secretary.'

Phineas found himself leaning forward to hear what his servant had gleaned. 'Pray tell.'

Ned rubbed his nose. 'Ye see, Your Lordship, the Hampford staff is waiting for you to ask Lady Rebecca out on a drive to the park. Yesterday she went driving with Lord Whitehurst and today she has a driving appointment with Lord Talbot. The Duchess of Hampford accepted for her daughter on both occasions. Mr Lawes was very specific on that point. I thought you ought to know that.'

He'd taken for granted that they would meet every morning in the park with or without a chaperon tailing behind them. *Ton* balls lasted until the early morning hours and if her mother was accepting invitations for her afternoons, Phineas should have realised that Becca would need to sleep some time.

His groom stood looking at him expectantly.

'Anything else, Ned?'

The groom took off his hat and held it in his hand. 'I were thinking you might be wishful for me to deliver a message to her ladyship about a drive to the park tomorrow. Your team of high steppers are a great deal better than Lord Talbot's showy horses. Mr Lawes also told me that Lady Rebecca is a capital whip and enjoys driving a team.'

Phineas should have thought of this himself. 'Very well. If you will make yourself ready, I will have a footman bring out a note to you.'

Ned plopped on his hat and grinned. 'I had another idea for you, my lord.'

'Did you now?'

'It happened upon me when I were eating luncheon in your house. You were in the music room pounding them keys and I thoughts to myself, it would be a grand romantic gesture iffen you were to write a song to Lady Rebecca,' he said, winking. 'Ladies like grand romantic gestures. Trust me. Mrs Jenks agreed to marry me after I sang a song to her in front of an entire pub.'

Phineas's lips twitched with amusement. His groom had clearly chosen the wrong profession, he was meant to be a matchmaker. 'Thank you again, Ned.'

With a nod, Phineas went into his house. The butler and the housekeeper met him with uncommon smiles. They were married to each other, but previously they had not been warm with their employer.

'Did you have a good time in the park, my lord?' Mrs Johnston asked.

'Good enough.'

'Shall I fetch a footman for you?' Mr Johnston asked. 'Ned mentioned that he would be needing to deliver something to Berkeley Square.'

Phineas breathed in. His staff had never tried to be friendly before now. They'd always kept their appropriate distance. But since he had met Becca, he had changed for the better. 'Thank you, Johnston. I will ring when I require assistance.'

He strode into his study and closed the door behind him, before opening the large envelope from Becca. No doubt Ned, Mr and Mrs Johnston, the scullery maid and all of his other servants were agog to see it. They seemed to be as interested in his love life as his groom. As far as he could recall, his servants had never before cared about his welfare beyond performing their required duties.

The off-kilter feeling returned.

A month ago, he would have nipped all their enquiries and impertinences in the bud. Phineas preferred the world not to get too close to him, whether the person was a royal duke or a servant. He'd carefully lived his life to ensure that no one came near him—ever. Yet the closer he allowed himself to become to Becca, the rest of the world seemed determined to follow.

Unable to resist his curiosity any longer, Phineas gently opened the large envelope and saw another lion drawing. The lion was wearing his tall beaver hat and standing in a cemetery holding an umbrella while raindrops fell all around. He held the umbrella slightly to the side of him and his furry part of his tail was around a little mouse with the same style of bonnet that Becca wore. Around the mouse were six black handkerchiefs on the ground. Glancing closer, he saw a snake and a spider. As usual, Becca had included herself and her two elder sisters in the caricature, but not the Duchess of Glastonbury. There was probably a good reason for that. He wished he knew what it was.

Underneath the sketch were two words: *Thanks, Fin*.

The other sketch had been playful and smart, but this one was truly a work of art. There was so much expressive emotion in the charcoal lines. He felt the little mouse's anguish, but also the gentle care of the much larger lion. Phineas had never thought of himself as a lion. He wasn't physically intimidating. He was slender and not much above medium height. He never boxed. It might ruin his perfect nose or bruise his beautiful face. He did not fence either. It seemed juvenile to play with sharp knives. And he no longer duelled with pistols.

But he was Becca's lion. A heady thought. Phineas's lips quirked up into a smile and he found himself grateful to his interfering groom. Taking out a sheet of hot press paper, he dipped his pen in the ink. He wanted to say a dozen things to Becca, but he also knew that reading was difficult for her. He tried to come up with the shortest possible message:

May I pick you up tomorrow at three o'clock for a drive in the park? Fin.

Pouring a little sand on the ink, he gently blew on the paper before folding it into an envelope and closing it with melted wax and the Norwich seal. He'd never before shortened his name to *Fin*, but he rather liked it. Or he liked it when Becca wrote it.

Phineas tugged the bell and gave the letter to a footman with the directions to be hand-delivered to Hampford House. He thought that all of his servants would be disappointed if they knew how short and direct the missive was. But he and Becca were not engaged—yet. It was not considered appropriate for unmarried people to send letters to each other. He was glad that Becca did not seem to think her sketches counted. Every one he received had made him feel light-headed and euphoric. As if he'd been in her joyful presence once more.

As he sat at his desk, it was hard to concentrate on his business matters. He kept thinking about her. Whitehurst wasn't competition. He was barely one and twenty. If that. His mother must have been pushing him to court Becca, a daughter of a duke, for he did not seem interested in her at the coming-out ball. The young fool.

Talbot, however, was a Corinthian. He dressed well as a member of the Four Horse Club and had a tall, athletic build. Younger than himself and his reputation was spotless—unlike Phineas's. Not that he thought the Marquess of Talbot had been a saint. He'd probably sowed the same wild oats and made comparable mistakes. He'd merely been smarter at not being the subject of gossip. Something, no doubt, his late father had helped steer him through before succumbing to his gout the year before. Phineas did not know whether, if his own father had lived, he would have bothered to help him in society. He might not have been taken in by the gull-catchers or nearly gambled out of his entire fortune by the Duke of York.

It was foolish to wonder.

His father had not spent much time in Phineas's company as a child or young man. If the man had intervened, it would have been because Phineas was his heir, rather than any warmer feelings. Not that Phineas could complain. Father had treated his illegitimate offspring worse. His will had not contained any provisions for his *natural* children. Phineas had provided for them out of his own purse. 'Ridiculous' is what Becca had called the fourth Earl of Norwich and Phineas thoroughly agreed with her.

There was a discreet knock at the door and Phineas found himself smiling as he told them to enter. It was Tom and Ned the groom. Tom wore his liveried coat and had an air of injury. Grooms were not supposed to come inside the house, or deliver correspondence to the master. It was *his* job. But Phineas doubted that the young and strapping footman, for all his inches on the groom, would have got the best of Ned in a bout of fisticuffs.

Ned handed the letter clenched in his hand to Phineas.

'Thank you,' Phineas said, bowing his head. 'That will be all.'

Tom lifted his nose in the air and began walking out of the room with great dignity. But Ned did not. His mouth hung agape and his black, bushy eyebrows were raised. 'Did she say yes, my lord?'

Phineas could have picked up his quizzing glass and sent Ned out with a snide remark. He chose instead to open the letter. Becca's response was even shorter than his:

YES.

Before he could share the happy news with his groom, Ned said, 'I'll have your horses ready and your phaeton shining tomorrow, milord. We got to make a good impression on her ladyship. Yes, indeed we do.'

The groom doffed his hat twice and left the room by slamming the door. Instinctively, Phineas jumped a little in his chair. With a sigh, he assumed that Ned had guessed the response based on Phineas's facial response to the letter. Or the one little written word that seemed to fill his entire body with warmth:

YES.

He hoped she would say it again when he asked her a most specific question in the near future. He'd only known her for less than a month, but he was already certain of his feelings. He wanted her. He cared for her. He wished for her to be his wife. How different these emotions were from his first proposal. Asking Lady Louisa had been prudent. He hadn't felt a whit of nervousness. Something told him that when he proposed to Becca that he would be a wreck of hope.

Becca allowed Shepherd to help her into her pelisse and bonnet. Lord Talbot would be arriving at any moment to take her for a drive down Rotten Row. And unlike the reluctant Lord Whitehurst, at least Terrence wanted to be with her. Although, like the Baron, he, too, had asked Mama instead of herself.

She was wearing a new blue net dress over a white underskirt. Her dark blue spencer and feathered bonnet matched the gown to perfection and her mother had even purchased her a reticule to complete the ensemble. Becca only wished that Phineas could see her in it. He appreciated clothes and Terrence didn't. But it did no good thinking about Phineas. It only made her more discontented with her partner.

Papa was sitting and reading his newspaper in the parlour when she entered. He glanced over the paper at her. 'Going somewhere, my dear?'

She slumped down beside him on the sofa. 'Driving with Terrence. Mama arranged it without asking me.'

Her father crumbled one side of the paper. 'With Talbot? What in the world is she thinking? He is a good sort, but not nearly clever enough for my daughter.'

Becca's heart sank a little in her chest. 'Probably that Terrence will never notice my learning deficiencies. He's proud of the fact that he isn't bookish. Not that I should scorn him, because I am not either.'

Papa fisted the other side of the newspaper. 'There is more to intelligence then reading, Becca. And the fellow would bore you to tears in less than a fortnight. I nearly wept after our one morning walk in the park.' He dropped the crumpled paper on the floor. 'I am going to go speak with your mother. Not even Talbot's five thousand a year is enough to make him worthy of you. At least bloody Norwich has brains.'

Becca gasped.

'You didn't think I'd notice six black handkerchiefs embroidered with the letter N? Do you take me for a dumb donkey?'

Smiling in spite of herself, Becca said, 'I think you are a very stubborn mule and that Mama is a lioness. She is going to eat you alive.'

Her father shrugged his shoulders, but his expression was sheepish. 'Probably, my darling. Do put in a good word for me in my eulogy.'

'I will,' she assured him as he left the room. Becca couldn't help but be touched that her father was going to stand up for her to Mama. Papa never sided with a child over his wife. He worshipped Mama and he respected her wisdom. However, Becca was certain that today would be her last drive with Terrence. Despite giving Mama her way ninety-nine times out of one hundred, when Papa decided something he was impossible to gainsay. Like a stubborn rhinoceros he sat down and refused to be moved.

When Lord Talbot arrived precisely when he was expected, it was impossible not to compare his looks to Phineas's golden ones. Terrence's features were regular and his countenance pleasing overall. He was also broader in the shoulders and his size complemented her larger figure. He bowed over Becca's hand and smiled, but it didn't reach his eyes.

'Lady Rebecca, how charming you look today and all grown up,' he said heartily.

Terrence was treating her as if she was a twelve-year-old girl and not a woman twenty years of age. But Becca was determined to be polite even if it killed her. And it just might. 'Thank you, Lord Talbot. You are looking all grown up, too.'

She wished that she hadn't known him when he'd picked his nose.

Becca allowed him to escort her out to his phaeton and to assist her inside the high-perched vehicle. He grabbed her waist clumsily and practically tossed her up into the seat. He clambered in beside her and took the reins from his tiger, a scruffy urchin who winked at Becca. She already liked the tiger more than his master. Terrence lifted his whip and cracked it over the horses' heads. He had a pair of matched bays that were pretty steppers and Becca noticed that he was a very good driver. He handled the ribbons efficiently as he weaved his team through the crowded London streets.

Once they reached Hyde Park and Rotten Row, Terrence turned his attention from his horses to her. 'If I recall correctly, Lady Rebecca, you are a very pretty whip.'

'Hand over your whip and I will show you,' she suggested with a false smile. She would more likely whip the man than his horses with it.

He guffawed as if she were a great wit.

Becca forced herself to smile again. This was going to be a very long drive and an even longer London Season.

Chapter Sixteen

Becca had not been in the park this morning, but Phineas did not mind. He would have her all to himself this afternoon.

After a light midday meal, Phineas had his valet brush off his glorious seafoam coat and shine his Hessians a second time. He took off his cravat that had become rather droopy and tied a fresh one. He even dabbed a bit of cologne behind his ears. Looking at himself in the mirror for nearly ten minutes, Phineas decided that his appearance could not have been improved upon. He put on his hat and left his house for the mews.

'You look as fine as fivepence, my lord,' Ned assured him.

'As does the phaeton. Thank you, Ned.'

Phineas's sporting vehicle appeared to have been freshly polished and his horses' hair shone as if they'd been recently brushed. He took a large step into the high-perch phaeton and reached out his gloved hand for the reins.

The groom handed the ribbons up to him. 'And don't forget, milord, to let Lady Rebecca have a turn handlin' the reins the way Mr Lawes suggested. Occasionally a lady likes to have the bit between her teeth.'

Touching the brim of his hat, Phineas said, 'I will not forget. Thank you, Ned.'

Reins in one hand and his whip in the other, Phineas cracked the lash above his horses' heads and they careened forward. They were a little fresh, but by the time he arrived in Berkeley Square, he'd taken the edge off them. A groom took their bridle and Phineas hopped out of his carriage to collect Becca.

The butler, an older man with a stern face, directed him into a front parlour to wait. Phineas saw an enormous pianoforte and couldn't resist taking a seat on its bench. He opened the instrument and ran a gloved finger across all the keys. It was well tuned and had a lovely, rich sound. Pulling off his gloves, he played the music from an opera. He lost himself in the song so much that he didn't even realise he wasn't alone until he played the final note.

'I thought you were Frederica for a moment,' Becca said, standing in the doorway. She was wearing a navy riding habit with two rows of golden buttons running down the front of her bodice and all the way to her hem. Over her burnished curls was a round hat the same colour as the habit with matching blue feathers. Her clothes perfectly complimented her lush figure and peaches-and-cream colouring.

Standing up, he saw a little colour steal into her cheeks. He loved that he made her blush. 'I hope you'll forgive the liberties I took.'

She raised her eyebrows and said primly, 'The trouble is that I would happily forgive any liberties you took.'

The adorable rogue. She knew more innuendo than any debutante should.

Taking his gloves in one hand, he strode over to her and closed the door behind her. He didn't want the benevolent butler to view their interlude. 'What sort of liberties did you have in mind?'

'Any liberty without hands.'

Becca had issued him a challenge and he was not about to fail it. He slanted his lips towards hers, not touching anywhere but their lips. Her mouth was sweet and moist and marvellous to taste. She opened her lips and he danced with her tongue. Her sweet innocence and her growing experience. This was the second time that he'd kissed her and she'd already become more adept at the art. She was clearly a quick learner and would surpass his own skills in no time.

With one last lick, Phineas broke the kiss.

Becca beamed at him. 'Your tongue is certainly an *education*, but we'd best get outside to your horses before the groom starts walking them up and down the street. Or poor Harper has a heart attack. He does not approve of us being alone.'

'Excellent points,' Phineas said, tugging on his gloves.

He opened the door for her and then offered his arm. Becca curled her hand around his arm and pressed up next to him as they walked. A most agreeable way to move.

The Hampford butler opened the door. 'Do be careful, my lady.'

She briefly touched the butler's arm. 'I always am, Harper.'

Happily, his vehicle was still stopped in front of the house with his groom holding the horses' bridles. Phineas placed his hands on each side of Becca's waist and helped her up inside the high-perch phaeton. She felt soft and curvaceous. He wished that he could have explored those curves more, but at least he had enjoyed a moment or two with his mouth.

Phineas climbed up after her and sat down. Their legs

were touching as he took the reins from the groom and tossed the man a coin. He flicked the whip and directed the horses into the road and on to the familiar path to Rotten Row. Trying to show off, he took a corner rather quickly and the phaeton tipped to be on only two wheels.

He should have felt embarrassed to be so ham-handed with the reins in front of Becca, but she'd taken his arm to stay in her seat and she had not released it. Phineas loved the feel of her holding him for support. No one had ever sought for him in that way. Even when they reached the park and their pace became sedate, she didn't let go.

'How was your drive with Lord Talbot?' The question was out of his lips before he'd thought it through. He was jealous, but he didn't want to appear jealous. Appearances had been more important than truths to his parents.

Pressing her luscious lips together, she shook her head. 'He told me that if I was a good girl, that he would let me hold the reins of the carriage in the park.'

He raised one eyebrow. He needn't have felt jealous at all. What a clunch. 'And what did you say?'

'I said if he was a good boy that I wouldn't slap his face.'

Phineas threw back his head and laughed harder than he had in his entire life. He laughed so hard that he found it difficult to breathe. It was a good thing that his horses were walking, because he could barely keep hold of the reins.

Her dimple peeped out from her cheek. 'Talbot chuckled, too, but I was being entirely serious. Why is it that so many men are under the great misunderstanding that because a woman has monthly menses, that she is somehow inferior to them?'

Becca's words sobered him. Scientific men and doctors might talk about the female cycle, but it was out of his depth.

He blinked. 'I do not think women are inferior to men in intelligence, or in abilities. I have it from my groom, Ned, that you are a capital whip.'

Her dimple was back out and she was smiling widely at him. 'Dear Ned. How does he go on?'

'The fellow has taken to matchmaking with considerable aplomb. He gives me advice daily on how best I should go on. This particular piece of knowledge came from Mr Lawes.'

She giggled. 'I thought it was from his wife.'

'No, I believe the best ideas are Ned's. His latest suggestion is that I compose a song for you on the pianoforte.'

Becca leaned against him in the carriage and his pulse quickened. 'I should be honoured, but you needn't waste your time on me.'

'There is nothing I would like to do more.'

She gave another gurgle of laughter that made his heartbeat thunder in his chest.

'I've been thinking about you. Every hour of every day,' Phineas said and it was true. Not just wicked thoughts, he wanted to know what she was thinking and how she was feeling at all times. He wished to be like the lion with the umbrella—her refuge in the rains of life.

'I think of you just as often, Phineas,' Becca said, but her countenance had turned sober.

His insides melted.

'I care for you Phineas. More than I have for anyone else in my life. And I should very much like to be courted by you. But I also know that I cannot live the way my sister Mantheria has. I will not marry a faithless rake. It would destroy me slowly.'

Phineas felt as if a bucket of cold water had been dumped on his head. He should have known that the Stringhams had kept nothing back about him. They'd called him a fortune hunter and a hardened gamester. Of course they would have shared with Becca his disreputable past for which he had no good excuses.

He'd repaired his fortunes. He'd stopped gaming for high stakes. He didn't have a venereal disease. He hadn't lived like a monk, but he'd never dallied with married women. Nor caused scandals since his salad days. But he hadn't been able to eradicate his reputation as a rake.

'I have not been a saint, Becca,' he said in a low voice. 'I have behaved like most young men, but I can assure you that I have every intention of being a faithful husband. You see, my father was not and the pain that it caused our entire family—'

Phineas didn't know how to finish the sentence. He was still paying for his father's selfish choices.

Becca's eyes were on her hands in her lap. 'I believe you and I hope that you didn't find my words too impertinent. I thought that it was important for us to know each other's expectations before furthering our relationship.'

He loved her honesty—even if it was often painful. He also loved that she believed him. Phineas didn't know how many of his acquaintances would take him at his word. No matter how many people he acknowledged socially on Rotten Row in the park. 'Would you like to take the reins?'

She didn't speak, but deftly took them from his hands. 'You still need to ask me fifteen questions.'

Phineas should have prepared questions, but he had not. His eyes passed a group of children playing with a dog. 'Do you prefer dogs or cats?'

'Cats. I have a lovely black feline that I named Witchhazel. But my brothers think that she is possessed by an evil spirit and simply call her *Witch*. And what about you?'

'Alas, I prefer dogs. I have half a dozen at Ridley Hall and I take them hunting, except for my pug, Pugsley. His run is the speed of another dog's walk. The lazy fellow rarely leaves his favourite cushion, let alone the house. Which leads me to my next question—do you prefer hot chocolate or tea?'

'There is nothing better than chocolate first thing in the morning. You?'

Phineas thought of something much better, but he was attempting to convince her that he was not a hardened libertine. 'Coffee.'

'That wasn't even an option,' she protested. She turned the team of horses down another park lane that led to the Serpentine.

'Next question: rivers or lakes?'

'For swimming or picturesque aesthetics?'

'First question and then second question.'

Becca wrinkled her nose. 'I prefer swimming in rivers to lakes. They aren't nearly as smelly. Although the water is always cold. And for your second question, the answer is the same as the first. Rivers, because the water is always moving and going somewhere new. Lakes are stagnant things.'

Phineas's life had been stagnant for years. Being with Becca made him feel fresh and new.

'Did you receive an invitation to Lady Lucas's musicale tonight?'

Phineas vaguely recalled receiving an invitation and he'd previously had no intention of attending. Musicales and other talent nights were usually tedious. And the debutante performers were mediocre at best. But he would endure a night of bad music for Becca's sake. 'I could look in for a few minutes if you'd like me to.'

'I shan't blink all night so that I won't miss your brief appearance.'

He smirked. 'I stepped into that one, didn't I?'

Looping the whip like a master whipster, she gave him another smile that he felt from his head to his toes. 'With both feet.'

And his entire heart.

Becca wished that any other sister besides Mantheria could have been her chaperon that night. Mama's head cold had returned and Papa was deathly allergic to society parties. Especially musical soirées full of young debutantes and single gentlemen. Not that Becca would miss his presence tonight. He was a bit of a whiner when made to go places he didn't wish to. Or, like her sister Helen, he would talk about embarrassing things like animal faeces or mating habits of different species that he felt were far superior to the human approach. She could just imagine him speaking for ten minutes at a time about whale song.

Frederica had originally offered to be her chaperon, but since she was currently casting up her dinner, Mama had thought it best to send Mantheria in her stead. Becca wished that it had been Helen. But her naturalist sister was almost as bad as Papa when forced to go somewhere she didn't want to and Helen wasn't at all musical.

Mama wanted Becca to make a few friends her own age and it would have been much easier without her exacting elder sister by her side. It was almost impossible for Becca to be herself next to Mantheria, even if her new evening gown was gorgeous. It was off-white silk with little black glass beads in a dotted pattern. The sleeves were short and puffed with a lovely scroll-like embroidery that was repeated on the flounce. She couldn't wait for Phineas to see her in it.

A servant offered Becca a glass of white wine and she took it. Before the goblet had reached her lips, Mantheria reminded her, 'Only a little sip. Wine goes straight to your waist.'

Lowering the glass without drinking it, Becca felt her mouth go dry. She wished that at least one conversation with her sister would not include a comment on her size. Mantheria was nearly the same height as Becca, but her figure was slender. Her hair was a similar golden shade to Phineas's. She took after Papa's side and was the beauty of the family.

Becca was the runt.

Except she wasn't little, as her eldest sister reminded her ever so frequently. Becca placed her glass on another servant's tray. She would have liked nothing more than to move to the side of the room, preferably into a dark corner. But Mantheria was speaking to Lady Lucas and, if she left her chaperon, Becca would never hear the end of it. Unlike Frederica and Helen, Mantheria did not have a sense of humour or fun. The rules of society seemed to be imprinted upon her very soul. She followed each of them with painful exactness. It still surprised Becca that her eldest sister had separated from her unfaithful husband eight years ago. The situation must have been unendurable for Mantheria to have broken the rules.

'Do you play the pianoforte, Lady Rebecca?' Lady Lucas asked politely. The older woman was dressed in a dark purple gown with a matching turban that made her head appear twice as large.

Swallowing, Becca tried to smile. 'I do not, my lady.

There was not much music in our home after my sister Elizabeth died at such a young age.'

Mantheria gasped and Lady Lucas coughed.

Becca had said the wrong thing. Not that it wasn't true, for it was. After Charles and Elizabeth, Mantheria's twin, died of scarlet fever, no one sang for years at the castle. Not even the servants. Elizabeth had been the songbird and no one wished to take her place.

However, it was also true that Becca hadn't been able to read with any reliability until last year. Not one of her governesses had ever tried to teach her the notes of the pianoforte. She'd only begun to sing a few years ago, when Miss Perkins had been their governess. And the way Frederica played the instrument made it impossible to sing to. She pounded the keys like a general at war.

'Becca,' Mantheria hissed out of one side of her mouth, 'this is hardly the appropriate place for such a personal discussion.'

'Forgive me, Lady Lucas. I did not mean to make you feel uncomfortable. What a lovely instrument you have. I am sure that all the other young ladies will be eager to show their skills upon it.'

The colour returned to the older woman's face and she smiled at Becca. 'My niece in particular, Miss Lucy Fraser, is very accomplished. I believe that you are old acquaintances, from Miss Victoria Clues's school, near Bath.'

Becca tried not to blink at the name of one of her childhood tormentors who had teased her mercilessly because of her reading difficulties. She'd left the school after only one month.

'What a delightful surprise for my sister,' Mantheria cut in, giving Becca a dirty look for not responding to their hostess. 'I am sure Rebecca would love to renew their acquaintance. It is so important for debutantes to make friends during their first Season.'

Lady Lucas's smile faltered. 'It is my niece's fourth Season, but I am sure that she will find the perfect match this year. Her dowry, shall we say, is not what it could be. Her own father would not have been able to give her another Season if it hadn't been for my husband's generosity.'

Becca found her tongue. 'Miss Fraser is lucky to have such a kind family.'

'If I may be frank, it is my dearest wish for my niece to become friends with you, Lady Rebecca. It would elevate her into the highest circles of society.'

Becca tried to smile, but she couldn't quite manage it. The woman only wished for her niece to be Becca's friend to raise her status. It was no wonder that Phineas had become disillusioned with society—they were more vicious than a murder of crows.

Mantheria nudged Becca in the stomach with her elbow. All Stringhams were elbowers. 'How kind of you. My little sister is eager to renew old relationships and make new friends.'

Becca tried to echo her sister's words, but her tongue would not allow her to make the syllables. She didn't want to be friends with Lucy.

'Lady Lucas, what a pleasure it is to see you. Thank you for the invitation,' Phineas said, sweeping the older woman an elegant bow. He was dressed in a silver suit of clothes that sparkled like a chandelier. He had diamonds on his cravat, his fingers, and even one diamond stud in his left ear. He must have had it pierced only hours before. He looked impossibly gorgeous and Becca felt as breathless as if she'd been elbowed in the stomach a second time.

'Lord Norwich, I did not receive your acceptance until

this afternoon,' Lady Lucas said, wagging her finger. 'I had almost given up hope on your attendance.'

Phineas took Becca's gloved hand and kissed it. Her body hummed in delight. 'With such company to be had, how could a mere man resist?'

He then took Mantheria's and Lady Lucas's hands. He bowed over them, as was correct, but did not kiss either of them. And if Becca had any doubts of his intentions, he took her hand and placed it on the crook of his arm, claiming her company. For the first time that night, Becca smiled and it didn't feel painful.

'My niece is going to play first,' Lady Lucas said, putting on airs. 'She is a most accomplished musician. Lady Rebecca unfortunately does not play.'

'As I am well aware,' Phineas said, insinuating that he knew her well. Although the subject of music had only come up once. 'But Lady Rebecca has the voice of an angel. Surely you can persuade her to sing, Lady Lucas?'

The older woman pointed her annoying wagging finger at Becca. 'You have been hiding your light underneath a bushel, my lady.'

Becca pinched Phineas's arm and he winced a little, but still smirked at the group. 'I am afraid that I have no one to accompany me. My sister Frederica is not here.'

Phineas showed his teeth, but Becca would not have called it a smile. Although he did appear amused at her anger. 'I shall accompany you myself, my dear Lady Rebecca.'

Lady Lucas clapped her hands. 'Then you two shall follow my niece to help begin the musical evening. Would five minutes be too soon to start?'

'Not at all,' Becca said through gritted teeth and the woman twirled away as if she were waltzing alone. 'I dare say it will not take more than four minutes to murder an earl.'

His smile this time was genuine, as was his laugh. It twisted up her insides and goose pimples formed on her arms.

'Becca, this is the second time you have put me to the blush in a matter of minutes,' Mantheria said, waving her painted ivory fan.

Phineas's eyes were on Becca, but he spoke to her sister. 'The fault is all mine, Duchess. I know that Becca does not like to be on display, but I couldn't resist the opportunity to hear her sing.'

'My lord, you should not be so informal with my sister's name,' Mantheria said primly from behind her fan. 'A young lady's reputation must be guarded at all times.'

'Then I volunteer to be her most devoted foot soldier.'

Becca pinched her lips together to keep from smiling, or worse, laughing at his joke.

Mantheria might have missed it, but Phineas didn't. 'I saw your smile, Lady Rebecca, there is no reason to try to hide it and you do not have a fan to conceal it like the Duchess of Glastonbury.'

'Phineas—Lord Norwich, I have never sung before anyone that wasn't family and, even then, it was never a solo. I don't have the voice for it.'

'Then I shall sing with you.'

'And accompany us?'

'Yes,' he said, leaning forward to whisper. His warm breath on her ear. 'We are going to be marvellous. Remember, I am always right... And look, you already like me a little bit more than you did only a few moments ago.'

Shaking her head, Mantheria clucked like a badly tempered hen. 'Lord Norwich, you are standing a great deal too close to my sister and whispering is *not at all the thing*.'

Phineas turned his gaze to her sister. 'We were just discussing what song to perform. What about "Early One Morning"?'

'I'd prefer "Adieu. Adieu".'

He gave her a half-smile that stole her breath a second time. 'An excellent choice, but not for the first number. What about "As I Walked Through the Meadow"?'

Before Becca could answer him, Lucy was introduced and began to play. They politely did not speak during her performance of the first song, or when she was asked to give an encore by her aunt. Lady Lucas came over after Lucy's two songs. Her wrinkled face was wreathed in smiles. 'Please allow me the honour of escorting you, Lord Norwich and Lady Rebecca, to my Broadwood Grand.'

Phineas placed his free hand over hers on his arm and gave her a reassuring smile, before dragging her with him to the new black instrument. He released her hand only to sit down on the bench and open it. The room fell silent and it was not only because of Lady Lucas's painful introduction. Everyone was looking at Phineas sitting at the pianoforte and the diamonds glittering on his fingers. Blinking, Becca assumed that he had never played in public before. Oh, why did he have to choose this very night to do so? And with her?

He glanced over his shoulder at her and the tightness in her chest loosened just a bit. 'Ready?'

'As death.'

Grinning, he turned back to the piano and began to play the most beautiful and intricate tune she had ever heard. His fingers moved over the keys in a way she'd only seen by professional musicians. The song that Phineas played she'd never heard before. It was like all the folk songs that she'd ever heard combined together in perfect dissonance. He changed keys and Becca recognised the melody to the song they were supposed to sing together.

Phineas took a deep breath before he sang.

As I walk'd thro' the meadows
To take the fresh air,
The flowers were blooming and gay,
I heard a fair damsel so sweetly a'singing
Her cheeks like the blossom in May.

Becca knew that her cheeks were redder than any blossom. Phineas sang with a beautiful tenor voice and kept glancing at her over his shoulder at her with soft eyes. No one in the room could be in doubt that she, Becca, was the damsel that he was singing about.

Said I, Pretty maiden, how came you here
In the meadows this morning so soon?

It was her part. Becca swallowed a mixture of fear and bile before singing,

For to gather some May,
For the trees they are all in full bloom.

Her voice was breathy, and not at all worthy of display, but Phineas looked at her as if he truly believed she sounded like an angel. Perhaps she might change her mind about murdering him after the song. He was simply too handsome to kill. Becca's pulse did not slow down until

Phineas played the last note and their performance was met with applause.

'Bravo, bravo!' Lady Lucas said loud enough for everyone in the large room to hear. 'Oh, do please favour us with another tune.'

Before Phineas could answer, Becca poked him sharply in the back with her own pointer finger. There would be no encore.

He chuckled as got to his feet. 'It would not be in the best interest of my health to continue. Besides, there are many beautiful and accomplished ladies here to present.'

Then, in front of everyone, he took Becca's hand and escorted her to a sofa in the back of the room with only space for the two of them. It was a poorly lit place and Becca thought it was perfect. Her pulse and heartbeat slowed down to their normal pace. Mantheria gave him a sharp glance from a chair a few feet away and he nodded back at her benignly.

Phineas was still holding her hand, so Becca squeezed it as tightly as she could. 'If you ever do that to me again, I will truly murder you.'

The awful, beautiful man simply smiled back at her until all of her anger somehow melted away. It was most unfair. 'Everyone begged for more.'

'Of your playing, not my singing.'

'I loved your singing.'

His words were a whisper, since Lady Amelia was singing and playing, but Becca thought that they were sincere.

'I do like to sing,' she said gruffly. 'But not in public. Never in public. I told you that I don't like being in the spotlight. You should have listened to me.'

'Then we will have to sing together in private. I have an instrument that is even larger than Lady Lucas's.'

Oh, dear.

Becca sniggered.

It was most unladylike, but she couldn't help herself. She'd grown up among naturalists and she knew more than most debutantes about male anatomy and the many nicknames given to a certain member.

Phineas blinked and then his eyes widened when he realised the euphemistic meaning of his words. 'Naughty, Becca. But you are not wrong.'

Becca had to cover her mouth with both hands to keep her laughter in. Sitting properly next to Phineas for an hour might just kill her.

Chapter Seventeen

Phineas heard a slight knock and Tom opened the door. The footman bowed to him and held out a silver tray with a hand-delivered note. He had hoped it was another sketch from Becca, not another letter from a respectable school matron sent first to Mr Walkley and then forwarded to himself.

He read the letter from Miss Eves and was most alarmed to see that it had been addressed to him specifically. Mr Walkley and Kitty had both been given strict instructions to never mention his name, or his connection to his ward. It would do neither of them any favours. He'd told Becca before that society's opinion was as fickle as the wind. But he didn't want Kitty to be blown away in a thunderstorm when society learned who she truly was. Illegitimacy was a taint that no amount of money could repair and Kitty didn't deserve that. She had had no control over the circumstances of her birth. His ward was an adorable scamp, who amused him as often as she exasperated him.

But there was nothing that he could do at this moment. He would send an express to Miss Eves after he returned home from his drive with Becca. He only hoped that Becca wouldn't catch wind of Kitty. At least not until he'd had time to explain the entire situation to her in person. It was too long and complicated for a letter. Phineas briefly considered telling her now, but a part of him worried that Becca would paint him with the same brush as his father—a careless rake, who only thought of his own pleasure.

The Stringhams' butler gave Phineas a cold stare when he arrived at Hampford House. Before the man could usher him inside, Becca swooped around Mr Harper. She was wearing a dashing red riding coat and hat that set off her colouring to admiration. And that infectious smile! Phineas longed to sweep her up into his arms and hold her tightly, but he couldn't in Berkeley Square. Especially not with her butler harping over them.

He held out his arm to her. 'Lady Rebecca, how beautiful you look.'

She grinned back at him as she placed her gloved hand delicately in the crook of his elbow. 'You look very beautiful, too. May I count the capes on your driving coat?'

Her teasing question caught him unawares and he chuckled. He helped her into the high carriage and sat down close to her. Phineas loved the feel of her curves against his body and the sweet fragrance of her skin. He wished to devour her on the spot and he didn't need to see the butler's glare to know that this wasn't the time or place for it. He had to earn her trust and then he could ravish her whenever he pleased with her full participation.

'How many questions have I asked you now?'

'Thirty-seven and I have answered them all honestly,' she said brightly. 'Although some were particularly difficult.'

'I shall only ask you easy ones on our drive.'

'Then I shall give you easy answers.'

Phineas drove slowly to the park. He wished to spend as

much time with Becca as possible. 'Your preferred monarch?'

'Queen Elizabeth I, of course. It is rumoured that she said she possessed the heart and stomach of a king. I have often wondered how they worked with the rest of her female internal organs.'

He chuckled at her wit. Only a simpleton would think that Becca wasn't very intelligent. 'Ideal day of the week?'

She breathed in deeply. 'I've always been partial to Thursdays. Although I cannot think of a good reason why.'

'Least ideal day?'

'Monday. Although Sunday is supposed to be the first day of the week, I cannot help but feel that the real beginning is on Monday. Which makes it rather tedious.'

Phineas enjoyed all his days equally if they included Becca in them. 'Are you a nighttime or a morning person?'

'An afternoon person when the sun is up and shining.'

He smiled. He enjoyed her company morning, afternoon, and nighttime. 'Favourite flower?'

'A pink rose. Like the one you gave me.'

'Second best?'

'I like the purple wildflowers that grow on the sides of streams. They are less finicky than a hothouse flower and adorn the world to make it lovely.'

'Much like yourself,' he said, unable to keep his eyes off her. 'Who is your dearest friend?'

She nudged him with her elbow. 'You are.'

Becca was his favourite person, too. She made every moment more joyful. 'Will you be at Lady March's ball this evening?'

'Yes.'

'May I have the first quadrille and the supper waltz?'

Her large blue eyes swallowed him whole. 'Yes.'

Three little letters arranged into one small word, but it meant everything to Phineas.

Lord and Lady March's ballroom was surrounded by tropical plants. It felt like dancing in a greenhouse and it smelled very good, too. Becca couldn't help but compare the lovely greens and bright colours of the flowers to the awful trophy heads at the Astley ball. She wished that other peers understood and respected the majesty of animals the way her father did. Mama had tried to convince him to come to this ball, but Papa had complained about a terrible toothache.

Her father's illnesses almost always coincided with a social event that he did not wish to attend. Becca was certain that Papa would be 'cured' by the morning. Unless Mama wished for him to make calls and then the pain would spread to his entire mouth. She couldn't stop her own lip muscles from smiling when she thought of her father's duplicity. She was certain that her mother knew of it as well, but she played along anyway. Probably because they loved each other. Her parents were not at all alike, but that didn't seem to matter. Their differences complemented each other.

Becca saw Phineas enter the ballroom and her breath caught. She'd never thought of it before, but Phineas was rather like her father. He was tall, slender and blond. He was more reserved with his emotions and he hid his true self behind his beautiful clothes, but he was a good steward to those in his care. And Becca was similar to her mother in face and figure, as well as in personality. She had her own interests, but loved her family dearly. Perhaps there was a reason that opposites attracted. It would be difficult for two people who were similar not to compete with each other for predominance in a relationship. Becca was more than happy to let her handsome peacock show off his turquoise feathers and watch appreciatively like a less noticeable brown peahen. She didn't want or need the attention of a crowd. She only wanted his.

Phineas swept Becca a most elegant bow and her pulse began to race. 'You are a vision of beauty, Lady Rebecca.'

Wick's dual string of pearls was around her neck and she was wearing a blue sarsenet gown over a white satin slip with short puffed sleeves. The neckline was low and nearly off her shoulders and decorated with a frill of blond lace. Around her waist was a sash of satin ribbon that ended in a front bow.

Becca gave him a full curtsy. 'If only every eye in the room wasn't already on you.'

One corner of his mouth quirked up. 'For once, my clever friend, you are entirely wrong.'

And she almost believed him. Phineas offered her his hand and she gladly accepted his escort to the centre of the ballroom floor. They had danced the quadrille together before and the steps came easily to her.

The dance was nearly halfway through when Phineas gave her a heart-stopping grin. 'What skill are you the most proud of?'

'Making you laugh.'

He obliged her by chuckling and spun away. When they met again, he said, 'The real answer, my lady.'

She tilted her head to one side. 'My ability to learn languages, especially since reading is difficult for me. I have had to learn almost entirely by sound and speaking.'

'You speak Latin and Greek.'

Their hands came together. 'And a little English.'

Shaking his head, Phineas laughed and continued to smile even as he moved away from her in the figure.

Becca was already grinning when she asked him the same question, 'What skill are you the proudest of?'

'I could tell you—but perhaps it would be more appropriate to demonstrate it to you once we are married.'

Naughty Norwich.

Becca blushed furiously and her mind went to many different wicked possibilities. She was grateful that they weren't waltzing and that she had time to recover and come up with a retort before she was able to speak to him again during the dance. But no suitable sally came to her lips.

Phineas had spoken of them being married as if it was something certain in the future. He'd never done so before. He'd said that he wished to court her, but courtship did not necessarily end in a wedding. Her stomach pooled with heat as he caught her eye from across the room. Becca had been right about him and her family had been wrong. Phineas was not toying with her. He did care for her and he intended to marry her.

It was everything that she'd ever wanted. She would never feel lonely again. She would be married to her best friend and finally be mistress of her own home and be able to make her own decisions. Becca was certain that she would make mistakes, but she knew that Phineas would help her. And that he would make mistakes, too. But they would work through them together. Her ducal family and royal connections could only help his Parliamentary career. She only wished that her family liked him better. It would break her heart if her marriage to Phineas created distance between them.

Becca wanted Phineas's heart and every other body part. Blushing, she felt her skin tingle with the need to touch his.

Intimacy with another man might have been intimidating, but not with Phineas. He was her best friend. She knew that he would be gentle and passionate and perfect. She trusted him with all of her firsts.

They bowed to each other at the end of the dance and Phineas dutifully took Becca back to her mama. She was sorry that they weren't dancing the second as well, but the best part of the supper waltz was that she would get to speak privately with Phineas during the dance and at the meal following.

Becca did not have much time to appreciate the decoration and flowers after Phineas left. Her mama was talented at finding her partners. Becca barely had a chance to catch her breath in between gentlemen and lords asking for her hand in the dance. Her mouth became quite dry and she could hardly wait for the small supper to get a drink. But at least her feet did not make any mistakes the way they had at her coming-out ball. Her friendship with Phineas had brought her confidence and a lady who could make the cold Earl of Norwich laugh was a much sought-after dance partner.

Phineas came up to claim his waltz with a glass of lemonade in his hand. He gave it to Becca. 'You appeared thirsty.'

She hoped that her face wasn't flushed from dancing and that Phineas was just being thoughtful. Becca *was* very thirsty and she downed the lemonade in one large gulp.

'Shall I fetch you another glass?'

'Oh, no. I should hate to miss a minute of our waltz.'

'Not as much as I,' Phineas said, taking the empty glass from her and setting it on a footman's tray. 'Shall we?'

Becca placed her hand in his and a feeling of rightness settled in her chest. They belonged together. They could have a rare relationship where they were both friends and lovers.

Phineas swept her into his arms for the waltz and held her rather closer than was proper, but Becca was in no mood to preach propriety. She liked when their bodies brushed each other during the movements of the dance. And she loved his scent and his warm sweet breath on her face.

'What political topics are you passionate about?'

'Politics?' One word that seemed to cool her ardour. 'You want to speak about politics in the middle of a ball?'

'I want to know everything about you.'

They twirled together in a perfect circle before she answered, 'I am passionate about animal welfare and believe that they deserve rights. God's creatures should not be kept in poor conditions, nor should they be killed for a man's pride or amusement.'

'You are thinking of Lord Astley.'

She nodded. 'And I am passionate about women's rights. I don't think a woman should lose control of her fortune and any possessions when she marries. Nor that she should be considered the property of her father or her husband just because she has a monthly cycle and can bear children.'

'I agree with you wholeheartedly.'

His answer pleased her greatly. 'And you, Phineas. What political topics are you passionate about?'

She noticed a little colour in his cheeks as he answered. 'Improved conditions in foundling homes and workhouses. We do not treat the poor or the parentless in our country very well at all and the laws that govern our policies were passed during the rule of your preferred monarch, Elizabeth I. They are outdated and not nearly generous enough. I am trying to push a bill through Parliament that increases government funding for foundling homes, for it is difficult to find private sponsors.'

With those words Phineas managed to steal the rest of her heart. There was so much more to Lord Norwich than what met the eye—although his physical form was quite enjoyable to look at. And given time, her family would see what a good person he was.

'That's wonderful, Phineas. You inspire me. I will spend more of my time and efforts helping the poor. I will talk to my family and I can assure you at least four more votes for your bill. How many more do you need?'

'Not counting your family's votes, two dozen.'

'I can get them for you,' Becca said, her expression earnest. 'I will simply ask my father, Matthew, Samuel and Mark to all persuade five people each. I am sure the task won't be too difficult for them and it is for a worthy cause.'

A surge of warmth suffused his chest. Phineas believed Becca that it wouldn't be too difficult for relatives to get the needed votes. Her brother and brothers-in-law were well liked, whereas Phineas was respected.

'Your help means a great deal to me. Finding people willing to support better funding for illegitimate children is difficult,' he explained. 'No child on my estates is without a roof over their head or the basic necessities of life and I have instructed the parishes under my jurisdiction to be generous to all in need, but there is more to do. The poverty in London and other cities is staggering. Especially among women and children. New laws need to be passed.'

'I agree.'

Phineas pulled her closer to him so that they were chest to chest. He whispered in her ear, 'How do you cope with life's uncertainties and challenges?'

This was another deep question that deserved more than

a flippant answer, although a joke was almost always what she reverted to when something was uncomfortable or too personal. Perhaps there was more truth in that than she had previously realised. 'With humour and hope.'

'And endless grace.'

'I believe that is more accurate for you, Phineas.'

Still holding her close, he said with a tender look, 'What memory from your childhood makes you smile?'

'Are you certain that Ned didn't come up with these questions?'

Phineas laughed in her ear. He was so very, very dear to her.

Becca grinned at him and at this particular memory. 'When I discovered a secret passageway in Hampford Castle that led from my bedchamber to my sister's and even out of the house. My brothers don't know about it and neither do my parents. I only told Frederica and Helen and we have kept it as a secret between us. And we have used the hidden door more often than we probably should have.'

'You might be the most scandalous of all the scandalous Stringhams.'

A chortle escaped her lips. 'And you, Phineas, what is a childhood memory that is dear to you?'

As if someone had blown out a candle, the light in Phineas's countenance was gone. Becca already knew that Phineas's childhood had been difficult and lonely and his parents' uncaring. She should have asked a similar question that brought up no painful memories. Maybe about his nurse.

Becca watched as a slow smile build upon Phineas's face and the light return to his countenance. 'My first year at Eton, Charles and I found a stray tabby cat in an alley by the college. Pets were forbidden in the dormitories, but we hid her from the other boys and the masters for the rest of the term. She liked to sleep on my feet and I would fall asleep to the sound of her purring. It was the most comforting sound.'

'What was her name?'

'Minerva.'

'After a Roman goddess. How flattering. She must have been a very fine feline.'

Smiling wider, Phineas shook his head. 'Minerva was not. She was missing an eye and part of her tail. I probably would have left her in the alley, but Charles was worried about her because there was blood on her fur. He ministered to her wounds and I sneaked her cheese. It irked him to no end that Minerva liked me better.'

'And what happened to Minerva?'

'She is still alive and probably the oldest cat in the entire world. Minerva is keeping the mice down at Ridley. Once I let her go on my estate, she returned to her feral state. Occasionally, she will come and let me pet her. But mostly she just stalks me when I am walking in the gardens and runs when I call her name.'

Her brother Charles had always loved animals. It didn't surprise her that he would not pass by a cat in distress. Becca's heart warmed and the feeling spread throughout the rest of her body. Charles's life might have been sadly short, but he had made a difference to both boys and beasts—and little sisters. She was grateful that Phineas had known him.

'I hope one day to meet Minerva.'

'She's not the only cat that I want to introduce you to.'

Becca raised her eyebrows and bit her lower lip to keep herself from chortling. 'I am duly flattered and eager to make the acquaintance of your pets and livestock.'

Phineas laughed and loudly, before asking her, 'What do you believe in that others don't?'

She was tempted to say *him*, but they were having far too much fun to bring in the black cloud of her family's disapproval. 'That animals have souls and therefore that they will go to heaven.'

'I fear Minerva may be more suited to the other celestial place.'

This time she could not keep in her laugh and he joined in with her. Becca noticed several eyes on them and she feared that the other members of the party were not merely eyeing their sartorial splendour. She and Phineas were being indiscreet with their feelings and the winds of society's disapproval would be coming for them if she didn't behave like a demure debutante. With great difficulty, she schooled her facial features to proper uninterest. The warmth in Phineas's eyes made it almost impossible to pretend indifference.

'What do you wish that you had more time to do?'

'Travel,' Becca said wistfully. 'I should like to see all of these gorgeous flowers in their natural habitats. My parents have travelled to Africa and America. I should like to go there, too, and then to Australia. I have heard that the flora and fauna is quite unique there. What do you wish that you had more time for?'

'Kissing you.'

She glanced over her shoulder and did not see her mother in the ballroom. The Duchess of Hampford was very tall and the large green feathers that she wore in her hair this evening made her easy to spot. 'It appears that my mama has become distracted. Perhaps we could slip out for a few minutes between the supper waltz and eating without her noticing.'

'Are you trying to compromise me out in the gardens, Becca?' Phineas asked sardonically.

'Yes. Thoroughly.'

'I was hoping so.'

Grinning, she allowed him to lead her through the rest of the waltz and then out the doors to the gardens. Phineas held her hand and guided her further into the darkness. He stopped behind the garden wall. The only light came from the ballroom, yet she could still see the lines of his handsome face. Phineas stood close to her, but he didn't kiss her.

Was he waiting for her to compromise him? Thoroughly?

Heart galloping, she leaned forward until she felt his warm breath against her lips. She wasn't brave enough to eliminate the slight distance between them. Closing her eyes, she waited for his mouth to touch hers. With one hand still cupping her cheek, his other arm wrapped around her waist and pressed her body against his firm one. His lips were soft against hers and all rational, scientific thought fled her brain.

She melted into his arms as he deepened the kiss. She did not try to think. The brain was quite an inessential organ for a kiss. She merely let her body feel. She was on fire. From the path of his fingers over her shoulders and back and then down to her waist. The moistness of his lips and his tongue stroking hers. The sensation of his rougher skin against her softer. The feel of her body against his hard muscles. Her heart beat wildly and her blood sang in her veins. Heat gathered in her woman's belly—it was most certainly not a king's stomach!

Phineas's kisses were deep and all-consuming. Her body shivered with pleasure and passion. Her mouth made a little moan of protest when he began to soften their kisses by degrees. She wasn't ready for this incredible moment to be over. She wanted more of Phineas. Nay, she wanted all of him!

He rubbed his nose against hers, which made Becca smile in spite of herself.

'Must we return to the ballroom so soon?'

Phineas brushed his lips against Becca's cheek. 'My dear one, if we do not, there may be unpleasant whispers about us.'

This time she shivered from the cold as she stepped back from Phineas. 'You're right. Mama would not like that at all.'

'Your mama will not like the fact that we have been absent either.'

Becca snorted. She most certainly would not. 'Hopefully she will think we were eating in the supper room.'

'I much prefer devouring you.'

Giggling, Becca allowed Phineas to escort her discreetly back into the house. She preferred kissing Phineas to eating supper as well. Becca reluctantly parted ways with him before finding her mother. She didn't want to further prejudice Mama against him. As predicted, the Duchess of Hampford was most displeased.

Mama's brow was furrowed and her colour was high. 'I have been looking for you everywhere. I searched the supper room and the ball room twice.'

Becca blushed as she lied, 'We must have just missed each other in circles.'

Her mother took her arm. 'Never mind. Mr Smoot is eager for an introduction and to dance with you. He has a large estate in Derbyshire.'

Becca was less eager, but she allowed Mama to tug her around the room and lead her to Mr Smoot. She curtsied to him and he looked her up and down as though she was a piece of meat. Perhaps when the *ton* called the London Season the 'meet market' they had actually meant 'meat'. Her belly churned unpleasantly for a debutante or a king as the lecherous Mr Smoot led her out to the set.

Chapter Eighteen

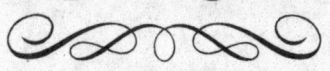

Becca looked at herself a second time in the mirror. Her green sprigged muslin dress complemented her blue eyes. The light material showed her voluptuous figure and the matching spencer were deceptively plain, but very expensive. Mama's tastes in fashion were always right. She asked Shepherd to put on her hat and tie the ribbon. Phineas was fastidious about his appearance and she wanted to look her best.

And she did.

Her skin was glowing this morning and it wasn't from Gowland's Lotion, it was from her growing feelings for Phineas. He thought she was beautiful and he made her believe it, too. Shepherd followed her down the stairs, presumably as eager to meet her own swain, Jim, in the park. But the footman was not waiting for them at the bottom of the stairs. It was her eldest brother Wick and he did not look happy.

Becca stepped down the last few steps and leaned on to her tiptoes to give her brother a kiss on the cheek. 'Isn't it a trifle early in the day to be making social calls?'

'This isn't a social call,' he said gruffly and handed her the newspaper.

There was a rough illustration with the inscription *The*

Duke's Daughter Tames the Rake. The sketch was crude and made her plumper than she was, but it was recognisably herself, and Phineas was drawn both overly tall and thin with a rope around his neck.

She took a deep breath and handed the newspaper back to him. 'Amateurs. My own caricatures are far superior.' She moved to walk around him and to the door where Shepherd was waiting wide-eyed with Jim.

Her brother grunted. 'Where do you think you are going?'

'On my morning constitutional.'

Becca wasn't about to tell her over-protective eldest brother that she planned to meet Phineas in the park and that she very much hoped to kiss him again behind an obliging tree.

There was a knock on the door and Shepherd and Jim moved aside. Becca expected it to be Alonzo, but it was Mantheria with Matthew in tow. No doubt they had also seen the gossip papers. This morning was becoming a regular family party.

'Have Mama and Papa seen the newspapers?' Mantheria demanded as she walked through the door, pulling Matthew with her. 'Becca's name is coupled in every gossip rag with that notorious Lord Norwich.'

Wick grimly held up his newspaper and Becca was surprised to see that Mantheria had three different editions that presumably also tied her name with Phineas's.

Matthew broke the tension with a loud chuckle. 'For once Norwich doesn't look prettier than a debutante. Perhaps I'll frame it and give it a glance every time I'm feeling low about myself.'

Mantheria was quick to swing her elbow and instinctively Matthew jumped just out of her reach. 'You are not taking this nearly seriously enough. Gossip like this could ruin Becca's Season and possibly even her good reputation. She might never find a respectable husband now.'

'Maybe she wants an unrespectable husband,' Matthew quipped.

Both Wick and Mantheria glared at him now. But Matthew didn't appear fazed at all. He never did what anyone told him to do. Becca envied him that.

'What's all this commotion?' Frederica asked from the top of the stairs. She had on her dressing robe and was carrying Arthur, who was rubbing his eyes with little fists. 'You woke up my son.'

It seemed to Becca that everyone spoke at once as Frederica descended the stairs like the Duchess that she was. Arthur reached for his uncle Wick who instinctively held the small boy and Frederica took the newspaper from his hands.

She only glanced at it for a few moments before she said, 'I shall go and wake up Mama at once. She'll want to nip this in the bud.'

Frederica swept back up the stairs and Becca decided that it was time to make her own escape. She walked quietly to the door, but before she could open it, Wick demanded, 'Where do you think that you are going?'

Becca attempted to appear innocent. 'As I already said, on my morning walk. The gossip can wait until I return.'

'Aren't you going to explain to the family why you are being singled out with Lord Norwich?' he asked, his disapproval evident on his face.

Mantheria clucked her tongue. 'Why did you dance with him twice last night and allow him to monopolise you for the entirety of Lady Lucas's musicale the night before?'

Becca gazed around the hall. Matthew gave her the smallest of winks of encouragement. 'I am twenty years old and this is no court of law. I do not have to explain myself to any of you.'

Wick exhaled before speaking. 'Perhaps it is *I* who should explain to you. Norwich is a fortune hunter and he proposed to Louisa eight years ago solely for her money.'

Becca was glad that Phineas had already told her of this incident and that she hadn't been blindsided by her brother. It was unpleasant to think that Phineas had once courted her sister-in-law, but since she'd been thirteen years old at the time, he'd hardly betrayed her. He hadn't even known Becca then.

Mantheria took one of Becca's hands. 'It is true, Becca. I believe that Lord Norwich is motivated by your dowry. Louisa was not the first or the last heiress that he has dangled after.'

She pulled back her hand from Mantheria's and clenched her fingers into tight fists. 'Did he propose to them all as well?'

'Not that I have heard rumour of,' Frederica admitted at the top of the stairs. Obviously, she had overheard most of the conversation. Samuel was beside her in his banyan. 'But he did dance and flirt with me before I married Samuel. And I can see how such a handsome gentleman could turn your head. You are so young and inexperienced.'

It wasn't her head, but her heart that was aching. She turned to her sister's husband who was walking down the stairs with his wife. 'Samuel, did you propose marriage to every young lady that *you* danced and flirted with?'

Her brother-in-law flushed. 'Of course not.'

'Then I do not see how Phin—Lord Norwich is any different. Besides, Mark flirted with Frederica and then he married Helen and no one seems to hold it against him.'

Clapping, Matthew came and stood beside her. 'Brava,

Becca. I should hate for my past sins to be a parlour discussion for any family—or rather, a hall one. And whether or not Norwich is after Becca's heart or her fortune, I can say with great confidence that the Earl is wealthy in his own right. He has invested in many of my business speculations and turned a good profit. And I happen to own the bank where he keeps his money. He's good with his blunt and he does not need Becca's dowry.'

Becca's legs shook against her fists. She was grateful to Matthew for standing up for her and Phineas. And she knew he was not lying. Matthew took money more seriously than anything else in the world.

Her brother gave her a side-hug. 'Farewell, beloved family. I much prefer a warm breakfast with my wife to cutting up Norwich's character.'

Matthew left the house and an awkward silence followed.

Grimacing, her eldest brother shook his head. 'You can tell me to mind my own business. Not that you've ever kept your nose out of mine. But, Becca, be careful. He's much older than you and known to be a *care-for-nobody*. I just don't want to see you hurt.'

'How can you blame Norwich for wanting to marry Louisa eight years ago, when you did yourself?'

'I loved her. He did not.'

Becca could not argue with that. Phineas had told her that he'd never loved anyone before.

'Norwich is a well-known gamester and a rake,' Mantheria said, her arms wrapped tightly around herself. 'Don't make the same mistake I did when I debuted. Don't be in a rush to marry as high a title as possible.'

Becca wanted to say that Phineas was nothing like Alexander, but that would be a lie. They were both handsome men, charming companions and witty conversationalists. She had cared for Alexander, but she wasn't blind to his faults as a husband to Mantheria. Becca didn't doubt her sister's sincerity. Nor her misery. Only a fool would choose to love an unfaithful partner. But Phineas had promised that he would be faithful to her and she believed him. He'd been honest with her about all of his faults.

Mama and Papa promenaded down the stairs in their dressing gowns. It was all that was needed to complete this family farce. Papa released Mama's arm and walked protectively between Becca and her upset elder siblings. 'A cheetah cannot change its spots, my darling girl.'

His words pierced the careful protection of her heart. She didn't want Phineas to change, but she did want him to be faithful to her. 'I believe that phrase refers to a leopard.'

'Really? Well, the term is true either way. Neither animal can change their appearance. The only animal that I know of that can alter their skin is a chameleon.'

'I know that. And I am ready to go on a walk,' Becca said quietly. 'I can see Alonzo standing in front of the house. No doubt he's heard our raised voices and is wisely waiting outside.'

Her father put his arm around her shoulders and kissed her brow. 'I hope you know how precious you are to me.'

'More precious than your ostrich?'

Papa chuckled and tweaked one of her curls. 'I adore your wit. In fact, I adore everything about you, Becca. And I am having a dashed difficult time letting you grow up. If I had my way, I'd keep you in the family nest for ever. But you were meant to fly. Nay, to soar. And I cannot clip your wings or keep you in a cage. Neither can your brothers or sisters, no matter how well meaning their interference.'

'Then treat me like an adult, Papa,' Becca said softly,

but loud enough for her meddling siblings to hear. 'Allow me to make my own decisions.'

Mama cleared her throat imperiously. 'And what about the gossip with Norwich? How do you intend to handle that without our assistance?'

'By ignoring it. I have done no wrong and neither has he. Driving in an open carriage in the park between three and five o'clock is perfectly respectable. I have also gone with Lord Whitehurst and Lord Talbot. Singing together once is hardly salacious. Neither is dancing twice with a man at a ball. There is no reason for such an uproar and the *ton* will find other debutantes to gossip about. It is only natural that as a daughter of a duke I would be singled out.'

The members of her family all made various sounds of disapproval. Tutting. Clucking. Groaning. Moaning. And harrumphing.

'Very well, Becca,' her mother said at last. 'You are an adult and we will respect your decision. However, I would beg you to be careful in your future interactions with him. It would not be a bad idea to avoid him for a few days and allow the gossip to simmer.'

'I am supposed to drive today with him in the park.' And go walking with him this morning. He was no doubt already waiting for her on the path.

'You will have to send your regrets,' Mama said. 'Tell the Earl that you are not feeling up to a drive.'

Her fingers were clenched so tightly that her nails were making crescent shapes on the flesh of her palm. 'But you said that *I* could make my own decision.'

'And so you shall,' her mother said. 'But what does a few days matter or one or two balls? Or visits to the park? You will meet Lord Norwich again soon enough.'

Becca thought that they might matter quite a bit. She

didn't want the lovely feelings growing between them to halt or to wither. But despite being a woman, she was not yet the mistress of her own house. Becca was still subject to the rules of her parents. Including her mother's ultimatum that she was not to go to the park.

Ned did not say a word when Phineas told him to saddle his horse after coming back alone from the park. He'd waited and waited and waited.

Something he never did.

For anyone.

Yet Becca still hadn't come. And he had only himself to blame. Foolishly, he'd wanted to share his music with her. He'd never performed in front of a crowd before and he doubted he would do so again. Phineas had further compounded his offence by sitting beside Becca for the rest of the evening. And dancing twice with her at balls. Their names were being coupled together in all of the gossip rags. It was unfortunate for Becca to be a target for gossip so early in the Season. And having her name attached to his would do her no favours in society.

Playing the pianoforte was his secret passion. That and writing his own music. Being self-taught, he'd learned the notes backward. The sounds first and then their placement on the musical lines. Earls weren't musicians, but when his fingers touched the ivory keys there was a sense of rightness that he found in no other place, with no other company—save for with Becca. She was beautiful, curved in just the way he liked best. She was kind and witty. She was loving. But it wasn't any of those things, nor all of them together.

He *liked* her.

And he didn't like anyone.

Not even himself.

After riding until his body hurt, he took a bath, changed into his favourite day wear, went to his pianoforte and opened the lid of his *instrument*.

A laugh escaped his lips.

Naughty, witty, darling, Becca.

He touched the keys—a dissonant chord. He usually invented his own music and today it was in a melancholy, minor key. Phineas played until the tips of his fingers were sore and still did not feel any better.

There was nothing for it. He would need to go shopping. A new ring or being measured for a pair of boots could at least give him some solace.

A knock on the door to the music room caused him to jump in his seat. His servants knew never to bother him when he played the pianoforte. There was very little privacy in being a peer and he guarded what little he had viciously.

'Come in,' he called sharply, in a tone of voice that would have put off most of his staff.

The servant who entered the room was none other than his butler, Mr Johnston, and he was followed by a second man: Mr Alonzo Lawes. Phineas's elbows hit the pianoforte's keys in surprise.

'Mr Lawes.'

Mr Johnston bowed and handed him a small envelope. 'This also arrived. If you need anything, my lord, simply ring the bell.'

Phineas watched the butler leave the room before he turned his attention back to Becca's former tutor. Surely he had come here for her.

'I'm sorry to disturb you, my lord,' Mr Lawes said, doffing his hat.

He got to his feet. 'Not at all, Mr Lawes. May I help you?'

'Your discretion would be most appreciated,' Mr Lawes

said, giving Phineas a large letter. 'A lady's reputation is delicate.'

Phineas was now certain that the paper Mr Lawes was holding was from her. He would give away a diamond for merely a glance from her. A word written in her hand. 'I would never hurt her. I can assure you of that.'

His expression was guarded, but he bowed. 'I'll leave you then, my lord. The Duchess of Hampford was not aware of my errand. However, she has informed her butler to tell you that the family isn't home for visitors for the rest of the week. And she has requested that I give you Lady Rebecca's regrets. She will not be available to go driving with you this afternoon.'

'Thank you, Mr Lawes.'

The secretary turned and left the room, closing the door behind him.

Phineas's hands felt sweaty as he opened the large envelope. It was the drawing of the back of a lion, sitting on a bench and playing Lady Lucas's grand pianoforte. It was another portrait of himself. Not only were his two paws involved, but his tail was also pressing the keys. The sketch was whimsical and charming. He would expect nothing less from Becca. He brought the paper closer to his face and found her mouse near his feet. Becca the mouse was smiling and standing on her two back feet and clapping her little paws. The snake and the spider were inside the pianoforte itself. Underneath the drawing was: *Fin-ished*.

It was a play on the misspelling of his name. But did it mean more?

He was not ready to be done with her. He was not sure that he would ever be ready to leave her. Becca inspired in him something that he'd never felt before—or if he had, they were pale imitations of this stronger feeling.

Phineas carried the piece of paper to his office and placed the sketch next to the others. He planned to have his secretary frame them all. Every time he saw the first drawing, he smiled. When he looked at the second sketch he laughed. And the third one, he loved. Phineas decided that he could become accustomed to smiling. To happiness.

He rang the bell and asked that his carriage be sent for. After the last two days, he deserved a ring, a new pair of boots and maybe a couple of jewelled pins. If he was going to wear his heart on his sleeve, he wanted to appear resplendent.

Chapter Nineteen

Mama fiddled with her necklace as they rode together in the carriage to that evening's entertainment. 'I do wish that you would give Lord Talbot a chance, despite what your father says.'

Becca smoothed a wrinkle from her violet ball gown. She'd missed Phineas cruelly. She had not seen hide nor hair of him in four days. Papa had decided to take her riding each morning to Richmond. And in the afternoon and evenings, her mother managed to pick entertainments where Phineas was not. 'Terrence is not a bad sort, Mama, but he is more interested in the sound of his own voice than he is in my answers.'

'There are more gentlemen in London than Lord Norwich and Lord Talbot,' Mantheria said, wringing her black gloved hands together. 'What about Lord Whitehurst? He has shown you marked attention.'

Rolling her eyes, Becca scoffed. 'At least his mother has. Perhaps she will accompany us on our wedding trip. What a merry party of three we will be. But, Mama, you should come as well. I dare say Lady Whitehurst likes you the best of the bunch.'

'*Rebecca,*' Mantheria chided.

Sighing, Mama raised her elegant shoulders. 'You are

right, Becca. Whitehurst does not seem to have his heart in it and I will no longer accept invitations or dances on your behalf.'

'Or Lord Talbot's?'

Her mother dropped her shoulders. 'Nor Talbot's. But be careful, dearest girl. We are not monsters, but your family that loves you. And we only want your happiness. I do not want to see you taken in by a rake, the way we all were with the Duke of Glastonbury. Alexander was just like Lord Norwich: wealthy, titled and older. He was a charming suitor to your sister and we assumed the best of him. That once he was married, he would give up his rakish ways and his mistress. But you know the truth. All of London knows the truth.'

With a heavy heart and two left feet, she exited the carriage and entered Lady Pennington's ball. Lord and Lady Pennington greeted Mama and Mantheria like old friends. Becca followed behind them, feeling cowed into submission and not at all like a woman who decided her own destiny. She stood silently as they were hailed by other friends and acquaintances. And she had no one.

The musicians began to play the quadrille and Becca saw Phineas coming towards her. He wore an exquisite emerald tailcoat that made every other man's coat look rather shabby in comparison. There was a large emerald on his finger and an even larger pin on his collar. He looked expensive and incomparable. Could she really bewitch, bedazzle and beset such a man?

Phineas executed a perfect bow. 'Duchess. Duchess. Lady Rebecca.'

Mama inclined her head slightly. 'Lord Norwich.'

Mantheria did not speak at all, but simply nodded haughtily. Phineas's mask of indifference was in place, but Becca knew him well enough to know that he was hurt that she had not seen or spoken to him in days. One small drawing had not been enough.

Becca dipped into a deep curtsy. 'Lord Norwich.'

He held out his gloved hand. 'May I have this dance, Lady Rebecca?'

Instinctively Becca put her hand in his—if only to let him know that she had not avoided him on purpose.

'It's my set with the fair Lady Rebecca,' Lord Stephen said, coming up to their awkward group. He was the younger son of a marquess and barely a year younger than Becca. Stephen wanted to be a dandy like Phineas, but he still looked like a schoolboy aping his older peers. His coral coat with several spangles was flashy rather than elegant. And his shirt points were so high that he could not turn his head from side to side.

Becca tried to pull her hand from Phineas's, but he gripped it tightly. 'May I have the supper waltz, my lady?'

'I should be pleased to reserve it for you.'

Phineas kissed the top of her glove before letting it go.

Her hand tingled where he'd touched and kissed her. She watched him go away and it felt as if he'd taken her heart with him. How foolish!

'By Jove! Lord Norwich is quite the out and outer, ain't he? I wonder if he'll show me how he ties his cravat. A work of art it is.'

'Perhaps you'd rather dance with him than me,' Becca said waspishly. 'I could arrange it if you'd like.'

Taking her hand, Lord Stephen guffawed. 'You are a witty one.'

Luckily, it was a country dance and Becca was not forced to speak much to Lord Stephen. And when she did, she only listened with one ear as he recited the shockingly expensive bills from his tailors. The young Lord was every single one of her preconceived notions about a dandy and Phineas was none of them. But she had to stop thinking of him and looking for him on the ballroom floor. Phineas did not join this set, nor the one after. Nor the two miserable ones with Lord Whitehurst. Becca did not see him again until he claimed her hand for the supper waltz.

She tried to ignore how her heart leapt in her chest and how her blood thrummed when he touched her hand. She closed her eyes when his hand encompassed her waist and Phineas drew her closer to him. How she longed to be in his arms again. To feel his devastating kisses on her lips. His hands on her curves, making her appreciate her shape for the first time in her life.

'Why are we *fin-ished*, Becca?' he whispered in her ear.

His hot breath on her skin made her entire body tremble with need. But how could she trust her own judgement over that of her mother's and Mantheria's? And of her elder brothers and her sisters? The forced parting had not cooled her feelings. If anything, she'd realised how much Phineas meant to her.

'Am I being a poor partner?' she countered. 'I suppose I am still in the doldrums from dancing with Lord Whitehurst for an entire set.'

'Did he ask you for the two dances himself?'

Becca managed a smirk. 'It was all very romantic. His mother asked my mother and then they both told us of their happy plans.'

'I dare say Lady Whitehurst and the Duchess of Hampford would be much happier dancing together.'

'But who would lead?'

Phineas laughed softly, but sobered. 'You can tell me the truth. There is nothing that I would not do for you.'

Becca tried to rally her wits and deflect the truth with humour. 'My family was not pleased about the coupling of our names in the gossip columns. Nor in one very mediocre caricature. Mama thought it would be best to not see each other for a few days so that the gossip would die down... I think she hoped our feelings would as well.'

'Have yours altered?'

His voice was tender, but she believed it was sincere. His eyes did not look cold for once, but like the burning blue wick of the fire. The hottest part of the flame.

'No.'

'Mine have not either.'

Phineas spun her around and not only were her mother and sister watching them dance, half of the people in the room were, too.

Becca sucked in a breath. 'We are garnering more interest than Miss Mary Anning's fossil bones.'

'Perhaps we should give them something new to watch and sit down for supper.'

'Would that be our second act?'

He took her elbow and escorted her to the supper room. Becca did not put much food on her plate. She could never eat much more than a few bites when Mantheria's beady eyes were on her. They sat down at a table and Becca's leg was right next to Phineas's—it caused her whole limb to thrum with a strange sensation. Becca wished that all the years she'd spent observing animals that she'd understood a bit more about the human heart.

'I was thinking more of Act I, Scene II.'

Becca raised only one eyebrow. 'Are we the fools that bring comic relief or the villains hatching an evil plan against the heroes?'

His lips twitched as if he were fighting a smile. 'I dare say your family is trying to convince you that I am a villain.'

'I've always preferred villains.' The words were out of Becca's lips before she could stop herself. She brought her hand to her mouth to cover it, but the words had already escaped.

Phineas rewarded her with one of his rare laughs.

Alas, Phineas's happiness and humour seemed to catch the attention of every person in the supper room. So many eyes were staring at them—most disapprovingly. Becca managed to eat a few bites and, despite the public scrutiny, she was sorry when Lord William Fitzherbert claimed her next set and Mr Rogerson the one after.

Her feet were sore and she was feeling out of sorts by the time she entered the carriage at the end of the ball.

'You're playing with fire by encouraging a rake,' Mantheria said, sitting beside her and smothering her with interference. 'And you will be burned, Becca. Why can you not trust me on this? Why will you not learn from my mistakes?'

There was a lump in Becca's throat that she could not swallow down. 'I suppose I have a fondness for rakes. I adored Alexander and I care greatly for Lord Norwich. He makes me feel beautiful and he asks me questions and listens to the answers.'

Phineas had said that he wanted to marry her and she wanted nothing more than to be his wife. To spend every moment in his glittering company. Becca liked who she was when she was with him. She was not the mouse of the family, but the star of her very own melodrama.

Mantheria took her hands into a pinching hold. 'Believe me when I say that such a man can be fascinating to flirt with, but you do not want to marry him. He may be faithful to you for a little while, but he will go back to his old ways. Everyone in society will know and whisper about it loud enough for you to hear. And you will be all alone with your misery. Becca, I am begging you not to make the same mistake that I did. Do not give your heart to a rake and a gamester. Once he has won your hand, he will be on to a new card. It is all a game to men like him.'

Mama put a hand on Becca's knee from across the aisle. 'I know that you think we are wrong, but, dearest, we are your family. We love you more than anyone else in this world and we want desperately for you to be happy.'

Becca winced. 'And you are sure that I will not be happy with Lord Norwich?'

'As certain as I am that letting Mantheria marry a rake was the greatest mistake of my life,' her mother said. 'I do not want to have two sad daughters.'

Becca's stomach hardened and an unsettling feeling swept over her entire body. Was she wrong to encourage Phineas? To kiss him? To care for him?

Foolishly, she'd believed that she could teach him how to love, the way he'd taught her how to kiss. But, no, Becca was only one of many ladies whom he'd admired and embraced. What if he eventually tired of her and moved on to the next woman? Like a bee sucking out the nectar from flower to flower. She'd thought that she could play the game of flirtation, too. But she'd been wrong. Every time she saw Phineas, she'd adored him more.

But he'd come to the funeral with several handkerchiefs just for her. Somewhere in his handsome chest, Phineas must care for her a little, otherwise he wouldn't have thought about her needs. Nor would he have purchased a mourning ring for her. But a man could feel affection and still be unfaithful. Alexander had been a great example of that. On his deathbed, he'd begged Becca to forgive his estranged wife. Despite everything, Alexander had cared for Mantheria.

But it hadn't been enough.

Would she be enough for Phineas?

Despite the scientific impossibility, it felt as if her heart was breaking.

Chapter Twenty

The following morning, Phineas scribbled in the next few musical notes on a sheet of paper. He had composed Becca's song and he knew it by heart, but he needed to write it down. Something that he'd never attempted to do before, but he wanted Becca to have a copy.

Even if she could not play it herself, maybe one of her disapproving sisters could perform it for her. It might even soften their opinion of him. Convincing the Stringhams that he was a worthy suitor of their beloved youngest daughter was proving to be an uphill battle. They did not care about his title, wealth, social status or his feelings. They wanted a man worthy of their daughter.

Phineas knew that he wasn't. He had made too many mistakes. But he also knew that he could make Becca happy. And that he was better for her than the fatuous Lord Talbot, the reluctant Lord Whitehurst, or the nincompoop Lord Stephen. Phineas would cherish and protect Becca with all the strength, cunning and intelligence that he possessed. There was nothing that he wouldn't do for her and eventually he could win around the strict Stringhams.

He heard a slight knock and Tom opened the door. The footman bowed to Phineas and held out a silver tray with mail that he'd paid to receive. His heart sank when he recognised the feminine handwriting on the top. It was from his ward, Kitty. He picked it up and thanked Tom. She had addressed it directly to him instead of to his secretary the way she'd promised to do.

The footman bowed a second time. 'Excuse me, my lord.'

Phineas raised his eyebrows. 'Was there something else, Tom?'

'Yes, my lord. I hope you don't find it impertinent. But have you told the lady that you love her? My sweetheart says that the words are just as important as the actions. That a lass wants to hear her man say them and often.'

Good heavens. Now even the footmen were giving him romantic advice. He ignored the urge to pick up his quizzing glass. Instead he smiled—it was becoming easier and more natural. 'Thank you, Tom. I will.'

The footman gave him one last bow before leaving the room. Once the door closed, Phineas dropped the note as if it were on fire.

He scribbled in a few more stanzas, before he sighed and picked up the note from his ward. He broke the seal. It was thankfully short:

Norwich,

I do not like school. Either come and get me by Saturday or I shall run away for good. That will teach you a lesson. And don't you dare send Mr Walkley. His wife pinches something awful and his daughter sticks her tongue out at me.

Kitty

Groaning, Phineas crumpled the missive in his hand. It would seem that Kitty was intent on making a scandal, despite how hard he'd worked to keep her name clean and respectable. Her association with him would do Kitty no favours. And the timing could not be worse. He was attempting to convince a ducal family that he was an honourable man and worthy of their daughter. He had Becca's heart and now he needed to prove his worth.

He stuffed the note into his pocket. Phineas had no choice but to go visit his ward in Bath and try to find her a new school as quickly as possible. Or take Kitty home to Winfield Park and wait until the autumn to find another respectable place. Even so the trip would take him several days and stir up a great deal of unwanted gossip.

Becca slipped on her black gloves and knew that she needed to pay a visit to Cressy. If she was not allowed to see Phineas, at least she would pay a call to another friend. And the poor woman was all alone now that Alexander had died. She hoped that Mantheria would still let her son Andrew visit Cressy, but she couldn't be sure. To the world Lady Dutton was the late Duke of Glastonbury's mistress. A scandalous person. But Becca saw that Cressy loved Andrew as much or more than any stepmother, since she had no children of her own.

When Becca told her mother that she intended to visit Lady Dutton, Mama had sighed, but insisted that she bring Alonzo, Jim and Shepherd. It would seem that chaperoning daughters was another duty of a Duchess's secretary. Becca didn't mind. She'd missed speaking with her friend.

'How are you liking your new position?' Becca asked once they were seated in the carriage.

Alonzo sat in the opposite seat next to Jim, who made calf eyes at Shepherd. Becca was delighted to see her stern lady's maid blush a little and almost smile. She never smiled at Becca, but she kept her clothing in excellent condition and she had quite a way with her hair.

'Very well, Becca,' he said with a familiar smile. 'I have even found a small house to let in Kensington. And I do hope that you will accept an invitation to the wedding.'

'I wouldn't miss it for the world, Alonzo. I am so delighted for your good fortune.'

The worthy gentleman blushed as red as an apple and beamed at her. 'I only pray that you are equally fortunate in love.'

Phineas.

She felt a sharp stab in her chest and thought that her heart might indeed break if she didn't see him soon. Lady Matthews had told her mother that Phineas had exited town in a hurry—which did not bode well for gossip. Everyone and anyone were coming up with reasons why the fashionable dandy would leave during the heart of the London Season.

She wished that Phineas had sent her a note before his departure, but since they were not formally engaged and Harper wouldn't admit him into the house, it would have been difficult to get a message to her. It took all of her considerable will to force a small smile for her happy and in love friend and the other pair of lovebirds.

'Would that we all were so fortunate.'

Jim smiled at her. 'Aye, my lady.'

Miss Shepherd's blush deepened and Becca thought that the other couple would be having the wedding banns called very soon.

When they arrived at Cressy's London house there was black crepe on the knocker. Her butler ushered Becca into a sitting room and her three companions happily to the kitchen where they could gossip with the other servants and eat biscuits.

Becca saw several changes in the sitting room. The light

blue curtains had been replaced with black ones. The two mirrors were covered in black cloth, as were all the paintings. And even the mahogany clock had been stopped at the time of Alexander's death. The very house seemed to mourn her dear friend's passing. She placed a hand on her chest and tried to massage away the pain of loss. At least Alexander was no longer bedbound and miserable.

The butler opened the door a second time and Cressy came into the room. She was wearing a black bombazine gown. The material was so dark and dull that it didn't reflect the light. Her brown hair had always been streaked with grey, but now it appeared to be entirely grey. Almost white. The poor woman looked as if she'd aged ten years in the last fortnight.

Rushing to her feet, Becca held out her hands to her friend. 'I should have come sooner.'

Cressy squeezed Becca's fingers and then hugged her tightly. 'I am grateful that you came at all, dear girl. I know that I have no claim upon you now. I am an old woman with a scandalous reputation. Hardly the best companion for a debutante. And I should hate it if the sticklers of the *ton* ostracised you for knowing me.'

Becca gave her friend a second hug—she'd lost at least a stone. The older woman felt frail. 'Cressy, you are a dear friend. And I am not your judge or jury. Neither is any matron of the *ton* who has their own share of sins. I do not care for their good opinions. I only care about you.'

They sat down together on a sofa.

Cressy pulled out a black handkerchief and Becca thought of Phineas. 'And I care about you, dear girl. Tell me all about your suitors. I only wish that I could see you dazzle the ballroom with your beauty and wit this Season.'

Unlike Mantheria, Cressy had never found fault with

Becca's waistline. But that was an ungenerous thought. Sighing, Becca shrugged her shoulders. 'Lord Talbot has been most particular in his attentions, but my cat is more interesting than he is.'

Laughing loudly, Cressy wiped at her eyes with her black handkerchief. 'Oh, how I have missed you, Becca. More than words can express. And your other suitors?'

'Lord Whitehurst may not fancy me, but his mother does greatly. What a jolly threesome we will be.'

Cressy let out another gurgle of laughter. 'Oh, dear. And I suppose he does what his mother says.'

Becca raised her eyebrows. 'Always.'

'What about Lord Norwich?' Cressy asked, folding the black handkerchief in her lap. 'I heard from my nephew that the Earl has been quite persistent in his pursuit of you. And I read about it in several of the gossip papers. I hear that there is even a wager in White's that he'll propose to you by the end of the Season. And that he even left town to fetch his family's heirloom engagement ring.'

The pinching in her chest doubled and she didn't answer directly. 'Lord Norwich is a well-known rake and my family has warned me against him. They do not favour his suit.'

Cressy took Becca's hand in hers. 'I sense Mantheria's influence in that answer. She is a very good person herself and has great difficulty accepting other people's flaws.'

Nodding, Becca said, 'Yes, Mantheria does not think that he'll be faithful to me and my parents do not like Norwich.'

'Did any of your siblings ask for your opinion when they chose their spouses?'

Becca snorted. 'No. But I did help push Wick along. He was so stubborn and anyone could see that he was head over heels in love with Louisa.'

'But the choice was his.'

'Of course it was.'

Cressy patted Becca's hand. 'And the choice of whom you love and marry is entirely yours, my dear girl.'

'But what if they are right? What if Phineas finds a mistress after we are married? What if I am not enough for him?' The older woman flinched at the word 'mistress' and Becca closed her eyes. Cressy had been Alexander's mistress for the better part of thirty years. It was a thoughtless and cruel thing to say to her. 'I am so sorry. I did not mean—'

'Do not worry, Becca,' she said with a sad smile. 'I know exactly who I am and what I have done. And I have paid a great price for loving Alexander and I do feel remorse for those that we hurt, like your sister. I shall always carry that on my conscience, but I do not regret even a moment of the time that we shared together. He was the love of my life and I loved who I was when I was with him.'

Her words struck a chord deep in Becca's soul. When she was with Phineas she thought that she could do anything. She felt bold and brave like a golden lion, rather than a little brown mouse. She felt beautiful, because she knew that he found her so.

'I l-like how Phineas makes me feel, too.'

Cressy raised her eyebrows. '*Phineas*. You call Lord Norwich by his given name? The relationship between you must have progressed more than I realised. Do you love him?'

'Yes.'

The older woman leaned closer to her. 'And does he love you?'

'I think so.'

'But you are worried because he has a reputation as a rake that he will not be faithful to you?'

She opened her mouth, but couldn't quite form the words. Closing her eyes and her lips, she nodded.

'I am hardly the arbiter of such a subject, but I know that your Lord Norwich does not have affairs with married women. More than one married woman has complained to me of him not only ignoring their lures, but treating them with contempt. Norwich appears to take wedding vows very seriously. I do not think that he will stray from you.'

'What of his past?'

'Do not take this amiss, Becca, but unless you intend to marry a boy straight from the schoolroom, your husband will have a past,' Cressy said drily. 'And even some boys start in the petticoat line at Eton. My late husband did. His eldest illegitimate child is older than I am.'

Lord Talbot and Lord Whitehurst's reputations might be spotless, but they were men and humans. Becca was certain that they, too, had made mistakes in their pasts. She doubted that either peer was a virgin like herself. But unlike Phineas, they were not as beautiful to look upon. Nor were their poor private choices known by the *ton*.

'You're right,' Becca said slowly.

'Only a fool would let go of you, Becca,' Cressy said, squeezing her hand one last time. 'And from what I know of Lord Norwich, he is no fool.'

Standing, she gave Cressy one last hug. 'Thank you, Cressy. I will bring Andrew with me the next time I come.'

'You are kinder than I deserve, dear girl,' she said with a mournful smile. 'And please ask Helen to visit me. I want to hear the catalogue of her symptoms. And the latest measurements of her stomach and breasts. For the sake of science, of course.'

'Of course.'

Becca began to giggle and Cressy joined her. They laughed so hard that Becca couldn't breathe.

Chapter Twenty-One

Phineas put on his hat and driving coat. The capes reminded him of Becca and the first day that they met. He'd thought that he was dreaming. His head was in the lap of a beautiful woman who was smiling down at him. The reality of Becca was even better than the fantasy. Everything about her was warm and welcoming and witty and wonderful. He would do nothing that might jeopardise his courtship with her.

Climbing into his high-perch phaeton, Phineas took the reins and easily manoeuvred the carriage through the streets of Bath to Miss Eves's School for Young Ladies. He'd chosen to stay at the George Hotel in Bath rather than to travel from his estate an hour away. The school was both expensive and well situated. Kitty should have nothing to complain about. Not that it would stop her from finding something not to her liking.

He handed the reins to his groom and went up the steps to the knocker. A servant let Phineas in and led him to a sitting room to wait. A few minutes later Miss Eves arrived. She was a small, diminutive woman with a great deal of white hair, but there were no lines on her face. He supposed that she was younger than she appeared. Her gown was simple and modest as was befitting of a woman who ran a school for young ladies.

Phineas got to his feet and bowed to the woman. She curtsied in return before saying, 'Won't you be seated, Lord Norwich.'

Gulping, he sat down. Speaking with her felt rather too much like being back at Eton—he'd hated it there after Charles died. 'I assume that you received a bank draft to thank you for your understanding and patience. And to invest in your wonderful school.'

Miss Eves sat in a chair opposite of him. Her back was as straight as a rod. 'Lord Norwich, I did receive your kind donation, but I fear not even a fortune would be able to persuade me to keep Kitty at my school. She is disrespectful, disruptive and entirely undisciplined.'

'She is only eleven years old.'

'Which makes her behaviour even more disgusting.'

Phineas gritted his teeth together. 'Kitty is a little girl. There is nothing disgusting about her.'

'I am not used to having base-born children in my school, my lord, and I shan't allow it again. No matter how much their natural fathers donate to the school. And I would not have this time if your secretary hadn't tricked me into accepting Miss Goulding by disguising her true parentage,' she said in the voice of a strict schoolmarm. 'I have my own reputation to worry about and I insist that you remove her immediately.'

If Phineas had attended Miss Eves's school, he would have run away, too. He felt a surge of sympathy for his terribly behaved ward. 'It would be my pleasure to do so. If you would have her trunk packed and send her to me at once.'

Miss Eves stood up and curtsied stiffly. 'Very good, my lord.'

'You have not been very good, Miss Eves. And for your information, Kitty is not my by-blow. She is my ward and if I hear any further slander regarding her good name, I will set my lawyers upon you and you will not have a brick left of your school when they are finished.'

The schoolmarm left the room with an indignant sniff.

It was a good quarter of an hour later before Kitty came in. She wore a blue pelisse with a matching hat. Black wild curls surrounded her square chin as she scowled at him as she sat down. Only a fool would believe that she was his daughter. They did not resemble each other in the least—except for in stubbornness, although Phineas had assumed the role of parent and guardian.

His half-sister looked remarkably like his late father. She had the same mulish expression as well. 'You received my letter, Norwich.'

He pressed his fingertips together. 'I did, Kitty. And I have told you dozens of times to call me Phineas.'

'I like Norwich better.'

Sighing, Phineas wasn't about to argue with her over a name. 'Very well. For the sake of discretion, we will go to Winfield Park and you will stay there until I can join you in the summer.'

'Where will you be?'

'At my London house.'

Kitty folded her arms across her chest. 'Then I shall go there with you.'

Phineas exhaled slowly. 'It would be disastrous for your good name if society learned of our true connection. We cannot draw attention to ourselves and you staying with me in London would be fodder for the gossips.'

She stuck out her square chin defiantly. 'What utter rot.

You draw attention to yourself with your clothes and your jewels. It's just me that you don't want on display.'

'I must be careful with my reputation and yours. How will you make a suitable match one day if your name is besmirched? If your true parentage is known?'

His ward stood up and flounced across the room as if they were in a staged melodrama. 'That's what you want, isn't it? For me to marry some stupid man and then become his problem instead of yours!'

He breathed in and out before answering her. 'I want what is best for you, Kitty. I have always wanted that for you. I wish for you to be happy. To have a husband and a home of your own. Is that so very bad of me?'

'I could have a home with you, my brother. And not just for the summers.'

'I am an unmarried gentleman, Kitty. It is not proper for you to stay with me in town.'

His ward snorted. 'I don't care about proper, Norwich. Either you take me with you to London or I am running away and this time I won't come back.'

What would Becca do?

Phineas rubbed his eyes and he knew the answer. 'Very well, minx. We shall go to London together and set the tabbies talking.'

Kitty eyed him suspiciously. 'You're not going to fob me off on Mr Walkley again, are you?'

He held up his hand as if taking a solemn oath. 'I will not. You can stay with me and I will find you a governess.'

'I don't need a governess,' Kitty said mulishly.

'But I need you to have one for my peace of mind and sanity.'

His half-sister chortled.

Miss Eves re-entered the room to inform them that Kitty's

trunk was packed and already lashed on to Phineas's carriage. Apparently, the schoolmarm could not be rid of his ward fast enough. Phineas thanked the woman and got to his feet. He began to walk towards the door when he felt Kitty take his hand. Instinctively, he looked down at her and she beamed up at him. She'd never done that before. A warm feeling covered his chest and a sense of panic. He didn't want to fail her the way his parents had failed him. But he did love her and he would try his best.

Over the next few days, Becca heard several more theories about why Phineas had quit London so abruptly: a duel gone wrong, a gambling debt unpaid and to see his baseborn children. Unlike many young debutantes, Becca knew how a child was created and that a man or woman did not need to be married to make one. But she reassured herself that Phineas would not have kept such a secret from her. Not when he intended to court her in earnest.

A small part of her was glad that Phineas had not been at Lady Carlson's dinner party last night. For Mantheria had embarrassed Becca in front of the entire table by saying, 'You've already had one glass of wine, Becca. I do not think that you should have another.'

There was an awkward hush over the table after her overly loud pronouncement. Becca could only hope that the other guests thought that Mantheria was stopping her from becoming inebriated rather than worrying about her waistline. Becca did not drink or eat another bite during the dinner. Her sister had made a nice night into a miserable affair and Becca was tired of it. If she could stand up to beautiful dandies like Phineas and demand to be treated with respect, then she could speak to her own sister. Even if she was a duchess.

Becca put on her favourite celestial blue gown and asked Shepherd to tidy her hair before she asked Harper to call for the carriage. She put on the mourning ring that Phineas had given her and a double string of pearls with matching earrings that were presents from Wick and Louisa. Phineas had taught her that clothes could be more effective than armour when going into battle.

'Where are you going, my lady?'

Harper was more than a butler—he also watched over her family as a friend. 'Only to Mantheria's house. I shall not be gone long.'

'Perhaps you would like Miss Shepherd or Jim, or both, to accompany you? I am afraid that Mr Lawes is at the factory with Her Grace.'

Becca shook her head. 'No, Harper. I want to speak to my sister alone.'

'What if Their Graces arrive home before you do?'

She felt a little guilty leaving the poor man to deal with not only one, but two duchesses. Mama and Frederica were an autocratic pair and would not stop pestering poor Mr Harper until they had all of the details.

'Tell them I will return shortly.'

Harper opened the door for Becca and escorted her out to the carriage. She got inside by herself and it felt nice to be alone. As a young unmarried woman, she was rarely given the opportunity to travel by herself. It felt as if she were caged, cribbed, confined and tightly corseted.

Animals only ate to live. Becca ate because she enjoyed it. She also ate when she was sad or upset, but mostly because food was one of the best parts of being a human. Over the last year, she'd learned to eat less and savour each bite more. She'd worked very hard to lose one stone, but no matter how hard she tried to reduce her size, she would never be willowy like Helen or Mantheria. Her shape was too different.

Phineas liked her curves and Becca did, too. She didn't want to resemble her sisters. She was happy to look like herself.

Pushing her shoulders back, she strode into her sister's house like a queen. The butler escorted her up the staircase and to the door of her sister's dressing room. Becca knocked before going inside. Mantheria sat on a stool in only her chemise and stays. Her beautiful flaxen hair was down over her shoulders. Her lady's maid had yet to arrange it.

'Becca, what are you doing here?' she asked with a wan smile.

Mantheria got up and gave Becca a hug in welcome. Becca returned the embrace stiffly. She knew that her sister loved her. And she knew that the words that she was about to speak would hurt Mantheria, but they would destroy Becca if they remained unspoken.

'May I speak to you privately?'

Her sister nodded and the lady's maid left the dressing room. Once she closed the door behind her, Mantheria asked, 'What do you need? Are you in trouble?'

Becca inhaled and then exhaled, before counting on her fingers. 'Firstly, I want to tell you that I love you. I do. Secondly, some of Alexander's last words were about you. Thirdly, he asked me to forgive you. Fourthly, I will forgive you. And lastly, I need you to stop making critical comments about my weight, my appearance and my behaviour. I am an adult now and I will choose how I look and the way that I behave.'

The expression of surprise on Mantheria's face was not feigned. Her mouth was slightly open and her eyes wide. 'I don't know what you are talking about.'

Becca placed her hands on her hips. '*"One glass of wine is plenty, don't you think?"* That is what you said last night in front of strangers. I was parched, but I couldn't drink even a small sip after your words.'

'Wine can lead to weight gain. As a naturalist you should know that.'

'But you would not have said that to Helen. Only to me. Your plump sister.'

Mantheria wrapped her arms around her own narrow waist. 'You're overreacting, Becca. I am only trying to help you be the best possible version of yourself and it is healthier to be thinner. You'll attract more suitors that way, too.'

'I like this version of myself and your intent has always been painfully clear—you think that I weigh too much.'

'One comment taken out of context means nothing. You've misunderstood my intent.'

Sighing, Becca shook her head. 'If only it were one comment, Mantheria. I could fill books with the number of gentle hints, little nudges and helpful words you've given me over the years. I will give you the benefit of the doubt and assume that you meant well, but your comments have hurt me and they are damaging to how I see myself. And how I feel. I will no longer politely accept them. If you continue to say things about my weight, I cannot allow you to be a part of my life.'

Her elder sister threw her hands in the air. 'I have just lost my husband and now you are threatening to cut me out of your life?'

Becca felt the urge to shrink and to apologise. To hide back in her mouse's corner. But Phineas believed in her and she desperately wanted to believe in herself. She glanced down at her beautiful gown and the black stone on her finger. They were magnificent. She looked magnificent and she didn't have to change for her sister.

'You lost your husband when I was still a child and you never tried to get him back,' Becca said. 'I overheard your conversation with him eight years ago. Alexander begged you to give your marriage another chance. He promised to do anything you asked him to and you said no. That you wanted a legal separation. I'm not saying that you were wrong at that time, or that Alexander was in the right, but you can't use him as an excuse for your bad behaviour any more. At least, not with me.'

'Becca, you don't know everything.'

'Of course I don't. I never assumed that I did. But I am only here because Alexander begged me on his deathbed to forgive you. He saw how you belittled and humbled me with your words. He suggested that I speak to you about it in Greece, but every time I tried to bring it up you did exactly what you are doing now. You make this conversation about *you*. This isn't about you. It is about *me*. About how I feel when you announce to the entire room that we should stop before we overeat, but your eyes are on me. It's the cutting hints that you speak as if they were general statements and not daggers directed at my faults.'

A tear fell down her sister's cheek and Mantheria reached a hand out as if to touch her. Becca stepped back from the physical contact. Her eldest sister brought the refused hand to her own neck. 'I am your eldest sister, Becca. It is my job to help you. I merely wanted to guide you the way I wish someone had guided me. I only want the very best for you.'

'I am an adult, Mantheria. A woman. I will probably always struggle with my weight. And I don't need you to point it out to me at every opportunity or mention the latest fashion for slimming. Trust me when I say that I am doing my best and that it is none of your business. I do not wish for your advice, nor will I welcome it in the future. I hope to see you tonight at Lady Grantley's ball. Farewell.'

Becca didn't breathe again until she'd left her sister's dressing room and slowly walked down the steps to the grand entry. The butler opened the door for her and she got into the carriage alone. Her chest was heaving as if she'd run from a bull. But she felt stronger than she ever had before.

She had fought her own battles and won.

Chapter Twenty-Two

Phineas could not remember if he had an invitation to Lady Grantley's ball before he went out of town. It didn't help that Kitty had decided to use the stack invitations to start a fire—at least it was in the grate. She also tried to 'help' in the kitchen and somehow managed to get flour on every surface. His French cook, Pierre, had spoken in quite colourful English and French, saying that his sister was not to be allowed below the stairs again.

Even his London butler and housekeeper were at their wits' end. Mr and Mrs Johnston had never experienced the joy of living with Kitty. He had not brought her to town before and the respectable pair seemed nonplussed when she slid down the banister and sang at the top of her lungs—entirely off-key. She'd also made a 'fort' out of the parlour furniture and her coverlet, breaking an antique vase worth over one hundred guineas in the process. Kitty had not been in his London house for an entire day before she'd caused mayhem in every aspect of his life.

Phineas loved his little sister, but he was grateful to have a break from her company. He left her in the reluctant care of Mrs Johnston. And he had it on Ned's authority that Lady Rebecca would be at this ball tonight. He'd intended on going to Lord Snow's party before he'd gone out of town. Not that he needed an invitation for admittance. Becca was right: earls didn't need invitations. Especially ones that dressed as beautifully as he did. Both Lord and Lady Grantley welcomed him effusively, as if he were the guest of honour. He inclined his head graciously and complimented the woman on her taste in decorating.

He walked further into their house. It usually took him a few minutes to find Becca hidden away in some discreet corner, wearing white. She was not hard to find tonight. Her crimson gown drew all eyes to her. No, it wasn't the colour of the dress, but how she wore it. The confidence in the line of her chin. How she held her head. Becca had always been beautiful, but tonight she was brave and bold. The Duchess of Glastonbury was a fool. A man did not want a bony woman in his bed—he wanted a lush, curvaceous one like Becca.

Phineas ought to have talked to a few acquaintances before coming to her side, but he could not do the correct thing. He'd dreamed about having her rosy lips against his and her arms entwined around his neck again. He wondered how soon he could ask Becca to marry him. They'd known each other only one month, but he felt as if it had been much longer. He wanted to spend every moment of every day with her. And every night, too.

She turned around as he approached, as if she could sense his presence. 'Lord Norwich, you are stunning in silver.'

He wanted to redden her lips with his kisses. 'May I have this dance?'

Becca opened the fan attached to her opposite wrist. 'Alas, dear friend, my dance card is a fan and it is already full.'

She opened it to show him and indeed every one of the sets had a name by it. Phineas took the attached pencil and crossed out Lord Whitehurst for the first waltz and put his own name in his place.

'Phineas, you cannot erase other men's names! It is not good *ton* and Mama will be so angry.'

'I will inform Whitehurst of his good fortune and mine.'

Her brow wrinkled with worry, but before Phineas could assure her that all would be well, Lord Russell claimed her hand for a country dance. Phineas did not like the man at all. His coat was loose about his shoulders—which meant he could be loose in all parts of his life. And his cravat appeared to have been through a meat grinder.

As he performed the steps of the country dance with Miss Fraser, he hoped that Lord Russell was equally as unappealing to her. Phineas and Becca's hands met only once, but it was worth dancing the entire set for. After Lady Amelia, he made himself ask two other ladies to dance, hoping to meet Becca in the figures. He watched her as she danced. Her cheeks were bright and so were her eyes, but none of her other partners knew her the way he did. Those men did not share her confidences, nor her sweet kisses.

At last, it was the first waltz. Phineas took her hand and then pulled her into his arms. His entire body seemed to tighten. He did not wish to wait even another day to propose to her. 'Try not to lead this time, sweetheart.'

A giggle escaped her red lips. 'I've warned you before. Helen and I always took turns leading and for the life of me, I cannot seem to follow very well.'

'I don't want you to follow me, Becca. I want you to be by my side. Always.'

He pulled her a little closer to him than was polite. He loved the touch of her. How she smelled of citrus and spice and everything nice. She was bottled sunlight coupled with sheer joy. Effervescent and addictive. His stomach bubbled as if he'd drunk an entire crate of champagne. She had that effect on him. He longed to make his declaration at this very moment, but he knew that Ned and no doubt the rest of his staff would be disappointed in him. Becca deserved something special for her proposal. Something memorable and romantic.

Phineas needed to give her the song that he'd written. The melody of Becca already played in his heart and haunted his ears. It would not be too difficult to finish putting those notes on a page. Although no tune could ever do justice to her.

The music ended and Phineas was slow to remove his hand from her waist. 'May I steal another dance?'

A pretty flush entered her cheeks and she used her dance card to fan herself. 'Phineas, if we are not careful we will cause a scene and end up in the gossip rags again. And my mother will be furious at us both.'

Reluctantly, he escorted her back to her mother where her new partner stood waiting. He did not want to relinquish her to this ungainly youth, but he did. And he even watched the sod dance poorly with her. Lord Eustace Herbert stepped on her toes twice in the first dance. In the second, the clumsy fellow tore her flounce, causing them to have to leave the dance floor. Becca's eyes met Phineas's. She winced as she held up her torn gown and walked to the retiring room with her mother.

Phineas knew that his heart had been lost irrevocably.

Becca and her mother stepped out of the retiring room after repairing her hem. She had learned how to sew from Louisa and was quite pleased with her patch-up job. The stitches weren't as small or as neat as Louisa's, but better than Mama could manage with a needle. Becca suspicioned that her mother had only followed her to keep an eye on her.

They were about to leave the retiring room when none other than Louisa entered it. 'I saw that your dress was torn.'

Becca pointed to her efforts. 'Already repaired.'

Louisa's cheeks were pink. 'And I observed you dancing with Lord Norwich. I have heard from Wick that he is courting you.'

Becca wished that everyone would mind their own business, especially those horrible people who wrote the gossip in the newspapers. 'He is.'

Her sister-in-law took her hand. 'There is something I must tell you.'

Becca's heart sank into her stomach with an unpleasant splash. 'I already know that he proposed to you, Louisa. I can only say that he has the most excellent taste.'

Louisa's face deepened in colour. 'No. That was not what I was going to say. There is no good way to share such news, but I have heard it from several reputable sources that Lord Norwich has a natural child and that he has brought her to live with him in London.'

She had heard the whispers, too, but Becca had ignored them. Surely Phineas wouldn't have kept such a large secret from her.

Mama took her hand. 'It is true, Becca. Alonzo saw the little girl and said that she is undoubtedly related to Lord Norwich. I assume her mother must have been a commoner, for Norwich obviously did not marry her. We tried to warn you about entangling yourself with a rake. He was always going to disappoint you.'

Pulling her hand away, Becca clenched her fists at her sides. She didn't want to believe them. But Alonzo did not have an imagination. He did not make up stories. He was honest to a fault.'

Louisa sighed and clasped her hands together. 'I am so sorry.'

'I can see how such a handsome gentleman could turn your head. You are so young and inexperienced,' her mother continued. 'But there are other excellent matches to be had and there is no need to settle for an offer this Season. There is nothing your father would like more than if you decided to put off an engagement and return for the little Season in the autumn.'

Becca didn't know what to think. Maybe she was as young and as foolish as her family thought she was. Perhaps that was why Phineas hadn't confided in her. He was treating her like a silly girl and not a grown woman. And all that she knew at this moment was that she needed to leave this retiring room. She couldn't breathe. It felt as if her chest was caving in. Unfurling her fan, Becca gave them a false smile. 'Ah, Lord Talbot is my next partner. If you will excuse me. As they say in the theatre, the play must go on.'

Her mother followed her to the side of the room and Lord Talbot came and claimed her hand for the dance. She kept her head up and her shoulders back and followed him to the ballroom floor.

Becca was in no mood for fools. Or for rakes. But he didn't seem to notice the difference. Opening her fan, she saw that her next set was with Lord Stephen.

'My dance, I believe,' Phineas said, taking her hand and bowing over it.

Despite the chaos and bitterness of her emotions, Becca almost laughed. 'Is your name Lord Stephen?'

'No,' Phineas admitted. 'But I have promised the young

buck to teach him how to tie a mathematical cravat in exchange for letting me steal his waltz.'

'Only one style,' Becca said, fanning herself with the dance card. 'A waltz with me should have been worth at least three intricate ties.'

Smiling in a way that made her heart gallop, Phineas swept her into his arms and they began to waltz. 'I missed you keenly while I was away, my dear one.'

Becca found it difficult to meet Phineas's gaze. She had missed him greatly, too, but at the moment she missed trusting him more. 'May I ask what called you away so quickly? It must have been very important for you didn't have enough time to tell me.'

'Estate business near Bath.'

Her heart sunk in her chest. She'd given him an opportunity to tell her the truth and he had obfuscated instead. 'Were you able to resolve it?'

'Mostly, but I did not come here to discuss that. I came to ask for your permission to speak to your father in the morning and then plan the most elaborate proposal known to man. Ned, I know, will want to help and so will my footman Tom... And I do not wish to be parted from you for even the smallest fraction of time again.

'I love you, Becca, as I have never loved another. You are the first person to see beyond my shell into the man underneath. I know that I am not worthy of you, but I will strive to become the best husband and father I can be for you.'

If it weren't for her very tight corset, Becca thought that her heart would have broken. Phineas loved her and she believed him. Every single word from his beautiful lips. And she loved him, too, but she didn't trust him.

'I have heard that you are already a father and that she was the reason you were called away so quickly.'

His hand on her back pressed Becca closer to him. His eyes widened as if alarmed. His expression was no longer cool and confident but panicked. 'It's not what you think. She's my ward.'

How much Becca wanted to believe him. How much she wished to prove to her family that she was a good judge of character after all. 'And why have you not mentioned her before? There has been ample opportunity.'

'Because I was a fool and I didn't dare risk your good opinion. I didn't want you to paint me with the same brush as my philandering father. Kitty is not my child, but my illegitimate half-sister. She was at school in Bath and I thought she would remain there until the summer. But Kitty wasn't happy and threatened to run away,' Phineas said, his hand holding hers rather too tightly. 'I had to make sure that she was safe... I swear upon my soul, Becca, I do not have a mistress. My rakish days were over the day I met you in the park.'

She believed him and it hurt even more. 'I do not blame you for your past before you knew me, but I cannot have a husband that I do not trust. And one that does not trust me with the personal details of his life. You should have told me about Kitty from the very beginning of our friendship.'

'You're right, Becca. I should have told you about Kitty. But I cannot go back and change the past. I can only offer you my future. And I promise not to keep secrets from you. Please forgive me.'

The musicians played the final note. Becca stepped back from Phineas and curtsied. 'There cannot be love without trust. And you were right. You are not worthy of me.'

Chapter Twenty-Three

The carriage ride home was uncharacteristically silent and Mama wasn't one to keep her thoughts to herself. Perhaps she was tired. Becca could barely keep herself from weeping buckets. She had received a proposal of marriage from the man that she loved and she had refused him. He hadn't trusted her and now she couldn't trust him. The pain cut through her heart as her eyes pricked with tears.

A footman assisted them from the carriage and into the house. She trudged up the stairs and to the door of her room. She intended to weep into her pillow once she was alone. Her hand was on the knob when she heard her mother finally speak.

'We need to talk.'

Becca hated when her family said that. She always felt as if she were in trouble. Probably because she usually was. Touching her neck, she recalled that Mantheria had not come to Lady Grantley's ball after all. Sighing, Becca would not allow Mama to rake her over the coals for standing up for herself. She was an adult and tonight she had made adult decisions. Even difficult ones like refusing to give Phineas permission to speak to Papa about paying his addresses to her.

'Very well,' Becca said, opening the door and letting her

mother inside her bedchamber. Her lady's maid was waiting and Becca thanked her and told her to go to sleep. Her mother wished to speak with her alone. Once Shepherd left, Becca lifted her head up. She was bold and brave.

'I know that you want us to treat my eldest sister as though she is made of glass,' Becca said, her voice low and gruff, 'but she isn't. Mantheria has made herself small enough to fit into the little box that society allows women. No matter what my size, I was never going to fit in that box. And I don't want to.

'I love my sister and I know that she loves me, too, but she has no right to criticise me or give me helpful little hints about my size that sting like digs into my skin. She makes me feel terrible and small. And I cannot help it that I read slowly and I spell atrociously. I have done my very best and I am clever. My weaknesses do not define me.'

Mama's face paled a shade or two. She took a deep breath before placing her hands on Becca's shoulders. 'Never try to fit into any mould, my darling girl. You were taught to forge your own path.'

'And Mantheria?'

There was a pained expression on her mother's face. 'I have noticed those comments as well and I should have put an end to them myself long ago. Forgive me, Becca. Being a mother to eight wonderfully different children has been more challenging than I anticipated. I didn't want to hurt one child and so I inadvertently injured another. You are right. I do treat Mantheria as though she is made of glass. I feel that her sadness is my fault. I should never have agreed to her marriage with Glastonbury and I should never have left my children when they needed me most.'

Becca had only been three years of age when her parents had first travelled to Africa to return animals to the wild and to study them. During that trip, her brother Charles contracted scarlet fever from Eton and brought it home to Hampford Castle. Charles and Mantheria's twin, Elizabeth, died while her parents were away. Becca couldn't comprehend how painful it was for her parents to learn that two of their children had died while they were gone. Their second trip to Africa was when Becca was twelve years of age. Herself, Helen and Frederica had been put in a select ladies' school. Frederica made dozens of friends. Helen none. And Becca only bullies.

'I do not blame you, Mama, for what occurred while you were away. Bad things happen to everyone. And I think Mantheria would be a great deal happier if she took responsibility for her own choices and mistakes, too, and stopped punishing you and Papa for them.'

Her mother pulled her into a tight hug and Becca felt her eyes fill with tears. She didn't like seeing her strong mother vulnerable. 'I love you all so much. I only want each of my children to be happy.'

Stepping back, Becca wiped her eyes with her red gloves. 'I love you, too, Mama. Mantheria's mistakes and her words are not your fault.'

'I was not a perfect mother,' she said, her chin quivering. 'Perhaps if I had spent less time at my perfume company and more time with my children it all might have turned out differently.'

'That's fustian, Mama. No one is perfect. You were always there when we needed you and watching you invent your perfumes and run a successful business allowed us to see how a person could succeed if they worked hard enough. Even a woman. A wife. And a mother.'

Mama rubbed her red eyes. 'I had come to offer you comfort and instead I am the one receiving it.'

'And I don't blame you for presenting Helen first, last year. Nor for my reading difficulties. But I do not like it when you treat me like a child.'

Her mother shook her head. 'Your learning challenges *are* all my fault and I should have told you this before now.'

A tear fell down Becca's cheek as she shook her head. 'You hired me the smartest man at Oxford University to help me read and I can now. Slowly.'

Mama's hand moved from her neck to her ear. 'No. I believe that your learning challenges are a hereditary trait that you inherited from me.'

Becca shook her head. 'That's impossible. You're brilliant with words and numbers.'

Her mother stepped closer, until she was near enough to Becca to wipe the tear from her cheek with a white handkerchief. Unlike Phineas's black ones, but she didn't want to think about him. Not now.

'You look so much like her.'

'Who?'

'My mother,' Mama said, her voice soft. 'She could not read or write. Even though your grandfather tried to teach her. She said the letters misbehaved and finally gave up trying to learn. But that doesn't mean that she wasn't intelligent. She helped your grandfather with his business and they made a fortune together. She was also the happiest woman I have ever known and no one could leave her company without smiling. My mother was the smartest, most loving, and generous person. Just like you, my darling Becca. You inherited your looks and so many of your wonderful traits from her.'

Her grandmother had died in a carriage accident when her mother was young. Not even Papa had ever met her. Becca had grown up only knowing her grandfather and her step-grandmother, a proper and prim lady who loved them all dearly. Mama had rarely spoken of her mother. Even now, it felt as if she was sharing something private with her. Something special that her mother had treasured secretly.

Her mother pulled her into another hug and Becca rested her head on her mother's shoulder.

'Please forgive me, Becca,' Mama whispered. 'I was trying to fix what I thought was my fault. I never meant for you or Mantheria to think that you had disgraced me, or that I loved you any less than my other children. And I do know that you have grown up and, despite wanting to remain my little girl for ever, I need to treat you like a woman.'

Becca pulled back, wiping at her eyes. 'Phineas—Norwich asked to pay his address to me at the ball, but I said no. You were right. He wasn't honest with me.'

'I am so sorry, sweetheart,' Mama said and she truly looked it. 'But there will be other suitors. You dazzle every room that you enter.'

Her mother kissed her on the cheek, before unbuttoning the back of Becca's gown and helping her out of her stays and into her nightgown. Mama took out the remaining hairpins and brushed Becca's curls before braiding them. And despite declaring that she was a grown woman, Becca allowed her mother to tuck her into bed as if she were still a child.

Becca woke up with sore and dry eyes. She didn't know how long she cried before she fell asleep. She loved Phineas—even with all of his flaws. But a woman and wife were at the mercy of a husband by law. Her money was his. Her body belonged to him. How could she trust him if he wasn't honest with her? Sniffing, she forced herself not to cry again. There was no use. There would be other suitors and other Seasons.

But they wouldn't be Phineas.

She wondered if he hadn't confided in her because he thought her too young to cope with the truth. But she was not. And that was partly due to her friendship with Phineas. His support had helped her become more confident and self-assured. Beautiful attributes that she had learned and would continue to build upon now that he was gone from her life. Wiping away another tear from her eye, Becca couldn't help but feel deeply saddened that Phineas wouldn't be a part of her future.

Shepherd brought Becca her hot chocolate and tactfully did not mention her bloodshot eyes as she helped her dress. There was a knock at the door and Shepherd left Becca to answer it.

'Your Grace, do please come in.'

Becca knew three duchesses: her mother, Frederica and Mantheria. She wasn't certain that she was ready to talk with any of them. None of them had approved of Phineas and she was in no mood for them to crow over her with their superior knowledge of his character. Or at Becca's youth and lack of experience.

'Shepherd, would you mind leaving my sister and I alone?' Mantheria asked.

'Of course, Your Grace,' Shepherd said, bobbing a curtsy. She turned to look at Becca. 'Just ring the bell when you are ready for me, my lady.'

Becca gave a little nod, her stomach roiling. Her sister was dressed in black from her hat to her boots. She wore full mourning attire for the first time since Alexander's funeral. She removed her black veil and revealed that she, too, had red eyes and puffy cheeks. For once, Mantheria did not look like the beauty of the family. Her complexion was blotchy and there were dark circles underneath her eyes, like bruises.

It was small of her, but Becca still didn't wish to have to apologise for saying how she felt. For standing up for herself.

Mantheria took a few halting steps and surprised Becca by kneeling before her. 'You have already been so generous to offer me your forgiveness, but I must apologise to you. My dearest sister, Becca, I have behaved unpardonably and I will do anything in my power to make restitution to you. I was too ashamed and stubborn yesterday to truly hear you. But once you'd gone, I knew what you said was true.

'I foolishly thought that, every time I pointed out your perceived flaws, I was helping you. That I was preparing you for society. I never once imagined that my words hurt you or made you feel as if you were less than the incredible person that you are. Never again will I presume to think that I know better than you about how to live your own life. You are a woman grown. Please forgive me.'

Becca's eyes filled with tears. 'Stand up, Sister. I love you and I have already forgiven you.'

Mantheria pulled her youngest sister into a crushing hug and tears fell freely from her eyes. 'Not just because of Alexander's request?'

Becca shook her head, a tear falling down her cheek. 'You are at fault, but then so am I. I should have told you how I felt years ago, but I behaved like a scared little mouse.'

Her eldest sister gave her another tight squeeze. 'You don't act like a mouse any longer.'

'Phineas taught me how to be a lion.'

Mantheria's smile faltered. 'I suppose you've heard the rumours around Lord Norwich?'

'Yes. And I loved him. But more than that, I loved who I was when I was with him,' she said, echoing Cressy's words.

Her eldest sister sniffled. 'I have never seen you happier or prettier. And perhaps we have all misjudged your Phineas. After my legal separation from Alexander, most of the *ton* snubbed me for the rest of the Season. But he didn't. Lord Norwich made a point of speaking to me when it was quite unfashionable to do so. His personality is not at all like Alexander's and I was wrong to suggest that he would behave similarly as a husband. For that, I am sorry as well.'

Becca took her sister's hands and squeezed them. 'He wasn't honest with me and I cannot have a husband I do not trust.'

Mantheria began to cry and Becca pulled her into a tight hug and comforted her.

Chapter Twenty-Four

'Why are you moping again this morning, Norwich?' Kitty demanded in the breakfast room. She was devouring bacon and eggs as though she'd never eaten before.

Phineas had drowned his sorrows for the last two nights with a bottle of wine and his head hurt something fierce. He had lost Becca because he hadn't had the courage to be vulnerable with her and tell her the worst truths about his father. About his own failings as a brother and guardian. 'The lady that I love turned down my proposal.'

Kitty spat out her juice on the table. 'She didn't! Why, all the maids at Winfield Park think that you're very handsome. They were always giggling over you. It makes me sick.'

'Thank you, Kitty,' he said drily and sipped the awful concoction that the housekeeper had made for his hangover.

'Well, why don't you ask her again?'

Phineas did not want to explain his romantic relationship with his much younger half-sister, but Kitty was like a dog with a bone. Once she caught on to an idea, she refused to let it go. 'She doesn't trust me.'

'Why not?'

'Because I didn't tell her about you.'

'That was badly done, but I find grovelling usually works rather well,' Kitty said, pointing a knife at him. 'That or asking so many times that the person finally gives in. You always give me my way by the fifth or sixth time that I ask you.'

It was a sad, but accurate pronouncement on his guardianship. Still, Phineas had been a fool. Becca had clearly been upset that night and now that some time had passed she might be willing to hear him out. His heart hoped she could forgive him. 'You're right, Kitty. I will ask again.'

'And I will come with you.'

He swallowed the noxious concoction too quickly and coughed. 'I am not sure that will help.'

Kitty continued as if he hadn't spoken. 'And then afterwards you can take me to get an ice at Gunter's for being so helpful. Sylvie Philips says that they are delicious. She claims to have gone there six times. She is such a braggart.'

'And so, too, will you be after I take you,' he said, walking around her and up the stairs to the master's rooms.

His valet was waiting for him with a hot bath prepared. 'Thank you, Ellis. Please see that my plain blue coat is brushed and ready.'

Ellis bowed to him and left the dressing room. Phineas climbed into the copper tub and mentally began planning his apology to Becca. He would beg on his knees for her forgiveness if necessary. His entire life, he'd wanted to love someone and to be loved. Phineas never explained the reasons for his actions to anyone. But he would not allow his pride, or his favourite pair of buckskins, to come between them. Sliding underneath the water, he knew that Becca wouldn't want fancy words—she'd want the entire truth.

When he climbed into his carriage an hour later, Phineas held the song he'd written for Becca and the hand of his sister. For the first time in London, Phineas was attired in his plainest clothes as if he were visiting his tenants in the country. He'd used no cosmetics to improve his appearance to cover the black circles under his eyes. He'd not slept well the previous two nights after Becca's rejection. He appeared as he truly was. Imperfect.

Phineas purchased a bouquet of pink roses before standing on the doorstep of Hampford House with Kitty by his side. For the first time in his life he was unsure of his welcome. Mr Lawes had said that the Duchess of Hampford had instructed her butler not to receive him or allow him to visit Becca for a week. More than that amount of time had passed, but he still wasn't sure he'd be accepted into the house.

Picking up the knocker, he rapped it three times. The older, disapproving butler took his card and at least directed him to the front parlour. He wasn't turned away at the door. 'I will see if Lady Rebecca is at home.'

'Tell her that Miss Kitty Goulding is here to see her,' Kitty said in her overly loud tone of voice. 'I don't have my own card.'

Phineas was certain Becca was in the house, but whether or not she would see him and allow him to explain was another thing. Maybe she would come for Kitty. He couldn't sit down, so he paced the room for several minutes and finally stood by the window looking out on to Berkeley Square. He watched his groom walk the carriage horses up and down the street.

'I've never seen you so nervous, Norwich,' Kitty said, a note of glee in her voice.

'Behave yourself, Kitty, or I won't take you for an ice.'

'Your threats mean nothing to me. You'll take me for an ice either way just so I stop nagging you about it.'

She was correct, but that didn't improve his humour.

***

Earls were not usually kept waiting and certainly not for over a quarter of an hour. He set his composition on the pianoforte. He heard the door open behind him and saw Becca enter the room alone. Her glorious locks were pulled back in a loose bun at the nape of her neck. Her day dress was white muslin with a pattern of little red cherries. Her neckline was high and her sleeves went all the way down to her bare wrists. She looked delectable. He wouldn't have minded taking a nibble of her.

Moving from the window, he held out his hands to her. All the words from his carefully prepared speech left his mind when her hands joined his. 'Forgive me. I have no excuse. I should have told you from the very start about Kitty.'

His half-sister put her feet up on the coffee table. 'You really should have, Norwich.'

He brought one of her ungloved hands to his lips and kissed it. His lips lingered against her soft skin a few moments longer than was proper—not that kissing her bare hand was precisely good manners. Hang propriety. He turned over her hand and pressed a kiss into her palm and then moved his lips to her wrist. 'Lady Rebecca, may I introduce you to my ward and sister, Kitty?'

His little sister did not stand, but gazed up at them. 'Half-sister, Norwich. I was born on the wrong side of the blanket.'

Phineas cringed. He'd told her years ago to stop using that phrase that she learned from her late nurse. Mrs Benning had been a good woman and very loving to his ward, but she'd also possessed a shocking vocabulary that his little sister had picked up. And Kitty liked to shock people and to put Phineas out of countenance whenever possible.

Becca, however, showed no sign of discomfort. She curtsied to his outspoken little sister. 'It is a pleasure to make your acquaintance, Miss Goulding.'

'You are pretty, it's no wonder why Norwich was blue-devilled the last two mornings… I am here to help you forgive my brother so that we can go and get ices. You can come, too.'

'What a nice treat,' Becca said, smiling. 'But perhaps since this is your first time in town you would like to have two desserts? Our cook has just finished the most delicious cake. Would you like to try some while I talk to your brother privately?'

At last, Kitty got to her feet. 'Yes. And, Norwich, don't forget to grovel. That's the most important part. Followed by nagging.'

'Thank you, Kitty.'

'If you'll come this way, Kitty,' Becca said, leading her to the door. 'Harper, there you are. Would you please take Miss Goulding to the kitchens and see that she is given a large slice of chocolate cake?'

'And a glass of milk,' Kitty added.

'Very good, my lady,' Harper said and Phineas saw Kitty following the butler before Becca closed the door to the parlour.

He met her gaze. 'Becca, I need to tell you everything. I have spent the last two nights tossing and turning, but only the truth will do.'

Becca pulled him to the closest couch and sat down beside him. She still held one of his hands. 'You can tell me anything, Phineas. Your confidences are always safe with me. And if you are also well behaved, you may have some cake, too.'

Leaning his head forward, he rested it against hers for a moment. His lips curled upwards at her quick wits. 'It is just hard to open myself to someone. I have never done this before.'

'You don't have to do anything you don't want to do.'

Lifting his head so that he could look into her beautiful blue eyes, he said, 'But I want to, my dear one, and Kitty will be terribly disappointed in me if I don't. I need you to understand why I did the things that I did. So that you'll forgive me and let me ask you the most important question so far.'

Becca nodded, a small, encouraging smile on her lips. 'Your fiftieth question.'

'I have already told you that I gamed away almost all of my inheritance after my father died and I might have, if a horrible woman hadn't brought a dirty little girl to my estate near Bath. She said that the scamp was my father's by-blow and that she'd only keep the child if I paid her what she was owed and what she was due for the next year.'

Her face paled. 'How old was she?'

'I don't know her exact birth date, but my housekeeper thought that Kitty was around two or three years old.'

'What a poor darling.'

Phineas swallowed heavily. 'Then the woman grabbed the girl roughly by her thin arm and said, "Smile for the man, Kitty." I am sure that it will not surprise you that my half-sister bared her teeth at me. I asked if Kathyrn was her name and the woman only laughed. She said that they called my half-sister Kitty because she fought with her fingernails—her claws. The poor child was covered in dirt and bruises, but she resembled my father greatly.'

Becca leaned forward, holding his hand tighter. 'How could your father leave his own child with such a person? In such awful conditions?'

'My father cared only about himself and I didn't want

to be like him. I paid off that horrible woman and I had my housekeeper wash Kitty. I knew then and there that I could no longer gamble my future away. I needed to be there for this little girl, for there was no one else. And I tried to take care of her the best way I knew how. I hired her a nurse and I even decided to find a bride during the next Season. A mother for her.'

She inhaled sharply. 'Louisa.'

Phineas sneered at his own stupidity. 'Yes. Lady Louisa was pretty, sweet tempered, and had a fortune that could put my messy affairs in order. I knew that she cared for your brother, but he'd said for years that he never meant to marry. I thought her the perfect solution, only to discover that she would risk her reputation, her place in society, all for this abstract idea called love. It seemed ludicrous to me at the time.

'By the next Season I had learned how to economise. I no longer wanted or needed a wife. Kitty was happy with her nurse and I left her to go to London for the Parliamentary seasons as my parents had left me. Then her beloved nurse, Mrs Benning, died suddenly last year and I found her a position at a good ladies' school. She was asked to leave. My secretary had her placed at two other schools, but none of them was a very good fit. She has high spirits and I never attempted to crush them the way my father did mine. I always wanted her to feel safe and loved.'

Becca breathed in sharply.

Phineas forced himself to continue. 'I tried not to be involved in the selection of the schools. I wrongly thought that no one would make the connection between her and me. I styled myself as her guardian, but still there were… are rumours that Kitty is my natural child. I had hoped by separating myself from her that she would not be tainted by my father's careless choices. But a week ago, Kitty sent me a letter that said if I didn't come and take her from her third school, that she would run away and never come back. I had no choice but to go to Bath.'

'And you brought her back with you to London.'

Sighing, he nodded. 'My father would have sent her to another school, but I thought about what you would do and so I brought her with me.'

One side of Becca's mouth quirked up. 'And the scandal?'

'I hadn't realised the gossip would spread so quickly, but I should have in London. I had every intention of telling you about Kitty and introducing her to you after my proposal. And my reasons were foolish for not explaining who she was to you before, but I sincerely thought at the time that I was keeping her name clean. But Kitty would rather tell the world that she was born on the wrong side of the blanket and claim a fallible brother, than to have a good name and no family of her own.'

Becca was fully smiling at him now. 'I learned about Kitty at Lady Grantley's ball and I was very upset with you. But I should have let you explain that night. It would have saved me buckets of tears and two days of terrible heartache.'

And Phineas two devilish hangovers.

He wrapped his arm around her shoulders, needing to be closer to her. 'Becca, no woman has touched my heart the way you have. From that first morning in the park and every moment since spent in your company, I have known a joy that I only hoped existed. With you I am finally able to be my true self. I don't have to hide behind my quizzing glass or my fine coats. I love you with all that is in me and

I would beg for a lifetime with you to show you just how special you are to me.'

She leaned forward and kissed the tip of his nose. 'Is this question number fifty, or are you simply mentioning again how besotted you are with me?'

Phineas got off the couch and kneeled down before her. 'Lady Rebecca Stringham, will you do me the great honour of becoming my wife?'

'Yes, Phineas. I love you. I love you with every major organ in my body and several minor ones as well. There is nothing in this world that I want more than to be your wife.'

In one swift movement, he was sitting back on the sofa next to Becca and kissing her passionately. She had said yes. Becca loved him. Her lips were warm and inviting. He could taste chocolate on her tongue. She must have only recently left her bed. The thought inflamed him.

Peeling off his gloves, he pulled the pins out of her hair and ran his fingers through the curls. His lady love was by no means a passive member of their embrace. Her hands explored the planes of his chest and then moved slowly up his back, then gripped his shoulders and pulled his weight down firmly upon her. There were no words for how wonderful Becca's body felt against his. Her large breasts, the curve of her waist and generous hips.

He ravished her lips and then made a trail of kisses to her neck, nuzzling her there. Her skin tasted sweet everywhere. 'I've wanted to kiss your wit for weeks.'

One of her hands moved to his hair and she ran her fingers through it. Mr Ellis would not be pleased, but Phineas didn't give a fig about his appearance. He only cared about how he felt—happy and deliriously in love.

'Is my wit underneath my ear?'

Phineas laughed and then nuzzled her neck. 'I haven't

yet discovered its location on your body, yet, but if you'll permit further exploration, I would be more than happy to search for it.'

Becca placed her other hand on the left side of his chest. 'I have found your heart and I would happily kiss it.'

'Are you trying to undress me again, my lady? The way you did the first day that we met.'

She blushed prettily. 'I was only making sure that you could breathe.'

He moved her hand to his rumpled cravat. 'I am having difficulty breathing at this very moment. Perhaps you should check my pulse.'

Leaning her head forward, she kissed his neck and nipped at his ear. He laughed in surprise.

'I think I found *your* wit!' she said with a gurgle of laughter.

'Minx,' he whispered before capturing her mouth again with his and tasting her tongue. Never in his life had he experienced such bliss. He could barely wait to bed her.

A knock on the door caused them to break apart. Phineas attempted to tidy his coat—his cravat was a lost cause. Becca straightened the lace around her neck, but nothing could be done with her hair that was falling down her back so fetchingly.

A footman opened the door for the butler.

'You called for tea and cake, my lady,' Harper said, bringing a silver tray into the room and setting it on the table in front of them. The footman followed him. 'Jim, why don't you stay with Lady Rebecca and shall I bring back Miss Goulding to keep her company? Her Grace would not like you to be alone with a single gentleman.'

'I am certain that she would object even more if I was alone with a married man,' Becca quipped.

Phineas chuckled and tried to cover it with a cough. He loved her clever humour.

The butler gave her a scolding look.

'I can assure you, Harper, that even Mama will not mind me speaking alone with a gentleman for a marriage proposal.'

Harper's face did not look at all assured—he eyed Phineas warily. 'Has His Lordship asked for His Grace's permission to pay his addresses to you?'

'I'm sure Lord Norwich would love to talk to Papa after our *private* conversation,' Becca said with the grace of a queen. She looked past the disapproving butler. 'Jim, fetch a bottle of wine and have Harper pour a glass for all the servants. A celebration is in order. For I am to be married.'

The tall, young man beamed at her. 'Very good, my lady.' He left his post by the door and hurried deeper into the house. No doubt to the cellars.

The older butler frowned and stood still.

Becca got to her feet, her hair charmingly messy, and her lips swollen from his kisses. She patted Harper on the arm. 'You are one of my oldest and dearest friends, Harper. Trust me to be alone with him and to make the best decisions for myself and my future.'

'It's Lord Norwich that I don't trust. He's a dangerous man.'

She nodded, moving her hand to his back and leading the butler out of the room. 'But I do trust Lord Norwich. And he would hardly have brought his little sister with him if he meant to ravish me.'

Phineas chuckled again. Becca was so clever.

Kissing his cheek, she pushed the bewildered butler out of the room and closed the door behind them. She came back to him and sat on his lap, her arms around his neck.

'Harper is very protective of me, because I am the youngest. He's known me for my entire life.'

He wrapped his arms around her waist. 'And I will protect you for the rest of your life, my love.'

'I don't want you to protect me. I want you to respect me.'

'Always.'

Becca's hands moved to his face and traced the line of his jaw, the curve of his thin lips, his nose, cheekbones, eyebrows and forehead. He closed his eyes and enjoyed her gentle ministrations. He was the more experienced lover of the pair, but she was teaching him things. New ways to feel pleasure and love. When her lips brushed against his tantalisingly, he knew that he would never be the same, cold and indifferent man. How could one sneer in the presence of such a person? Becca was all light, joy and love. She burned brightly in his arms as she kissed him.

Her fingernails gently scratched his back and he jumped.

She pulled away from him. 'Oh, dear, I should have been more careful with your beautiful coat.'

'It's not that,' he assured her, moving Becca off his lap and walking away from the sofa. 'I am growing too overheated for the parlour and certainly for a gentleman whose little sister is in the house.'

Phineas went to the windows on the other side of the room, taking deep breaths. He'd never lost control of his body before. And judging from how Becca was smiling at him now, if he came any closer to her, he would lose it again.

Her smile slipped a little. 'My family will grow to like you, Phineas. They just don't know you the way I do. You are nothing like Alexander. I know that you will be faithful to me. And I know that I will love you every day of my life.'

Phineas thought of his own wretched family. 'It is unfair to ask you, but may Kitty live with us? I know that her presence will always cause pernicious gossip from society about her origins, but if I try to send her to school again, she'll simply run away.'

'Of course Kitty must live with us. I only forgave you as a courtesy to her.'

His mouth felt dry. 'You are too good for me, Becca.'

'I was angry and wrong, Phineas. You are worthy of me and I am worthy of you. And we are our best selves together,' she said lovingly. 'Do you know Aesop's fable of the lion and the mouse?'

Phineas knew that the Stringhams loved animals, but he wondered why she would bring up such a thing now. He tried not to sneer as he mentioned his own father and mother, 'No, my parents did not read or tell me stories and my nurse was not literate.'

Slowly, she stood up and came towards him. Every part of his body longed to pull her into his arms and claim her as his own. Phineas's hands clenched into fists at his side. He would not behave like a libertine. At least until after they were legally wed.

'One day, a lion caught a mouse by its tail and was about to eat the little mouse whole. But the mouse begged the lion to show her mercy and promised that in future that she would help the lion. Now the lion was a large and fierce and powerful beast. How could such a small, scared and powerless creature help him? But the mouse insisted that some day the lion would need her help and so the lion let the little mouse go.'

'The lion probably wasn't in the mood for mouse.'

'He didn't have the right white sauce on hand,' Becca agreed with a little laugh. 'Now, let me finish the fable. One day the lion found itself caught in a hunter's net. Its large teeth could not bite through the rope to get him free.

His fierce claws could not cut his cords. And not even his powerful strength was enough to escape. The lion was certain of his own death, until he heard the voice of the little mouse. The mouse had returned to fulfil her promise. She was small enough to climb between the ropes. She was scared enough to shred the cords with her teeth. And she was powerless enough to remember the need for friends. Together they escaped to freedom.'

Phineas could no longer keep his hands to himself. He touched Becca's face, cupping his hand around the curve of her cheek and the line of her chin. 'That is a beautiful story, my love. But how am I the lion and you the mouse in this tale?'

Her blue eyes sparkled as she smiled at him. 'You are clever, my handsome lion. You helped me find my confidence. You helped me no longer be a little mouse. I stood up to my sister and to the rest of my family. I demanded to be treated like an adult and it is not perfect, but they are trying. And now it is my turn to help you, with your half-sister.'

'I cannot make Kitty behave. No matter how hard I try.'

'You are speaking to a young lady who was also asked to leave school,' Becca said, her eyes dancing with merriment. 'We do not have to make Kitty behave. We simply have to love her.'

'Love solves everything?'

'Unconditional love does. At least everything that is important.'

Phineas had never known such love before and he realised that it *did* change everything. He could be vulnerable with her. He could tell her anything and Becca's love would never alter. How lucky both he and Kitty were to have someone like her in their lives. Someone who accepted them as they were and loved them anyway.

A worthless rake.

A base-born daughter.

'May I play a song that I wrote for you before we take Kitty for ices?'

'Of course!' she said with an adorable giggle. 'Ned would be terribly disappointed in you if you didn't make the song a part of the proposal.'

'His matchmaking skills are seriously lost on a groom,' he said, sitting at the piano bench. Phineas felt the warmth of her smile in his very soul as he played Becca's tune on the pianoforte. It was light and lilting and lovely. Just like his soon-to-be bride.

He played the last note and turned to see her reaction to his song. She leaned down and pressed her lips softly against his. 'It was perfect. Thank you, Phineas.'

Getting to his feet, he couldn't resist pulling her back into his arms. He pressed his lips harder against Becca's and she slightly opened her mouth. He parted her lips with his tongue and stroked it against hers. He was lost in the sensations and textures of her velvety skin, her satin lips and her clever tongue. Becca moved her hands against his firm chest. His heart was truly pounding now. Then she slowly slid her hands up around his neck, pulling him closer to her. He deepened the kiss and the experience felt entirely new.

Unconditional love changed everything.

Breathlessly, he broke the kiss, but made a trail of hot kisses from her lips to her neck. His blood thrummed with need for her. His knees felt strangely wobbly as he nuzzled Becca beneath her ear.

She giggled. 'Lucky me. I get to keep your wicked tongue and your heart!'

And Phineas got her humour and happiness for the rest of his life.

Epilogue

Becca insisted that they be married at the chapel in Hampford Castle. She wanted to go home one last time before she wed Phineas. And as much as she knew her groom would have preferred their ceremony to be in the fashionable St George's Chapel with all the *ton* gazing in awe at his sartorial splendour, he'd acquiesced, saying, 'I will marry you any time. Any place. As long as you'll have me.'

Shepherd arranged Becca's hair for her wedding, placing little white flowers all around her honey-brown curls. She wore a white slip underneath her wedding dress of silk gauze in the colour of Maiden's Blush Rose. The gown had a low neck, delicate embroidery on the bodice and flower cup sleeves. Becca had never before felt more beautiful. Not in spite of her curves, but because of them. She no longer needed to feel small. Her breasts filled out the front of her bodice quite nicely and the slightly lower waist of the skirt emphasised the shape of her hips. She could hardly wait for Phineas to see her in it. No doubt he would give her a new ring to match the gown. He loved giving her jewels and, after today, it would no longer be scandalous to accept them.

Opening her perfume bottle that her mother had made just for her, Becca dabbed it on the inside of her wrists and the back of her neck. It was the most perfect scent in the world: witch-hazel, orange citrus and leaves. The combination of all her favourite things.

'Is there anything you need, my lady?'

Becca touched the diamond necklace around her throat with matching earrings that Papa had given her. She shook her head. Her lady's maid left the room, just as the tapestry on her wall moved and a door from the secret passageway opened. Helen was the first to come out, followed by her other four siblings.

Wick shook his head bemusedly. 'How could you three little girls have discovered a secret passageway and not told us about it?'

Before today, only Frederica, Helen and Becca had known about the passageway and the hidden door that led outside the castle. Being both clever and naughty children, they had wisely not shared the existence of a secret passageway with their elder siblings. They might have put a stop to their night-time shenanigans. Sharing it with them now felt like a final goodbye to her childhood.

Frederica laughed, holding her small belly. Her countenance was bright and no longer green. She looked like her usual beautiful and determined self. 'How else were we going to get spiders into your beds?'

Matthew gave a full body shiver. 'And snakes.'

Helen placed her hands on her own growing belly bump. 'Oh, stop! I haven't done that in years.'

Her ball snake, Theodosia, slithered out from underneath the tapestry, causing Mantheria to shriek. To her own surprise, Becca had missed the snake, but not as much as she'd missed living with all of her sisters. Helen's home was now a castle in Scotland and Frederica's a palace. Mantheria's Glastonbury estate was only a few hours away from London, but it wasn't the same. Nothing would be the same again and Becca allowed herself to mourn the change in her family for a few moments.

A caterpillar had to give up crawling in order to fly.

Mantheria placed a light hand on her shoulder. 'Becca, you look like a princess.'

Frederica touched her other shoulder. 'No, a queen!'

Pushing them both aside, Helen shook her head. 'You all think too small. Becca looks like an empress—*Rebecca the Great.*'

Becca got to her feet and hugged her three sisters. Next, she hugged her brothers. First, Matthew. And then Wick. She had always been his favourite and he hers. She hoped her obstinate brother would eventually warm to Phineas and Kitty.

Her siblings had gathered in Helen's room before her wedding a year before, but it still felt special to have them here with her. To feel their love and support for her own marriage. They surrounded her as they walked together from her room and down the main staircase. She was to be married in Hampford Chapel in her own home.

When they reached the door of the chapel, one by one they left her to go stand by their spouses and families. Wick with Louisa and their four small sons. Mantheria sat next to Andrew and Kitty—who were about the same age. Matthew and Nancy attempted to wrangle their two wiggly daughters. Elizabeth and Samuel both held little Arthur, who was playing peek-a-boo with Grandfather and Grandmother Stubbs who were sitting behind him. Helen and Mark were huddled together.

Phineas was standing in the front of the chapel with Lord St Albyn by his side. The two dandies were gorgeous by themselves, but together in their silver outfits they dazzled the entire room.

Mama gave Becca a kiss on the cheek and then pulled the blush veil over her face. 'I love you with all of my heart, dearest girl. Promise me that you will visit us often.'

Tears sprang to Becca's eyes as she nodded.

Papa, who was wearing a new tailcoat and trousers that actually fitted him, stood beside her. 'You can still change your mind, Becca. You know that, don't you? Your mother and I will take you anywhere in the world that you want to go. Isn't that right, Selina? Africa? America? Asia? Australia? Think of all the animals that we could see in their natural habitats.'

Her mother rolled her eyes. 'Theophilus. This is not the time.'

'I am completely in earnest,' Papa insisted, his blond hair looking greyer than ever.

Mama gave her husband a kiss on the cheek and then went down the aisle to sit by Helen and Mark.

Becca linked her arm with her father's.

He patted her hand. 'As you know Matthew wrote the wedding settlements. Nothing is final until the vows have been said. Norwich can't even sue you for breach of contract.'

'I love Phineas, Papa,' she said, leaning her head against his tall shoulder. 'And I want to marry him.'

Papa sighed heavily. 'You can't fault a father for asking.'

Becca grinned as Papa led her down the aisle. Some of her earliest memories were in Hampford Chapel. Mostly of her father snoring during the services or Mama's shushing them to be quiet. It didn't matter that Phineas owned three estates, Hampford Castle would always be home to her.

All the servants and staff had come to see her wedding.

Becca had never seen the chapel so overflowing with people. Mrs Mary Wallace, her old governess, pushed up her now foggy spectacles. Beside her in the pew were two well-behaved small children with their arms folded reverently. The next row held Mrs May, the Hampford housekeeper who smiled through her tears. Even Mr Harper had his starched white handkerchief out. Alonzo and Cassandra Lawes held hands. And Becca spied Miss Shepherd sitting suspiciously close to Jim the footman. She would have to ask Phineas to hire Jim, for she did not want to split the pair up. Love was too precious to waste. They passed by her grandparents and the rest of her family. Including her niece Lady Susan, who kicked her father Matthew and yelled, 'I hate church! I want to see the animals!'

Susie's escape was blocked by Grandfather Stubbs's cane. He then swept the little girl up into his arms and promised her a piece of chocolate. Becca remembered being held by all of her family. She'd been the youngest child and babied by each of them. Despite marrying Phineas today, Becca knew that she would always be a Stringham. That the bond between them would not weaken over distance or time. They were a tight pack.

Chaplain Wallace began the service and Becca didn't hear a word. All she could see and think about was Phineas. His golden hair gleamed in the light from the stained-glass windows. He had worn his silver tailcoat and he sparkled as bright as any jewel. He was smiling widely and looked handsomer than ever. And she loved him with all her heart.

All his broken pieces.

And he loved all of hers.

Phineas was heartily sick of shaking hands with his friends and acquaintances. He wanted nothing more than to run off with his luscious bride. He should have known that the Stringhams would not let a fellow off so easily. The Duke of Hampford shook his hand and then pulled him into a death-grip embrace that might have been considered a hug, if the expression on his face hadn't been so threatening. Then the rest of the family proceeded to hug him—something that no one had attempted since his nurse. The Duchess of Hampford even kissed his cheek.

Lord Cheswick squeezed him painfully and probably wrinkled his beautiful silver coat from Weston.

Cheswick's wife, Louisa, embraced him. 'Love is worth waiting for, Lord Norwich. You were wise to hold on to your heart until Becca debuted. You two are perfectly matched.'

Rakes and dandies did not blush, but Phineas felt the colour rise in his cheeks. He'd once proposed to Louisa and he hadn't loved her. 'Thank you.'

Lord Trentham pulled Phineas into a hug and patted his back jovially. 'Now that we are brothers, I cannot wait to share with you the family rate in the business. I have several speculations that I think you'll be most interested in.'

Lady Trentham pushed her husband's shoulder and then she embraced Phineas, too. 'Beware, Lord Norwich. Matthew charges for snobbery.'

Phineas gave a breathless laugh and he was ready to be hugged by the Duke and the Duchess of Pelford and then Lord and Lady Inverness. Even the next generation of Stringhams covered him with hugs and kisses and sticky hands. He hadn't much experience with children, but when the smallest babe licked his cheek, his heart felt fuller than ever. Phineas was finally a part of a loving family. What he'd always missed having.

Smiling, he watched his wife receive the same attentions. Becca's face was covered with kisses. Each person told his bride that they loved her as they showered her with affection. Phineas would continue to do so as her husband. She was *his* beloved.

A hand touched his shoulder and he turned to see Kitty. She still had black corkscrew curls, but Lady Glastonbury's maid had arranged them becomingly. But the greatest change was that his naughty sister was smiling. Grinning widely from ear to ear.

Instinctively, Phineas pulled her into a hug like he'd just received from all of Becca's family. Like himself, Kitty stiffened momentarily before squeezing him back as tightly as Lord Cheswick. It was their first hug, but it would not be their last.

He attempted to say the three words that came so easily to every member of the Stringham family. 'I love you, Kitty.'

His eyes filled with tears as Kitty smiled wider and hugged him close to asphyxiation. 'I love you, too, Norwich.'

Once he was able to detach himself and his beloved coat from his half-sister, he said, 'We will be back in a fortnight to bring you home. Try not to cause too much mayhem for the Duke and Duchess of Hampford.'

Becca gave Kitty a second hug. 'Nonsense. Our castle was made for mayhem. And you are my newest sister and sisters are precious things.'

'Almost as precious as husbands,' Phineas said, holding out a hand to his bride.

She placed her fingers in his. 'And families. I have a present for you, Kitty.'

'But it's your wedding,' Kitty pointed out.

Her lady's maid handed Becca a paper, she smiled at it,

before giving it to Kitty. His little sister snorted and then started to cry.

'Oh, no! Kitty I am so sorry,' Becca said, blanching. 'I thought that you would like it.'

With tears streaming down her face, Kitty shook her curls. 'I love it.'

Phineas held his breath until he saw Kitty turn the paper around. It was one of Becca's caricatures. He saw himself as a lion in his best wedding clothes marrying a mouse that was of a similar height and between the two of them was a naughty kitten that had Kitty's smile. They were underneath a wedding arch and he could see a snake in the grass for Lady Inverness. A spider dangling from the top of the arch for Lady Pelford. A little songbird perched on the side for her late sister Elizabeth. And flying in the sky was a butterfly: Lady Glastonbury was finally a part of Becca's drawings.

Kitty flung herself into Becca's arms and his bride hugged her tightly and kissed the top of her head. 'Our first family portrait. We will have a proper one done very soon.'

'Thank you, Becca.'

'You're very welcome, Kitty.'

Phineas's energetic little sister then showed her new drawing to each person, one at a time. Kitty wasn't just getting a sister. The Stringhams had welcomed her with open arms. She now had grandparents, aunts and cousins to love her. It was everything that Phineas had ever wanted for his little sister. All that he hadn't been able to give her.

Becca slipped her hand into his. 'I have hugged and kissed everyone at least three times. I believe it is time to escape.'

He kissed her brow and then her cheek. 'Would that we could, my love. But the door to the courtyard is blocked by your numerous family members and I believe your mother planned a wedding breakfast in the grand hall.'

'We are not going that way.' Becca tugged him towards the front of the church and a side door. Having only stayed one night in the castle, he didn't know precisely where she was taking him up the back stairs and down a long hall. His bride opened the door to a bedchamber that he assumed was her room. Two walls were a lovely shade of pink and the other two were covered by ancient and, no doubt, priceless tapestries. It was impossible not to notice the enormous canopy bed in the middle of the room. His heartbeat thundered in his chest. Phineas would have to wait until tonight to make her his.

Becca put her arms around his neck and brought her soft lips to his. But there was nothing soft about her kiss. Her breasts were pressed against his chest and her lush hips against his. Phineas could not think. He could only feel her tongue entering his mouth. Her fingers running through his locks. Her kisses on his neck and then her teeth nibbling on his ear. Every part of his anatomy was on fire and they were in a castle full of wedding guests with the door unlocked.

With all that was left of his self-control, Phineas stepped back from his bride. Becca merely stepped forward with her lips tilted towards his. He couldn't resist kissing her deeply, but managed to say it against her mouth, 'We cannot, my love. Everyone expects us.'

Becca kissed the line of his jaw. 'I promise you that they don't. None of my siblings attended their wedding breakfasts. We are a hot-blooded family.'

His usually sharp brain was not functioning as well as other organs at the moment, but he managed to understand that his presence was not needed at the party. He placed his hands on the dip of her back and pressed her body harder against his. She rubbed up against him like a cat and the sound she made was almost a purr of satisfaction. Phineas's control was entirely lost and his daydreams had not been close to the delicious reality of making love to his bride.

Becca tiptoed to kiss him on the nose. 'But we had better go now.'

He blinked. His mind was completely blank. 'Where?'

She grinned at him. 'On our wedding trip. I asked for your driver to meet us around the back of the castle. Come with me.'

Bewildered, he watched Becca put on a blue velvet cape and then pull back one of the enormous tapestries that covered an entire wall to reveal a hidden door. She opened it and stepped into a dark and frankly sinister passageway. With one hand she beckoned him to follow. Instinctively, Phineas entered the dark passage and Becca closed the door behind him, making it even dimmer. She put a delicate finger on his lips. 'This is a secret way out of the castle that is only known by a handful of members of the family. You are now a fully-fledged Stringham.'

Phineas kissed her finger and then sucked on it.

Becca grinned. 'Come, my love.'

Holding hands, he followed her through a narrow passageway and down a steep set of stairs to a wooden door. Becca unlatched it and they came out of the castle behind a rather large bush. Even in the light of day, Phineas would not have noticed the secret entrance. He did, however, notice his chaise and four ready to take them to his estate only a few hours away.

He opened the door for his bride and she eagerly climbed inside. Phineas thanked his driver and closed the door behind him, pulling down the window coverings. Becca giggled as he took her into his arms. She responded with a passion that inflamed him once more and he didn't mind when she pulled off his cravat and began unbuttoning his waistcoat. She tugged his shirt out of his trousers and placed her hands on his bare chest. Phineas could not breathe. He did not want to. It was all too wonderful. He could hardly wait to touch her delicate skin too and to make Becca his in all ways.

Phineas kissed her neck and admitted, 'We need to slow down, my beloved. I cannot take your innocence in a carriage.'

Becca blinked at him and then smiled. 'That's all right, my love. I will take yours.'

He laughed softly before allowing his determined bride to ravish him.

* * * * *

*If you loved this story, make sure to read the
previous books in Samantha Hastings's
The Scandalous Stringhams miniseries*

The Marquess and the Runaway Lady
Debutante with a Dangerous Past
Wedded to His Enemy Debutante
Accidental Courtship with the Earl

Author Note

I'm delighted to share Lady Rebecca Stringham's story! She is the youngest daughter of the Duke and Duchess of Hampford. Becca has been a favourite of mine for several books and I am so excited for her to be the heroine this time.

Lord Norwich—Phineas—was first introduced in *The Marquess and the Runaway Lady*. Norwich is inspired by real dandies like Beau Brummel, who had considerable power during the Regency era. They swayed both society opinion and fashion.

In 1810 Miss Mary Anning (1799-1847) and her brother found the first known Ichthyosaurus specimen near Lyme Regis. Mary excavated it. In 1817 Lieutenant Colonel Thomas Birch bought several of the Annings' collection of fossils, bringing them to national attention as described in this book. In 1842 Sir Richard Owen first used the word 'Dinosauria' which is Greek for 'terrible lizard'.

Unfortunately, dyslexia and other learning struggles were not understood in the early nineteenth century. People like Becca, who had difficulties reading, were thought to be 'dunces', or unmotivated, and in some cases medically deficient. In 1887 Rudolf Berlin, a German ophthalmologist, coined the term 'dyslexia'.

In the same way that Becca does in this story, I have

struggled with my weight and my self-esteem based on the measurement of my waist. Persons of size often experience micro-aggressions from friends and family who think they are 'helping'. Becca's feelings are similar to my own, but everyone experiences body perception differently. I hope that, no matter your size, you realise that your worth is great and your possibilities are endless.

Phineas's Fifty Courtship Questions

1. What is your favourite colour?
2. What is your favourite card game?
3. What is your favourite dance?
4. Which of your siblings are you the closest to?
5. What is your favourite flavour of ice cream?
6. Do you like to swim?
7. Who is your favourite artist?
8. Who is your favourite composer?
9. Do you like to sing?
10. Do you play the pianoforte or another instrument?
11. Do you prefer walking or horse riding?
12. Can you drive a carriage?
13. Which parent are you closest to?
14. Do you speak a foreign language?
15. Do you enjoy travelling?
16. Which food do you dislike?

17. Which food is your favourite?
18. What is your favourite holiday?
19. What is your favourite gemstone?
20. Do you prefer to wear rings or necklaces?
21. Are your ears pierced?
22. What is your favourite footwear?
23. Are you afraid of any animals?
24. What makes you angry?
25. Do you like hats?
26. What is your favourite season?
27. How many children do you have or do you want?
28. What names did you give your children or what would you like to name them?
29. What was your favourite childhood toy?
30. What is the name of your favourite childhood pet?
31. Do you prefer dogs or cats?
32. Do you prefer hot chocolate or tea or coffee?
33. Do you prefer rivers or lakes?
34. What is your idea of a full life?
35. What does happiness mean to you?
36. What lessons has life taught you?
37. Are you afraid of anything?

38. Who is your favourite political leader or member of a royal family?

39. Which is your ideal day of the week?

40. Are you a morning person or an evening person or an afternoon one?

41. What is your favourite flower?

42. What is your second-favourite flower?

43. Who is your dearest friend?

44. What skill are you the most proud of?

45. How do you cope with life's uncertainties and challenges?

46. What political topics are you passionate about?

47. What memory from your childhood makes you smile?

48. What do you believe in that others might not?

49. What do you wish that you had more time to do?

50. Do you love Phineas? And if you were Becca would you marry him?

Harlequin Reader Service

Enjoyed your book?

Try the perfect subscription for Romance readers and get more great books like this delivered right to your door.

See why over 10+ million readers have tried Harlequin Reader Service.

Start with a Free Welcome Collection with free books and a gift—valued over $20.

Choose any series in print or ebook. See website for details and order today:

TryReaderService.com/subscriptions